RAVEL

LAKE HAVEN BOOK 2

By D.M. Simmons

Copyright © 2021 by D.M. Simmons

Book design by D.M. Simmons

978-1-7376302-2-7 (paperback)
978-1-7376302-3-4 (eBook)

Published by Foggy Day Publishing

For those whom fate has brought together

CHAPTER ONE

EVAN LEANED AGAINST THE RAILING AND LOOKED AT me, lips pulling into a luminous smile. The news was out. We were engaged and the runaway train that was our mothers, had left the station. They'd dreamed about this moment since the day we were born and there was no containing their excitement.

"Have you picked a date?" my mother gushed.

"And Laney," Evelyn added, eyes dancing. "The dress...what about the dress?"

"I haven't thought about either yet," I laughed. "This *just* happened."

"Yes, but you must have some idea," she countered. "All girls fantasize about their wedding."

Best friends Marina Thomas and Evelyn Davies loved weddings and gowns and beautiful events. But that had never been me. Dresses and parties

1

had always been Lisa's thing; *my* beautiful best friend that preferred glitz and glamour to our small, seaside town. But she was no longer here, and since she died, things had changed. *I'd* changed.

I now *was* the kind of girl that dreamed about weddings and fairy tale endings, and mine was simple...living happily ever after, with Evan.

"I have some thoughts," I admitted, meeting his smile; my stomach tumbling the way it did whenever our eyes met.

Evan was my heart. My world. My reason for living. But it hadn't always been that way. Once upon a time we were two of five—Lisa, Timmy, Caleb, Evan, and me—and the close-knit friendship we'd all shared, had been my everything. But in the blink of an eye it was gone, and everything changed.

Had I'd known the camping trip we'd taken the summer before our senior year of college, would be the last time the five of us were together, I'd have done everything differently. I'd have believed Evan and I were strong enough to weather Lisa's anger and told her about us before the trip. But foolishly, my need to protect her, like always, had been greater than any need I had for myself, and I'd regret that decision, for the rest of my life.

Lisa was like my sister. It didn't matter how

selfish and stubborn she'd been. I'd loved her, nonetheless. It's why we'd argued that horrible night. She'd felt betrayed; hurt that I'd not trusted her enough to tell her the truth. And I'd been nervous; worried my heart would break apart the friendship I'd cherished so dearly.

But I *had* trusted her. Of course, I had. I'd just been scared of the lie that Evan and I had been keeping and what it would do to our group. It's why I chased after her when she ran to Caleb's car, desperate to make things right.

Sometimes, however, the universe has plans that are out of our control, and we must live with our decisions, no matter how hard we wished we could go back and do things over.

The accident that claimed the lives of she, Caleb, and Timmy that night, changed my world forever. But while a life without my friends may have once been unthinkable, I remembered something when my heart stopped, and I walked the line between life and death. Every fiber of my being was in love with Evan Davies. Always had been. And that world I'd experienced, where I'd lived months in seconds, was meant to remind me of that truth. It's what brought me back. *He* pulled me back.

Evan was home. My safety. All I knew to be true in life. For him, I came back, and would, every time.

"Well," my mother continued. "You must know *when* you want to get married."

I looked over to Evan, shaking my head. "Are you listening to this?"

"Oh, I am," he grinned, the happiness in his eyes undeniable.

"Laney," Evan's mom continued, "don't underestimate how long it takes to find the perfect dress. No planning can begin, really, until you have it. The entire wedding is built around the bride."

"Oh Evie, you're right," my mother smiled at her friend. "The dress really does determine whether you'll have an intimate gathering, or formal event, or..."

"Seriously?" I looked from my mother to Evelyn.

"Yes," they said in unison.

"Well," I laughed in response. "We haven't talked about dates yet. And I definitely haven't thought about a dress. It's only been what..." I looked down at my watch. "An hour?"

"Well darling," Evelyn cooed. "All I'm saying is don't wait. Start looking now."

"And..." my mother added, "you'll want to think about the kind of wedding you'll want to have, *before* you start looking...to guide your search."

"Oh Mare, you're right," Evan's mother looked

4

to mine, nodding.

"Do you two want to plan the entire wedding?"

"Could we?" they asked in harmony, turning back to me.

"No," I laughed again, and the two pretended to pout.

"Okay," my mother eased, taking a sip of champagne from the flute in her hand.

"Fine," Evelyn agreed, doing the same. "But at least pick a date so we can put a hold on the hotel."

Evan's family owned Aqua Luna, Lake Haven's five-star hotel. Nestled along the water's edge, the sprawling property was reminiscent of the seaside resorts of the past. It was grand, yet inviting, and hosted countless weddings over the years, and I knew Evelyn would love nothing more than for Evan and me to get married there.

"When we have a date, we'll let you know," Evan reached for my hand, giving it a squeeze.

Evelyn Davies was a force of nature. She had the kind of aplomb that came naturally but wasn't overbearing or obnoxious. If there was anyone that could make our wedding perfect, no matter what we decided to do, it was her. She was like a second mother to me, and I trusted her implicitly. Still, he'd only just slipped the ring on my finger, and my head was still spinning, and knowing this, Evan

5

jumped in to save me.

Being with Evan filled me with a confidence I didn't know I was capable. However, while I was no longer the unassuming girl I'd once been, it didn't stop him from being overprotective. He'd always been in my corner, and since the accident, more than ever.

"Okay, okay," Evelyn held up her hands in mock surrender, but I knew the reprieve would be short.

We knew our mothers' excitement would be great. It's why Evan and I decided to stop by my parent's house first, then his, before heading home to celebrate privately. But as the sound of laughter greeted us, as we came up my parents' back walk, something told us not only did they already know, but had already begun celebrating.

"So, how did you know?" I asked once the barrage of questions subsided.

"Mothers know these things," Evelyn winked.

"Someone had to have told you."

"When Evan started asking questions about Grandma Davies' ring last year, I knew," she said easily. "And naturally, I told your mom..."

"Last year?" I looked over at Evan. "When we were in New York?"

While originally, Evan and I had gone to college

on different sides of the country—he in North Carolina, and I in Los Angeles—once we got together, being that far apart was no longer an option. We wanted to spend our last year of school together. But, before we could make plans, the accident happened and put life on hold, indefinitely.

That summer had been long—my recovery a balance of one step forward and two steps back—and when fall rolled around, neither Evan nor I were ready to go back to school. We were both still grieving, especially Evan, who took Timmy's death particularly hard. The two may have been cousins but losing him, was like losing a brother.

However, by the time winter came, we *did* start to talk about our last year and when we might return. Only, neither his school, nor mine, seemed right. Our dads had suggested New York University, and Evan and I agreed it was perfect.

With both of them being alumni with friends in high places, it was easy to transfer in time for the spring semester. And before we knew it, we were unpacking our stuff in the small apartment we rented off campus, and beginning our final year of college, together.

Evan and I thrived in New York. There was comfort in anonymity, and in that city of millions, we were able to breath, and heal, and both of us began to enjoy life again. So much so, that instead of coming home for the summer after that first semester, we stayed in the city, and had a summer unlike any.

But when we finished our last semester that following winter, we were both ready to move back home, and start the next chapter of our lives. To think Evan had been planning to propose all this time...

"You're quite the planner," I smiled.

"You have no idea," he winked.

Looking at the smile on Evan's face, there was no denying he was happy being back home. I didn't have the heart to tell him it hadn't been as easy a transition for me.

At first, it felt good to be back in Lake Haven. I missed its tree-lined streets and the smell of salt in the air. We even rented a place on the water, at the edge of town, spending our days making it ours, and nights listening to the buoy bells rocking gently in the cove. Then one night, they began. Nightmares...ominous sleep stealers, leaving no memory of their story, only a dark and lingering foreboding.

When the first one happened, I chalked it up to nothing more than too much coffee and not enough sleep. But when another one hit and then another—sending me shooting up in bed, covered in sweat—I couldn't ignore that something else could be causing them, and had a feeling I knew what it was.

Being back in Lake Haven was no doubt stirring up emotions I thought I'd moved past. I would never *move on* from the deaths of my friends, only forward, and in moving home, my heart had taken a step backwards.

Yet, I didn't tell Evan about the nightmares. He thrived being back in Lake Haven, working at the hotel with his father, and the last thing he needed was to worry about me. Besides, everyone had nightmares, and what weight did a couple of bad dreams carry, really, when you had a love like ours?

"So...it was mother's intuition that told you today was the day?" I pushed the nightmares from my mind and turned to Evelyn.

"Not intuition," she said simply. "Your father."

"Dad?"

"Yes honey?" my father answered, stepping onto the back deck where we had gathered, a bottle of champagne in each hand.

"It was you?" I asked, not sure how much more I could drink. My cheeks were already warm, thanks to the two glasses I'd already consumed.

"Me, what?"

"How did you know?"

"Know what?" he asked, pretending to be confused.

"I told him," Evan whispered. I turned my head, his face inches from mine. "I asked for his permission."

"You didn't," I grinned.

"I did."

"Why?" I asked, swallowing over the lump in my throat.

"What wouldn't I do for you, Alaina Thomas," he said softly, eyes locked on mine.

"Young Davies is a gentleman," my father set one bottle down, and then popped the cork of the other.

"Oh, what does it matter how we found out?" my mother said excitedly as my father filled each of our flutes. "You two are engaged!"

"Cheers to that!" Evan's dad agreed, happily.

"Oh Laney," my mother's eyes filled with tears. "You are going to be the most beautiful bride."

"I second that," Evan wrapped his arm around my waist and pulled me close, kissing the top of my head.

Our mothers gripped each other's hands with tears of joys in their eyes; a prayer whispered between them years ago, finally answered.

"This is going to be the wedding of the decade," my mother said proudly.

"You mean century," Evelyn corrected, and clinked her flute against her best friend's.

"To Evan and Laney," my mother lifted her glass, proffering a toast.

"To Evan and Laney," everyone repeated, and we held up our glasses.

"To us," Evan tapped his glass against mine, as our parents laughed and talked excitedly with one another.

"To us," I smiled back.

How I'd managed to have my happily ever after, despite all that had happened, was a question I'd asked, too many times to count. But today, I'd decided, I would not think about any of it. Not the accident, or the past. Not even my nightmares. Today, I wanted only to be in the moment. This incredible, beautiful moment, that I never wanted to end.

CHAPTER TWO

LATER THAT NIGHT AS EVAN AND I LAY CURLED UP ON the couch at home, I stared at the ring on my finger, reality sinking in. We were engaged and I felt like the luckiest person in the world.

When we set out on our run this morning, I had no idea it would turn out the way it had. I'd assumed we'd be home quickly so we could take the boat out for the afternoon. With the official end of summer only days away, Evan liked being on the water as much as possible. Little did I know, it would become the most unforgettable day of my life.

While originally, Evan and I wanted to get home to celebrate on our own, spending the day with our families felt right. Neither he, nor I, declined when my mother invited us to stay for dinner, and as we sat around my parent's dining room table hours later, listening to stories we'd heard at least a dozen times, I felt happier than I ever had. I could still taste the pepper on my lips from my mother's baked crab and hear the laughter in my mind.

"You alright?" Evan asked.

"Mm-hmm," I nodded dreamily and snuggled up closer to him. To love, and to be loved…there was no other feeling like it in the world.

"You've been quiet ever since we got home."

"Big day," I smiled to myself and looked down at the ring on my finger for the dozenth time.

Being with Evan filled me with a kind of peace I felt only when we were together. I was content when it was just us, and if life were only moments like this, it would be more than enough.

"Do you like it?" he asked.

"Like, is an understatement."

I didn't know much about jewelry, but knew the ring was special. The round diamond was the color of the sky, and sat atop an antique platinum band, surrounded by a halo of delicate diamonds.

"You know…that ring has quite a history."

"Oh?" I asked, looking up.

"My great-great-grandfather gave it to my great-great-grandmother in 1857."

"It's over one hundred and fifty years old?" I asked, stunned. To think it had traveled through time and was now on my hand, gave me goosebumps.

"The ring is, but the stone is much older." I raised my eyebrow in question. "My great-great-grandfather found that stone along the banks of the Zambezi River when he was a captain's apprentice on one of Queen Victoria's ships. Although, it didn't look like that."

I sat up, surprised to hear a story I hadn't before. Evan's family had been in Lake Haven for generations and like other families with roots in the town, their history was well known. I knew Evan's great-great-grandfather had come from England and spent his early years on the sea but didn't recall having ever heard about his time in Africa.

"You're great-great-grandfather was literally, in the middle of Victorian England," I marveled.

"That he was," Evan nodded. "He was pretty far down the ladder, though."

"Doesn't matter where he started. Look where he wound up?"

"True," Evan smiled. "He learned everything he needed to know about ships during that voyage, and when he returned home, he went out on his own. Started with one small boat and then another. And the rest, is history."

Evan's great-great-grandfather had started the

shipping company that the Davies family had owned and operated for generations. While at one time, it'd been the most successful company in the area, his family sold it around the time Evan's father was born, when the old ways began to grow obsolete in a changing world. Real estate became their new family legacy, and that which Evan was born into.

The Davies were one of the most prosperous names in Lake Haven and given their role in helping build and shape the community, featured in the Visitor's Center alongside other families who also played a part of Lake Haven's history. Like my own, who established the town's first printing press and newspaper.

However, while the Davies may now be about land, a love of the sea ran in Evan's blood. He was most comfortable on the water and had sailed from the time he could walk.

"The familiarity doesn't end there," Evan said, mischievously.

"Oh?" I asked and he smiled. "Well, go on," I encouraged, wanting to know more.

"Well, it wasn't until he'd met my great-great-grandmother that he'd learned of the treasure he'd found that day on the Zambezi River. He didn't have a lot of money when they met, so he brought the stone to a jeweler and asked them to turn into a ring for the woman that stole his heart."

"He turned it into a ring for her?" I asked, lacing my fingers through his.

"A voice in his head that day on the river said to pick it up...that one day it would change his life. And it did. The jeweler told my great-great-grandfather the stone he'd found was a blue diamond, one of the rarest, most priceless stones on the planet. And...that's why gave it to her. She was his treasure, and their love, priceless."

"Wow," I exhaled, the story leaving me breathless.

"There's more."

"Really?" I asked, eyes widening.

"After he'd proposed, my great-great-grandmother insisted they sail back to Africa and return the stone to the river. She believed it belonged back where he found it, and this caused quite the argument between the two. But of course, unable to refuse her, he agreed."

"This ring?" I held up my hand.

"Same one."

"So, what happened, because obviously..." I pointed at my finger.

"Well, mid-way into their journey, they hit a horrible storm, and the Atlantic current pushed them here."

"That's how they arrived in Lake Haven?"

"It is," he nodded.

"That's not the story they have in the Visitor's Center."

"Family secret," he winked. "And my great-great-grandmother never took this ring off after that and called it their good luck charm. Any other ship would have gotten lost in that storm, but not theirs. My great-great-grandfather however, believed it was the sea that protected and guided them to Lake Haven. That's why he loved this town and the water so much. And...it's why he spent the rest of his life in service to both."

"Why didn't you ever tell me this story?"

Evan exhaled and rubbed the top of my hand with his thumb. "I guess because when they locked the ring in the safe, their story was locked away, too."

"Why would your family want to lock such a beautiful story *and* ring away?"

Evan leaned his head back on the couch and exhaled. "My grandfather was an only child, and his father before, which made it easy to pass the ring down to each son. But when my father and uncle were born, there were two boys, and then they each had a boy...."

Evan's voice trailed off, but he didn't have to say anything more. I understood. With he and Timmy's dad each having a son to whom the ring could belong, they'd decided to put it in the safe, instead of it becoming a point of contention, the way heirlooms could be.

"When Tim passed, my father talked to my uncle, and he agreed to give the ring to me," Evan said, as if reading my mind. "But what my dad and uncle don't know, is that Tim told me years ago, he wanted me to have it."

"He...what?" I sat up straighter.

"He thought I should give it to you."

I stared at Evan speechless. "How could he know we would ever be a thing?"

"Because *I always knew*. I never told you this, but Tim knew about us before the camping trip."

"How did he know?"

"Because I told him." I stared at Evan, needing an explanation. "He knew since we were kids that I cared about you. But when we finally did get together, I told him because I thought he could help keep the peace that weekend if we wound up telling Lisa and Caleb."

I understood Evan's rationale. If anyone could've been the glue that kept us together, it'd have been Timmy. He'd always been the peacemaker. I should've known however, that everything's eventual. Including friendships, we think are unbreakable, no matter the glue that's holding them together.

The truth was, the five of us were growing apart. I could feel it. We all could. But I'd hoped the trip we'd taken every summer since we were kids, would remind us of the good times that came before and bring us back together.

I also hoped they'd see that if we found happiness, it was more important than 'the rule;' the pact we made as kids and joked about over the years, and yet, taken seriously enough, that none of us had considered breaking it. Until Evan and me.

Then again, we'd been breaking the rule since before it even began. He'd always liked me, and I, him. And technically, it was Lisa and Caleb who had broken it first, the night of my birthday, the winter before the accident when we all went to Bangor for the weekend.

Lisa hadn't admitted it then but finding she and Caleb passed out in bed together the morning after their night of drinking, she didn't have to. It was obvious. And when we argued the night of the accident, and I threw it in her face, she didn't deny it. Instead, she claimed it wasn't the same thing as Evan and me. And she'd been right. We were beyond definition and would've changed the dynamic of our group. But a part of me hoped our friendship would've been strong enough to weather that change.

Hope, however, could be futile. And thinking about what could have been, was pointless. It was too painful to think about how different things might've turned out, had Evan and I just been honest with one another, years ago.

"I don't know what to say," my eyes searched his, filled with love and melancholy.

"You don't have to say anything," he said softly. "I've waited my whole life to give this ring to you. You are *my* treasure. There is nothing I want more than to marry you, and protect you, every day, for the rest of my life."

"Being married won't protect me from the world," I placed my hand on his cheek.

No matter how hard the accident may have been for me, I'd never know what Evan went through that night, as he sat on that road, holding me, waiting for the paramedics to arrive. But I knew it stayed with him, and no matter how strong or confident I'd become, he'd always worry about my safety.

"I will spend the rest of my life trying," he tucked a strand of hair behind my ear.

"You're stuck with me, Davies. I'm going to marry you and grow old with you. And…if our mothers have their way, we'll be married tomorrow."

"Well, that doesn't sound so bad," he smiled, and I did too, liking the sound of it. "I'd marry you tomorrow if I could. But, when we get married, and what kind of wedding we have, is up to us. Actually, it's up to you. Whatever you want, it's yours."

"You," I looked into his eyes, falling into them as always. "I just want you."

"You always have me. That will never change."

He leaned in and kissed me, and my pulse accelerated the way it always did when our lips met. He was my first kiss, and my last, and I'd never tired of his touch. In his arms I came alive and was where I most wanted to be.

Climbing onto his lap, our kiss grew deeper as he moved his mouth expertly from my mouth to my neck. "Thank you for saying yes," he whispered.

"Thank you for asking."

"Do you know how long I've waited for this?" he pulled back, eyes searching mine.

"Apparently since last year," I said cheekily, the smile on his face making me melt. Evan had always been good-looking, but the last couple of years had been good to him. He'd matured and was now handsome, not to mention unbelievably sexy. Yet, his heart was the same, and it was that, which I'd loved most.

"Longer," he corrected.

"The year before that?"

"Forever," he pulled me closer.

"That's a long time," I grinned, running my thumb along his lower lip. I too, had changed these past few years. My desire for him, filled me with powerful combination of want and need that I wasn't afraid to show.

"I mean it," he said with more urgency, locking his eyes onto mine. "I've never wanted anything more. You're everything to me."

"And you, me."

"So, we're stuck with each other?"

"Forever," I confirmed, looking down again at the ring on my finger.

"Are you sure that you like it?"

"I love it. Even more so now that I know its history."

"Good," he exhaled. "I was nervous you may think it's too much."

"Well, it is," I laughed. The ring was large on my slender finger and shifted to the side, due to its size. "But it's perfect. *We're* perfect."

We sat that way in silence as he looked at me and I at the ring on my hand.

"You alright?" he asked when I grew quiet. I nodded but didn't say anything. "They would be happy for us," he said softly, tipping my chin up.

Of course, Evan assumed I was thinking about our friends. They were with us today, as they were for any special moment or milestone. But surprisingly, I *hadn't* been thinking about them just now. Something else was bothering me.

No matter how happy I was, I couldn't ignore the feeling that things were too good to be true. We'd fought to be where we are. We deserved to be happy after everything we'd gone through. So why did it feel like something was out there, threatening to break my world apart, all over again?

Then I'd remembered...*Dean*.

I'd completely forgotten about seeing him earlier, and as his name crashed into me, the root of the foreboding was clear.

The shy former classmate I'd once known, had showed up in that life I'd lived when my heart flatlined. Only, he'd been a completely different person than he'd been in school. He was mean and aggressive, and possessed a deep-seated loathing for Evan that didn't make sense. Every time he was near me, it filled me with fear.

I never told any of this to Evan, however. There was no point. Dean's presence in that world I'd experienced had been nothing more than an obstacle meant to remember my heart's truth. I hadn't seen or thought of him since the accident. Yet, out of nowhere, on the best day of my life, there he was. The timing was strange and raised a flag.

"You think?" I pushed Dean from my mind and turned my thoughts back to our friends.

"They loved you," Evan smiled. "They'd want you to be happy."

"Us..." I corrected.

"They would want *us* to be happy," Evan nodded.

I leaned in and rested my head against his chest. "I'm sorry."

"For?"

"Ruining the moment," I pulled back.

"First, you don't ever have to apologize to me."

"And the second?"

Evan reached for the hem of my shirt and lifted it overhead, tossing it to the floor. "It's time for us to celebrate."

I smiled and did the same; my raw and primal need taking over, pushing everything from my mind. This love was perfect. And our future would be, too. To hell with any monsters that dared rear their heads.

He wrapped his arm around my waist and pulled me close; everything fading away. And that night, as we lie curled up together, sound asleep, no bad dreams haunted me. The only thing I experienced, was a deep, blissful, uninterrupted sleep.

CHAPTER THREE

I PUSHED OPEN THE DOOR TO MY MOTHER'S SHOP, THE bell overhead jingling as I stepped inside.

"Mom?" I looked around, the familiar smell of glass cleaner and wood polish filling my nose.

"I'll be out in a minute," she called from the back.

I made my way to the sales counter and set my bag down, looking around. The shop hadn't changed. It looked just like it did when I was a kid.

While it was common in Lake Haven for businesses to stay in the family for generations, that wasn't the case with my mother's store. She started the business because it was her dream, and she took pride in serving both the community and visitors that flocked to it with hospitality, as if it been there for generations, like the others.

I had fond memories of the time I'd spent here over the years. Like most children of Lake Haven business owners, I'd worked at the shop on weekends and holidays growing up and knew my mother's routine well.

Today was Monday, which meant she would spend the morning returning client calls, and mail from the weekend would go untouched until tonight.

As a respected antiquities dealer, she had clients up and down the Eastern Seaboard, and she used Mondays to focus on their needs after the bustle of the weekend, her busiest time of the week, especially during the summer.

I grabbed the stack of mail next to the register, and organized it into two piles, just as I'd done hundreds of times: items that needed attention, and those that could wait.

"Well," my mother smiled at me brightly when she finally made it out of her office. "Good morning, future Mrs. Davies."

"Good morning," I smiled. It was the first time anyone had called me that, and it sent butterflies fluttering in my stomach.

"Has it sunk in yet?" she asked.

"It's starting to," I used my thumb to move the band of my ring, adjusting it so it sat on top of my finger.

"It's just beautiful," my mother stared at it, eyes

dancing.

"It's pretty incredible," I agreed.

"Leave it to Ev," she said wistfully.

"Were you surprised?"

"Not really," she smiled. "Everyone knows how that boy feels about you."

"Did you ever think that maybe we would never get together?"

"Oh honey," she leaned against the counter. "Growing up, you two were always in your own world. A fool could see how he felt about you. And you lit up whenever he was around. But I could see your heart was ...cautious."

My mother was right. I had been careful. I was always more concerned about what my friends wanted; their happiness and needs, coming before mine.

"Did you really not know he was planning to propose?" she asked.

"Not at all. I mean, we've talked about the future...but I didn't think he would propose just yet. I mean, we're so young."

"Well," she mused, pulling the stack of mail that needed attention towards her. "Your father and I were already married at your age."

"That's true," I nodded, forgetting my mother and father got married days after they graduated college. "I guess I forget we aren't kids anymore."

"You and me both," she laughed.

As my mother worked her way through the stack of mail, I leaned an elbow on the counter and looked out the window. Billowy blue-grey clouds had started to move in, a sign that a storm was on its way.

"Are you meeting up with Tony and Sam tonight?" she asked.

"Yeah," I nodded.

"That should be fun."

"We always have fun together."

Evan and Tony Spencer had played baseball together since they were kids. He was a classmate we both knew and grew up with. Sam Hamilton and I, however, had a class or two together in high school, but weren't particularly close. This was mostly because in those days, I focused on the four which had been my world—Caleb, Evan, Lisa, and Timmy.

If there was an upside to tragedy, however, it was its ability to bring people together, and that had been the case with Tony and Sam. They'd been there for both Evan and me after the accident, and our friendship continued to grow while we were in New York. They'd visit us from time to time, and when we moved back to Lake Haven last winter, it felt as if the four of us had been friends for years.

It was easy to be friends with Tony and Sam. We always had fun, whether grilling in our backyard, or a night out, and our friendship had grown even stronger since we moved back.

"I'm sure they're anxious to celebrate with you," my mother continued as she looked through the mail. "Are they excited?"

"They will be," I nodded.

"Will be?" she stopped and looked up.

"They don't know yet."

"Really?" she asked, clearly surprised.

"Nope," I shook my head. "You and Evan's parents were the first to know."

"Well," she smiled softly. "That makes your old mother feel good."

"You're hardly old."

"True," she reached out and pinched my nose.

"But I am old enough to not be pinched," I swatted her hand away.

"I know," she smiled, eyes tearing up. "My little girl is all grown up and getting married."

"Oh mom, could we not do sentimental? I haven't had my coffee yet."

"Too much champagne yesterday?" she winked.

My mother and Evelyn were professional wine drinkers, so it was no surprise she was fully functional this early.

"No…" I grinned. "We went to bed late."

"All the excitement of the day?"

"Not exactly," I smiled coyly.

"Oh, you!" My mother hit me on the arm with an envelope as she realized what I was inferring.

"Hey," I laughed, "you brought it up."

"Oh, honey, I remember those days."

"Eww, mom, stop," I covered my ears.

"No," she rolled her eyes. "I'm not talking about that. I'm talking about those first days after getting engaged. The butterflies in your stomach…the newness of the ring on your finger. The smile you can't seem to shake. Oh Laney," she sighed, "you're so lucky. Aren't you looking forward to shopping for a dress, and picking out your cake, and well…all of it?"

Of course, I was excited, but I didn't think I was ready for round two of wedding talk just yet. Her voice had raised two octaves in the last minute and I could only imagine what she would be like when we were actually knee-deep into planning.

"Well, even if you won't let on how excited *you* are, your families are *thrilled*. Which, speaking of… I'm glad you're here. After you two left last night, Evie and I got to talking."

"And?"

31

"And… we'd like to throw you and Evan an engagement party."

"But we celebrated last night."

"Not a family celebration…one to share the news with everyone."

"But everyone knows."

"They don't," my mom countered.

It took me a minute and then I understood what she was saying. Lake Haven may have been a small town, but like any community, there were social layers, and both my family and Evan's played a role.

"Oh, come on," I groaned.

"Hear me out," she held up a hand. "I know you've never been particularly fond of a fuss being made over you, but you and Evan getting engaged is a big deal."

I exhaled, tuning out my mother's ruminations about the importance of generosity and social graces. I'd heard it my entire life and didn't care for any of it.

While my mother was not from Lake Haven, she'd come to love the town as if she were. She and Evelyn were on their fair share of committees and knew everyone. Not to mention, the hundreds of business contacts Evan's father had, being a respected real-estate developer, and my own, through his work at an established publishing house in New York City, and member of the advisory board for Lake Haven's newspaper, *The Current*.

"Did you hear me?" my mother asked, seeing I'd drifted off.

"Yes, I heard you."

"And?"

"And...you want to have a party."

"Is that a bad thing?"

"It's not the best thing."

"Cold feet?" she mused playfully.

"Never," I snapped.

"Woah," she pretended to surrender. "I was just kidding."

"Well don't be ridiculous."

"Okay," she reached for the second stack of mail, and began flipping through advertisements and mailers from businesses in town.

"What?" I asked when she grew quiet.

"Hmm?" she asked, keeping her eyes down.

"There's something you want to say."

"Nope," she pressed her lips together.

"Mom. There is nothing in that stack but random ads."

"Maybe I need this," she held up a black and white postcard-sized mailer.

"A two-for-one oil change?" I looked at the flier in her hand, amused.

She sighed, put the card down on the stack, and pushed it aside. "I just thought it might be fun to have a party. Something to take your mind off things."

"Off what *things*?" I scoffed.

"Never mind."

"No," I pushed back. "What do you mean?" She looked and me, saying nothing. "Mom," I pressed, "clearly there's something you want to say."

My mother took a deep breath. "I am your mother," she said finally.

"Yes," I nodded. "And?"

"For nine months your heart beat next to mine."

"Your point?"

"My point is that I know it as well as my own. So, I know when something is wrong."

"What could be wrong?" I laughed. "I just got engaged. Things are amazing."

My mother tapped her finger on the counter and looked at me. "I'm calling your bluff."

"We aren't playing poker."

"Alaina?"

"Mother?"

"I've been wanting to say something, and then yesterday happened, and, well..." she trailed off, but I motioned for her to continue. "I was just going to say, that you've seemed tired lately."

"Well, the four of you drank Evan and I under the table last night," I laughed. "And I told you, I didn't get much—"

"I'm not talking about last night," she cut me off before I could finish. "I've noticed it for a while, now."

"Noticed, *what*?"

"That something is troubling you."

"Nothing is troubling me," I pushed back.

"Well, I think there is, and I think I know what it is."

"Is that so, Detective Thomas?"

"It is."

"And what, pray tell, may that be?"

"I think, being back here may be harder on you than you're letting on."

Her brutal accuracy surprised me, but I remained stoic. I didn't want my mother to know she was right. She'd already worried about me enough for one lifetime.

"It's a little strange being back home," I admitted, choosing my words carefully. "New York and Lake Haven are very different."

"Yes," she nodded, "I'm aware."

"And Evan has been working hard, and me too,

with my new job." It was an answer, but not an answer. I could've been a politician.

"And now, there's the engagement," she added, studying me.

"Right," I smiled. "And that."

"Is it too much?"

"The engagement?"

"All of it," she clarified. "Engagement, work, being back here. Don't get me wrong," she added quickly. "I love having you back home. And I'm thrilled beyond words for you and Evan. I just worry that it might be too much for you."

"Life is too much sometimes," I admitted. "But I just got engaged to the most incredible person on the planet. What do I have to be stressed about?"

"Life has changed, and it will continue to, and it may be stirring up things in your mind that you don't even realize. Maybe if you had an outlet," she suggested.

"Like?"

"Someone to talk to."

"I do, Evan."

"No honey," she smiled. "Someone trained, with the experience to—"

"Are you talking about a therapist?" I straightened.

"Now Laney," she tried to interject, but I

continued.

"Are you kidding me? You do remember what happened the last time you encouraged me to talk with someone, *right*?"

I knew something happened to me when my heart stopped, but the therapist my parents encouraged me to talk to hadn't believed me; looking at me disapprovingly as he scribbled on his notepad the words of his diagnosis, after our first, and what would be, only session — *manifestation of an illusionary state as a coping mechanism for loss.*

The unbiased ear, whose job was simply to listen, hadn't been that at all. He was a skeptic, likening my near-death experience to a dream; a place of my mind's creation, to help deal with the death of my friends. Not to mention, he resented my faith in the power of love and belief it is what saved me.

Patient confidentiality prevented him from sharing any of this with my parents, however. They never knew why I didn't go back, only that the session had been a failure, and from then on, the only person I'd ever talked to about that night, was Evan.

How could I trust anyone with my feelings, when all I saw in the eyes of the one person I did see and who was supposed to help me, was disbelief?

"I wasn't thinking of a therapist," she said softly, seeing how irritated I'd become.

"Then what *are* you saying?"

"I was thinking more like a group...where you can talk with others who have gone through what you have."

"Oh mom," I closed my eyes, the idea of sitting in a circle, bearing my soul, sounding completely unbearable. "I don't need counseling."

"No honey," she sighed. "I'm not talking about counseling. I'm talking about meeting with others who have experienced something like you have. I've been doing some reading," she fingered the crystal pendant, hanging from her neck. My mother was not a religious person. Neither was my father. But the way she wrapped her hand around the rock, told me she believed in something. "Post-traumatic stress in sole survivors can take years to manifest," she continued. "It could explain the anxiety you are feeling."

Sole survivors. Post-traumatic stress. What was she saying?

"I'm not anxious" I replied crisply.

"Maybe being home is—"

"I'm fine!" I snapped. My mother straightened and stared at me, eyes wide. "I'm...sorry," I took a deep breath; the fact she'd been able to read me, hitting a nerve.

If my mother knew I hadn't been sleeping well, and there might be more to it than just a couple of nights, tossing and turning, surely Evan would have noticed, as well. I was more concerned about this, than the idea of her suggestion I see someone.

"I just think it could be helpful," my mother said quietly.

"I'll think about it."

"You will?"

"Yes," I grabbed her hand, and gave it a squeeze. I didn't want to fight with my mother. I loved her and knew she was only trying to help. "Now," I changed the subject. "Weren't you saying something about a party?"

"Really?" her eyes lit up.

"Why not," I smiled. "Parties are good, right?"

And like that, I'd managed to successfully derail any further talk about therapy. My mother squeezed my hand back and began sharing all of the ideas she and Evelyn discussed after Evan and I left last night.

"So, you'll talk to Ev and let me know?" she said finally, after talking nonstop for ten minutes.

"I will."

"Good," she nodded happily.

"Thank you," I said as she tidied up the sales counter.

"For?"

"Caring about me."

"Being your mom is the job that matters most to me in this world."

"Speaking of jobs," I grabbed my bag. "I need to get to work."

When life changes in the blink of an eye, something happens to your dreams. They can change, or die, and that's what happened to my dream of becoming a doctor.

After the accident, I still wanted to help others, but was no longer interested in spending years in school. Something about the unpredictability of life made me feel like I should be living, not studying.

When the beloved guidance counselor at Lake Haven High School announced her retirement this past spring, it was serendipitous. As a pre-med student my degree was in psychology, and what better way was there to help people *and* use my degree, than by working with students at the high school.

I'd been nervous when I submitted my application. I met all the requirements and already knew everyone at the school but knew there were other qualified applicants. Still, I was thrilled when they called to tell me I'd gotten the job and spent all summer meeting with teachers and staff—and when the new school year started a couple of weeks back, I was the new guidance counselor at Lake Haven High School.

The phone in my mother's office began to ring and she looked towards the back.

"Go get that...I'll talk to you later."

"We're good, right?" she hesitated.

"Of course," I smiled. "Why wouldn't we be?"

"Okay," she exhaled, obviously relieved with my answer. "I'll give you a call tonight and we can talk more about the party."

"Great," I laughed, knowing I'd opened the flood gate.

"Oh, Laney," my mother asked as she stepped around to the other side of the counter. "You never said why you stopped by?"

"I was going to see if you wanted to grab a coffee with me before school."

"Oh," she smiled wider. "I wish we could have."

"Me too," I nodded to her office. "Go get that. I'll talk to you later."

"Okay," she waved. "Bye honey."

As I gathered my things, the bell over the front door jingled. Hearing my mother now deep in conversation, I decided to help the incoming customer before leaving.

Setting my bag back down on the counter, I smiled and turned, preparing to greet them. But my planned welcome fell short, as I laid eyes on the person walking through the door.

CHAPTER FOUR

DEAN ENTERED MY MOTHER'S SHOP, A SLICK GRIN pulling at his lips, and the combined weight of trepidation and déjà vu slammed into me. I stumbled backwards, hitting my back against the counter, sending a glass paperweight that had been there forever, rolling off. It fell to the floor and shattered, scattering broken crystal fragments across the floor.

"I hope that wasn't valuable," he stopped and looked down.

I closed my eyes, hoping my mind was playing tricks on me, but when I opened them up again, he was still there.

"You okay, Thomas?" he asked, eyeing me curiously.

I nodded, my voice trapped in my throat like a fly in a web, and bent down, turning my attention to the broken crystal scattered around my feet.

It was him on the overlook yesterday, I thought, my mind racing.

"Be careful," Dean bent down and reached out. I pulled my hand back instinctively and froze; his presence paralyzing me. *Why was he here? What did he want?*

I couldn't breathe. Couldn't hear anything, but the sound of my heart, pounding in my ears. Then a pain shot through my hand, snapping me out of the daze.

I looked down, slightly confused for a moment, then understood the source of the pain. The sharp edges of a piece of crystal were digging into my skin. I'd been so shocked to see Dean that I'd grabbed it and not even realized.

I dropped it to the floor and stood up quickly.

"You're bleeding," he looked at my hand, brows pulled together with worry.

"It's...fine," I said numbly, finally finding my voice.

"Let me help you," he reached out again.

"I said, I'm fine," I flinched, as my pulse started to race.

"You need to elevate it."

"What?" I asked, my pounding heart, making it hard to breathe.

"Your hand...you need to elevate it to slow

down the bleeding."

"Right," I shot back; irritated by his having to point out the obvious.

I hurried around to the other side of the counter, fumbling around underneath for something to wrap around my hand. Finding a roll of paper towels, I set it down and pulled off a handful, hastily.

"Make sure to apply pressure," he instructed as I patted my hand carefully.

I mumbled and kept my focus on my hand, sneaking a peek at him from under lowered eyes. Tall and built, with a tattoo on his arm, this Dean was eerily similar to the one in my near-death experience. Only, his blonde hair had grown out and not buzzed short, which made him appear less menacing, and eyes, not as steely.

"What are you doing here?" I asked as the bleeding began to subside.

"It's been a while, hasn't it?" he smiled, answering my question with one of his own.

"I'm not sure how long it's been," I said tersely.

"Keep it elevated," he nodded to my hand. "It will help with the pain."

As if in response to his comment, my hand began to throb. "It doesn't hurt," I lied.

"You're different than I remember," he continued, smiling slightly.

"We're not the same people we were in high school."

"No," he cocked his head to one side, "we're not."

"Why are you here?" I asked, his presence unnerving me more than it should.

"This is still a shop, is it not?"

"It is," I tossed the blood-soaked paper towels into the trash and tore off another handful from the roll.

"Just, wanted to see if things had changed."

"Since high school?"

"No," he looked around. "Since the last time I was here."

"You've come here before?"

"Sure," he turned his attention back to me.

"When?"

"While I was home…on leave."

"So, you're still in the service?"

"Are you keeping tabs on me, Thomas?" he grinned.

"No," I shot back, a little too quickly.

"I'm kidding," he held up a hand. "No, I'm not in the service anymore. And you?"

"Am I in the service?"

"No," he laughed. "Do you live here, or are you visiting?"

"Why?"

"Just making conversation."

I was visibly on edge and angered by the effect he was having on me. "I moved back last spring," I clarified, taking a breath.

"After college?"

"Yes."

"Was it hard?"

"Was *what* hard?"

"Moving from California to Maine?"

"How did you know I was in California?" I straightened.

"You do remember who my mother is?" he laughed.

Everyone knew Katherine Danvers. She had fiery red hair and a laugh you could hear a mile away. She ran the gift shop in town that sold t-shirts with slogans like 'Will You Be My Maine Squeeze?' and 'I Left My Heart in Lake Haven.' She was best known, however, as the town gossip, and had no doubt filled Dean in on everything there was to know about all his former classmates, myself included.

"Not to mention," he continued. "Everyone knew you were headed to California. You wanted to be a doctor if I remember correctly?"

"Right," I pulled my hand to my chest.

"How is that going?"

"I...don't know."

"Not well?"

"No. I mean, I didn't go to med-school."

"No?" he asked, surprised by the admission. "Why not?"

There wasn't a person in town that didn't know about the accident. It rocked our town. For months after, I couldn't go anywhere without pitying eyes following me. It's partly why New York had been so healing. No one knew us there. To anyone Evan and I passed on the street, we were just two people. But here, we were the two that lived, and I could see it in everyone's eyes.

The upside of everyone knowing your business, however, was exactly that—no explanations were necessary when Evan and I left Lake Haven, or when we returned. But everyone knew, and no one said anything, unless we did.

Dean closed his eyes, realizing his mistake. "Alaina...I'm...sorry."

"It's fine," I dismissed the apology and cleared my throat. "I work at the high school now."

"Yeah?" he asked, clearly surprised. "Well, that's cool. Good for you."

Dean grew quiet as he looked around again. "So, how long are you in town for?" I asked, remembering he'd never answered my question.

"It depends."

"On?"

"How things go."

"Like?"

"Oh, you know. Life...and work," he shrugged. I nodded and said nothing. "It's nice to know though, the more things change, the more they stay the same."

"Meaning?"

Dean pointed to the wall behind me, and I turned, looking at a picture of Evan and me hanging with dozens of other family photos. "You and Davies still close?"

"We're engaged, actually."

"Ah," he looked at the ring on my uninjured hand as it held the damaged one close. "Congratulations. Although, I will say, it's not a surprise."

"Why do you say that?" I asked a little too defensively.

"The two of you have always been, attached at the hip. Like I said," he smiled, "the more things change, the more they stay the same."

"Continuity is nice."

"Can be," he agreed. "But, sometimes, life changes, and there isn't anything we can do about it."

I understood the sentiment, more than I cared to admit, but I couldn't help but feel as if there were a deeper meaning to his words. If I cared to know what he was implying, I'd ask. But I didn't. My hand was beginning to ache, and I was done with what felt like a hide n' seek conversation.

"Well," I said as if he were a customer that I was greeting for the first time. "I was about to close up, so if there is something I can help you with…"

"No, no," he nodded. "I won't keep you. Just…stopping by to say hi."

"Okay," I looked to the door, not sure what else to say.

"It was good to see you, Alaina," he smiled. "I'll…see you around."

And without another word, he turned and left, bell overhead jingling as he closed it behind him.

I stared after him, not sure any of what just happened was real. Then my mother's worried voice filled my ears, and I knew it had.

"Laney, goodness!" she exclaimed as she came out from the back.

"What?" I asked numbly, staring at the door.

"What happened?" she looked at the blood-soaked paper towels in my hand.

The entire time Dean was here, I'd felt the

50

adrenaline coursing through me, fueling me with strength. But once he left, it vanished, leaving me cold and dazed.

I turned to her, searching for words. "I...um..."

"Honey..." she looked at me concerned. "You're as white as a ghost."

"Something...fell," I said lamely.

"Clearly," she looked at me, brows pinched.

I looked down and guilt slammed into me as I saw the bloody piece of crystal on the floor scattered among the rest of the broken paperweight. "Oh mom," I remembered knocking it off the counter. "I'm so sorry."

"Well," she exhaled and placed a hand on her hip. "There's no use crying over spilled milk."

"It's not milk, mom. There's glass, everywhere."

"It's crystal," she corrected. "Waterford, specifically."

"I'm...sorry," I said again. I knew it was valuable. She'd had it as long as I could remember.

"Sweetheart it's fine," she held the back of her hand to my cheek. "But you're not. You're cold and clammy."

"Let me help you clean up," I offered, reaching for the paper towels.

"No," she grabbed a dustpan and hand broom from under the counter. "I'll clean this up. Why don't you go to the bathroom and tend to that hand?"

"Are...you sure?" I swallowed.

"Yes," she waved me off. "Go. I'll get this."

I made my way to back of the shop, and once inside the bathroom, pressed my back against the door and exhaled. I couldn't believe I'd seen Dean Danvers for a second time in just twenty-four hours. Nothing for two years, and then bam, suddenly here he was, stirring up old fears that I thought I'd buried.

Once I'd steadied my breathing, I turned on the faucet and washed the blood from my hand and when done, rifled underneath the sink for something to wrap around it. Finding nothing but a handful of Band-Aids, I pulled a fresh paper towel from the holder on the wall, folded it into a square, and placed it on my palm; sticking a Band-Aid on each side to keep it in place. It would have to do until I could clean and wrap it properly.

When done, I looked into the mirror to remind myself who I was, and the reality of this world. *You saw Dean*, I said to my reflection. *So what?*

The person I saw just now was different from the one in the world where I'd feared him. Not to mention, I was no longer that girl. The one who was afraid of her own shadow. Afraid, of Dean Danvers.

I hadn't been her in a long time. If anything, I was angry at myself for how he'd unraveled my confidence simply by showing up.

"Better?" my mother asked when I returned a couple of minutes later. The floor was spotless, all evidence of the broken paperweight, gone.

"Much," I smiled. "By the way, where is your First-Aid kit?"

"I got rid of it. Everything was so old."

"Well, you might want to get another one," I held up my hand.

She eyed the paper towel I'd affixed to my hand with Band-Aids. "Are you sure you're, okay?"

"Yeah," I exhaled. "I'm fine."

"You do look a bit better," she hesitated.

"All that blood got to me, I guess."

"Well, then, it's probably good that you didn't go to med school," she said lightheartedly.

"Right," I laughed once in response.

"Do you want to tell me what happened?"

"Freak accident."

"That's it?"

"Yup," I nodded.

"Alright," she exhaled. "Glad it wasn't your other hand. I'd hate to see that beautiful ring of yours covered by a bandage."

I looked down at my ring, relieved to see it

flashing back brilliantly at me, unmarred by blood — a beacon, shining bright in a storm.

"Well," I grabbed my bag with that hand. "I've got to get going. I need to go home and get this cleaned up before heading to the school."

"Oh honey, you're going to work?"

"Sure. Why wouldn't I?"

"Your hand."

"It's just a scratch."

"Scratch?" she scoffed.

"I'll be fine," I leaned in and kissed her on the cheek.

"Okay," she watched me dubiously.

"I'll call you later."

"Sounds good," she waved.

"Love you," I waved back over my shoulder, forcing a lightness I didn't exactly feel. My hand was starting to hurt more, and even I knew it was more than a scratch.

"Love you, too," she called back.

As I walked to the car, the sound of the ocean and birds overhead soothed my frayed nerves and lifted my spirits. But after climbing into the driver's seat and starting the engine, Dean came crashing back into my mind — *Are you keeping tabs on me, Thomas?*

I threw the car into reverse, backed out of the

parking spot, then put it into drive; anger building all over again as I waited for the cars to pass.

Damn you Dean Danvers, I seethed, as I pulled onto the road, and made my way home. This was my life, and I wasn't about to let anything, or anyone, derail it.

CHAPTER FIVE

EVAN GREETED ME AT THE DOOR WHEN I ARRIVED home ten minutes later, the smile on his face fading, as he saw the bloody paper towel in my hand.

"What happened?" he asked clearly alarmed, as he shut the door behind me.

I tossed my bag and keys down on the entry table. "I cut my hand."

"Looks like it was more than that."

"It's nothing," I sighed as he motioned for me to follow him to the kitchen. "Looks worse than it is."

The larger cuts had started bleeding again, thanks to my having gripped the wheel, all the way home.

"Let's see what we're dealing with," he pulled out a stool from under the counter.

"I'm fine, really," I insisted, taking a seat, and holding out my hand.

Evan gently peeled off the soiled paper towel, eyes widening as he saw my lacerated palm. "Oh wow. What happened again?"

"I…dropped something."

"A set of knives?" he asked, trying to be funny.

"Ha, ha," I rolled my eyes.

"Stay there," he instructed, and went to the pantry to grab the First Aid kit.

"We should drop that off at my mother's shop," I said wryly as he set it down on the counter and turned on the faucet.

"Why?" he asked, adjusting the temperature so it was lukewarm.

"Nothing," I sighed, the lack of supplies in my mother's shop unimportant.

"Let's get that cleaned up," he motioned for me to join him at the sink.

After holding his finger under the water to make sure it wasn't too hot, I lowered my hand into the stream, gritting my teeth as it hit my skin—each laceration feeling like it was being forced apart, as the blood washed away.

Once clean, Evan dried my hand gently, and examined it again more closely. "The smaller cuts aren't bad, but this big one may need a stitch or two."

"I'm not getting stitches. It's just a cut."

"Uh huh," he opened the First Aid kit and removed a bottle of antiseptic, small pack of cotton balls, sterile pad, and a roll of gauze.

"Will that hurt?"

"It may sting a bit," he unscrewed the cap and opened the pack of cotton balls, dousing one.

I bit my lip in anticipation, as he reached for my hand and pulled it to him gently. "Ouch," I hissed, pulling it back after he pressed the cotton ball onto on the first cut.

"I said it might sting."

"That's not a sting. That feels like I was stuck with a hot poker."

He pulled my hand back to him and blew softly. "This better?"

"I guess," I nodded stubbornly.

"Doing, okay?" he asked as he applied antiseptic to each of the cuts.

"Yeah," I inhaled, breathing through the pain.

"You sure?"

"I'm...irritated."

"Why?" he asked, and I nodded at my lacerated palm. "Accidents happen. But do you want to tell me what *really* happened?

"It was nothing."

"Well," he screwed the cap back onto the bottle of antiseptic and returned it to the kit. "I'd say it was something."

"I knocked something off the counter at my mother's shop."

"What do we owe her?" he winked and reached for a sterile pad.

"*You* don't owe her anything," I watched as he placed it down on my palm, grabbed the gauze, and then began wrapping it carefully around my hand. "I'm the one who feels awful."

"I'm sure she forgives you," he offered me a sympathetic smile.

"She does, but it was obviously important to her. She's had it forever."

"The paperweight on the counter?" he asked, looking up.

"How'd you know?"

"How many times have I been to her shop?" he laughed.

"Good point," I nodded.

"Well, I'm sure she's more worried about you than the paperweight," he continued.

"She was," I admitted. "But still, I feel guilty."

Evan nodded with understanding; guilt a currency of which we were both familiar. "Well, there's nothing to feel bad about now because would you check this out," he reached into the kit for the medical tape, ripped off a piece, and secured the gauze in place.

I assessed my hand, impressed. "Maybe you should've been a doctor."

"Right," he smiled, and put everything back into the kit and returned it to the pantry.

"What do I owe you?" He looked at me and grinned, and I knew well what he was thinking. "Later," I smiled, my cheeks warming. "But how about my mother?"

"I'm sure she doesn't want anything."

I remembered her suggestion of a party. "Oh, she does."

"Oh?"

"And honestly, that's the only way she'd want me to repay her." He looked at me, puzzled. "Our moms want to throw us an engagement party."

"Oh yeah?" he brightened.

"You like the idea?"

"A party could be fun," he nodded.

"Not you too?" I groaned.

"Not me what?" he smiled.

"You like the idea of having a party?"

"Laney," his smile grew wider. "I can't remember a time I *didn't* want to tell the world how I felt about you. So yes, I'm fond of the idea of having a party so I can shout it from the rooftops."

"Well, when you put it that way," I blushed.

"Maybe, let them have this one win?"

"You mean, second."

"What else do they want?" he asked, lifting an eyebrow.

"You know they won't be happy until we pick a wedding date."

"Well, like I said last night…it's up to you. If you want to plan everything, down to the day and time we say our vows, then that's the way it will be."

"I guess it could be fun," I admitted, thinking about the engagement party from Evan's point of view.

"A night about us? What's not fun about that," he winked.

"Okay, I'll call her later and give her the good news."

"Great," he leaned back against the counter.

"Any dates off the top of your head? For the party that is."

"Now that, I'll have to check on."

"Things heating up with the expansion?"

"That's why I'm still here," he nodded. "Had an idea this morning and decided to work on it some before heading over to the hotel."

Evan had been pitching his father on the idea of expanding the hotel for years, and as soon as he began working there, put together a formal proposal. The plan included the addition of private cottages and amenities, including a full-service spa, and a commitment to using local resources, not only in its construction, but once completed.

Evan's father loved the idea and put him in charge. He'd worked on it every day for the past few months and was due to present the plans to City Council at their next meeting.

"That's why you're here," I smiled, the pain in my hand subsiding. "I was wondering…"

"About?"

"How it is you always manage to be there when I need you."

"Magic," he winked.

Magic, I smiled, looking out the kitchen window. From here you could see down to the water, and if the windows were open, hear the waves lapping against the shore. There was no doubt, Lake Haven was magic.

"Penny for your thoughts?" Evan asked.

I wondered if I should tell him what really happened at the shop. Realizing it would mean I'd have to tell him *why* Dean unnerved me to the point I'd gotten hurt, I decided not to, and instead, told him about my mother's other idea.

"My mother thinks I should see someone."

"About?"

"Well not someone," I clarified and turned back to him. "A group...for people like me."

"People like you," he repeated.

"Survivors," I clarified, and waited for his response.

While that night forever changed our world, it also turned Evan's greatest fear into a reality. As he held me in his arms, waiting for the paramedics to arrive, he felt the moment my heart stopped. For a handful of seconds, he lived in a world that I did not, and that moment, while brief, would forever haunt him.

Seeing, however, that he was listening and not reeling, I continued. "She thinks it may be helpful to talk with others who experienced what I did."

"Okay," he considered the comment, rubbing a hand across his chin, eyes pensive.

"You think it's a bad idea."

"Didn't say that."

"You think it's a *good* idea?"

"I didn't say that, either."

"Well, what *do* you think?"

"It's not about what *I* think. It's what *you* think."

"I don't know," I considered his answer. "Maybe she's right. Maybe it *would* be good to talk with others who've gone through what I have."

"All of it?" he asked, raising an eyebrow.

"Now that, I'm not sure."

I'd never planned to tell anyone but Evan about my near-death experience and didn't think I'd change my mind anytime soon.

"I am curious, though," he continued.

"About?"

"Why she made the suggestion now, after all this time?"

There was no way around telling Evan *why* my mother suggested I see someone, without telling him that she'd noticed I wasn't sleeping well. And I hadn't decided that I'd tell him at all. I hoped the nightmares would just go away and they would become a non-issue.

But, when I'd accepted his proposal, hadn't I'd also accepted the idea that life was no longer about he or me, but we? Didn't he deserve to know?

"She's…concerned about me," I answered carefully.

"Does she have reason to be?"

"She…got the impression I haven't been sleeping well."

"And?"

"And…I told her with the exception of last night, there was some truth to it." He shook his head and grinned and my lips tingled with the memory of last night.

"Laney," he shook his head, his grin fading.

"What?" I asked, wondering why his expression had changed.

"I know," he said softly.

"You know...what?"

"I know you haven't been sleeping well." I tried to protest but he continued. "I know," he said again.

"How long have you known?"

"We share a bed, Lanes. I know when you're tossing and turning." I bit my lip and looked down. "Why didn't you tell me?"

"I didn't want to bother you."

"You are never a bother."

"You know what I mean. I'm the *last* thing you need to worry about with everything you have going on with the hotel."

"Laney," he exhaled. "You are the *first* and *only* thing I should worry about."

"You can't go through life worrying about me all the time."

"I can worry about you as much as I want."

"You know what I mean."

Evan looked to the window; lips pressed together. "I should have thought about how being back here might affect you. I mean, it's certainly hit me a time or two."

"It...has?"

"Sure," he turned back to me, eyes soft. "How can it not. New York was so different. When we were there, it was just you and me. But being back here," he paused. "There are memories, everywhere."

I nodded in agreement, Evan saying perfectly, what I'd been afraid to.

"Do you know why it's happening?"

"No," I shook my head. "But *something* is...and I wish I knew, what."

"Could it be working at the school...being back there?"

"I don't think so," I shook my head. "They started *before* I got the job. And the thing is...it doesn't bother me to be there. It feels good, actually."

"What are they about?" Evan asked, curious.

"Nothing, really."

"Nothing?"

"Nope. They're just...darkness. I don't know," I sighed. "Maybe she's right...I've focused so much on the loss of *them*, and never really dealt with the seriousness of what happened to *me*."

"Only you can answer that question," Evan came over to where I stood, and wrapped his arms around me and held me tight, resting his chin on my head. "But I do know, whatever you decide, I support you."

I was surprised how well he was taking this conversation, given how hard the topic of my heart's stopping had been for him in the past. I leaned into his chest and inhaled, filling my lungs with his scent.

I didn't know why I had been so afraid to tell Evan about my nightmares. As always, he'd understood. "How do you do it?" I asked.

"Do what?"

"Understand me without fail."

"It comes naturally."

"Ah," I nodded, knowing well the intrinsic nature of our hearts. "And the past?" I pulled back to look at him. "How do you ignore it?"

"I don't," he said simply. "I remember, and then I focus on the good, and make every moment count. Just as I know they would've wanted."

"Is that why you proposed?"

"I proposed because I love you."

"And I said yes because I love you."

"And that, my love, is the best good there is." Evan's eyes searched mine. "This is home. Our past, present, *and* future. We can't run away from what happened. Not when there is so much good in the past."

"I feel that way, too," I nodded. "That's why I

want to do whatever I can to figure out why these nightmares are happening and make them go away."

"How about from now on, when a memory hits, we share it? Maybe, talking about the past will help in some way."

"Deal," I agreed. "And my mother's suggestion?"

"It's up to you. Only you know what you need."

"I need you."

"You already have me."

I laid my head back against his chest, looking out the window, watching the heavy branches of the maple tree in the backyard, twist in the wind. They bounced up and down like giant hands controlling the strings of a puppet; autumnal leaves, fluttering with the movement.

"Think we're in for an early winter?" I asked, eyeing the changing sky.

Evan turned his head, also taking note of what looked to be signs of a storm coming in. "Not sure. But I hope whatever's brewing isn't anything major."

"Me too. I'd love to take the boat out this week."

Evan would spend every day on the water if he could and loved that I'd come to enjoy sailing as much as him.

"If winter does come early," he looked down at me and smiled, "we'll just have to figure out something else to do to pass the time."

"Like?" I teased.

"Unpacking."

"Unpacking?" I scrunched my nose.

"Those last few boxes in the corner of the garage won't unpack themselves."

"Right," I laughed.

"Did you think I was talking about something else?" he laughed back.

"You're ridiculous."

"I'm serious," he smiled wider. "Once those are unpacked, then we will be officially moved in."

"Didn't that happen when we signed the lease?"

"It did. But unpacking all our baggage will make it official."

"You mean boxes."

"Right," he corrected, the skin at the corner of his eyes folding as he laughed again.

"You're amazing you know that?" I beamed, thanking whatever was responsible for making him mine.

"I'm not that great," he shrugged.

"Oh, you are. You always know what to say to make me feel better."

"Well, the way I see it, we're in this together. I

got your back."

"And I got yours."

"So, with that in mind, do me a favor?" he asked.

"Anything."

"If that hand gives you any trouble at school, go get it checked out."

"I will."

"I mean it."

"I promise," I tipped my head up to kiss him.

"Don't you have work to do?" I whispered as his lips lingered on mine, and he pulled me closer.

"Yes," he mumbled.

"I need to get going or I'll never leave."

"And that would be bad?" he ran his hand up my back.

"Yes, because you have work to do, too. We can pick this back up, later."

"Promise?" he pulled back, eyes flickering.

"Would I lie to you?" I winked.

Evan followed me to the front door and opened it, handing me first my bag, and then my keys. "Drive safely. Try not to aggravate those cuts."

"I will."

"And remember," he smiled. "You and me."

"You and me," I nodded, then kissed him one last time, and walked out the door.

CHAPTER SIX

WHEN I FINALLY MADE IT TO SCHOOL, THERE WAS A folder waiting on my desk. A new student had transferred and as part of the orientation process, it was my job to review their classes, answer any questions about the school, and show them around campus.

"So, Niña," I set the folder down, greeting the girl on other side of the desk. She was petite, with tawny skin, chestnut colored hair, and deep brown, heavily lined eyes. "Welcome to Lake Haven. How are you settling in?"

I could only imagine how difficult it was being the new kid, especially in a town as small as Lake Haven. Most kids had grown up here together and cliques were abundant.

"Aren't you a bit young to be a school counselor?" she asked, peering at me with scrutiny.

I was growing used to the candor of teens and had come to learn two things in my first weeks on the job. One, they'd rather talk about you, than themselves. And two, those who acted tough, were usually, not.

"A lady never reveals her age," I smiled. "But I went to school here. In fact, I spent my whole life in this town. So, if there is anything you'd like to know, just ask."

"Man, that sucks," she sat back, slinging one leg over the other, revealing a chunky heeled boot.

"Not really," I countered. "There's something to be said about growing up in a small town."

"Like?"

"Well," I clasped my hands together and rested them on the desk. "It's easy to get around and there's always a smiling face."

"Aces," she replied blithely.

"And this is a great school," I continued. "We have lots of clubs, and sports, and there is always something going on."

"Like?"

"Well, I did a little of everything when I went to school here. I ran track and was editor of our high school yearbook."

"Not into either," she crossed her arms.

"Well, we also have incredible beaches and

hiking."

"Are those clubs?"

"We have a nature club, and they take regular hikes."

"California has the best beaches," she exhaled. "And I prefer music."

"You're from California?" I looked down again at her enrollment forms. I hadn't been able to review her file as thoroughly as I normally would, thanks to this morning's chaos. I'd barely hung up my coat before the school secretary was knocking on my door to show her in.

"Los Angeles," she replied.

"LA?" I looked up.

"Heard of it?" she asked wryly.

"As a matter of fact," I cleared my throat, "I lived there for three years."

"Oh yeah?" she straightened, showing sudden interest.

"In college."

"Went all the way across the country for freedom, huh?"

"No," I laughed. "Moving was my best friend's idea."

"You left for a friend?"

"I did," I nodded, words from years earlier, echoing in my mind. *It is what best friends were for, right?*

"Did you like it?"

"LA? It was okay," I responded carefully. But the truth was, I didn't like it. Not at all.

The City of Angels that Lisa thought was perfect, had been anything but to me. I never felt comfortable there. The smog and heat—the way everyone appeared perfect but were deeply flawed—created a strange heartbeat for the city, which felt as if it were always trying. Trying to be more, do more, have more. I spent more time wishing I were home when I was there, than anything.

"Did they like it?" Niña asked. "Your friend?"

"She did," I smiled, remembering the way Lisa dove head-first into the waves the first day we went to the beach in Santa Monica.

"Why did you move back?"

"How about, you tell me more about yourself," I said instead. "What are you interested in? We could find something you'd enjoy. We're only a couple of weeks into the school year and most clubs are just starting."

"No thanks," she slumped down in the chair again. "I don't plan to be here long."

"Oh?"

"Nope," she continued, emphasizing the word at

the end with a pop.

"Well," I closed the folder, deciding I'd take a better look at her file after our session. "Why don't we try to make this first day as bearable as possible, hmm?"

"Looks like that will be *pretty* impossible," she looked to the window. The clouds were growing darker, and I worried the looming storm would be here before we knew it.

"Maine does have some pretty harsh weather," I agreed. "But hopefully, this storm will come and go."

"And if it doesn't?" she challenged.

"Well, then, I guess you better buy a coat," I smiled. "Now, why don't we take a look at your schedule."

Niña stared at me for a moment, then reached into the pocket of her hoodie and placed a slip of paper down on my desk, pushing it to me with her finger.

I read her class list, impressed. "AP English, AP Art History, AP Spanish... I had a couple of these teachers, and I can tell you, they're pretty terrific. Although, I didn't take Spanish."

"No soy fan de Española?"

"Jai appris le François à l'école. Wow," I laughed, easily switching back to English. "They're right. Once you learn a language, it stays with you."

"Spanish is my father's native language, so it's kind of impossible to forget."

"You speak it well. I'm sure Mr. Cervantes would enjoy having you in the Spanish Club."

"Why not," she shrugged. "As they say, until death it is all life."

"Don Quixote," I nodded, easily knowing the quote.

"You're familiar?" she asked, lifting an eyebrow.

"Some parents tell their children stories as a way of teaching life's lessons. My dad uses quotes from his favorite writers well, all the time."

"He was an interesting man, Cervantes. The writer, not the teacher," she clarified.

"Don't know much about him," I admitted.

"He was poor most his life, and most of his work written in the years before his death."

"Isn't that the case with most great writers?" I handed her back the slip of paper.

"You have a point," she agreed, matter of fact. "What happened to your hand?"

"Nothing," I moved it to my lap. "Just an accident."

"What kind of accident?"

"The kind that never should've happened."

"Sounds like there's a story there?"

"Not really."

"Does it hurt?"

"It's fine, thank you for asking. Now," I shifted the conversation back to her for a second time. "How about I give you a tour of the campus?"

"If we must," she exhaled and got up, slinging her backpack over her shoulder.

"Great," I got up from the desk and grabbed my phone. "Shall we?"

Niña was quiet as we made our way down the hall, barely acknowledging when I pointed out the cafeteria, gym, and library. "It's a pretty easy campus to navigate," I said fondly, remembering how it had once been new to me, too. "You should get the hang of it pretty quickly."

"It's small," Niña looked around.

"I'm sure its smaller than your school back home, but it's a fun place."

"I wish I were there, now," she said wistfully, looking around.

I stopped and turned to face her. "Would you mind if I offered a little advice?"

"You're the teacher."

"Sometimes life changes and it can be really hard. But sometimes, that change can lead you someplace new."

"Is that from one of those motivational posters in

the office?"

"Are you talking about the one by the front desk with the kitten hanging from a tree that reads, 'hang in there'?"

Niña's lips pulled slightly upward, and while it wasn't a smile, it wasn't a frown, and I considered it a win.

"Give it a chance," I suggested.

"I guess it is the task at hand," she exhaled.

This girl was either old for her age or left to manage the world on her own for a while. Either way, the result was an overly confident young woman that felt she should be anywhere but exactly where one her age should be.

"Why don't we meet for the next few weeks...until you get settled?" Something told me this student could use a bit of guidance.

She opened her mouth to answer, but the bell overhead rang, and doors up and down the hall began flinging open, students pouring out.

"Perfect," I smiled as the sound of lockers opening, and excited voices, filled the hall. "You're just in time."

Niña followed my eyes across the way, to a door covered in multi-colored flyers. "There?" she pointed, looking at the classroom in dissatisfaction.

"That's your AP Spanish class."

I stood with her, waiting for the last student to exit, and once the classroom was empty, knocked on the door and introduced her to Mr. Cervantes.

He welcomed her to the class and the two began speaking with one another in Spanish, and when done, she took a seat, reached into her backpack, and removed a black notebook.

"See you Friday," I called out as I prepared to leave. Sticking her finger up in acknowledgement, she opened the notebook and began scribbling.

As I started my way down the hall, it was hard not to feel the infectious energy of the students around me. The nervous laughter of the girls, and the loud shouting of the boys, was like the fountain of youth. It reminded me of being a teenager, and the excitement of those years.

Just before turning the corner, I stopped to look at the oversized trophy case on the wall, filled with awards and photos from years past, including one from an assembly the year we graduated. I didn't have to look hard to find the five of us because I knew where we were in the picture. We were always together, and I remembered that assembly well.

Placing my hand on the glass, I warmed with the memory of that day; the feel of Lisa's shoulder pressed against my arm on one side, and Evan's leg pressing against mine on the other.

"You going to miss this?" Evan whispers in my ear over the thunderous roar of applause shaking the walls of the gymnasium.

Seconds earlier, Lisa jumped up from her seat next to me and ran to the center of the court, pom poms waving.

"You have no idea," I turn to him, his eyes intent on mine.

"Then don't go," he says simply; words clear, despite the noise around us.

"We have to graduate," I shake my head and smile.

"That's not..." he looks at me then stops as music fills the gym, cutting him off.

Lisa and the other cheerleaders have started their routine, triggering whistles and hollers from everyone around us.

Pulling my hand back, I reached into my pocket and grabbed my cell phone to call Evan.

"Hey," he answered on the third ring.

"Busy?"

"Never for you. What's up?"

"Remember the spring assembly, senior year?"

"The one where I started to ask you not to go to LA?"

Evan and I once spent the night sharing all the

times that we had wanted to tell the other how we felt over the years. The list was long and began in elementary school and continued through to college.

The assembly had been a big one for Evan. It was the first time he'd actually begun asking me not to go to California. Only, he didn't finish, and had gone on to wonder for the next three years, what would've happened if he had.

"That's the one," I nodded.

"Is that picture still in the trophy case at the end of the main hall?"

"Yep," I smiled. "How'd you know?"

"That's the legends case and the assembly they presented Tony with his All-American award. And, I might add, the year our team took state. First time in thirty years."

"Was that last part supposed to be an imitation of Principal Edwards' voice?"

"Did it not sound like it?"

"Um, no," I laughed. "Never do that again."

"That bad?"

"Worse."

"Okay," he laughed back. "Man, that seems like so long ago."

"It does," I agreed, looking up and down the hall. It was growing quiet again as doors began closing and classes resumed.

"Still there?" Evan asked.

"I'm here."

"You, okay?"

"Mm-hmm," I stepped back from the case. "Just...thought I'd call."

"Memory?"

"Yeah," I exhaled. "But a good one."

"Are you sure?"

"Yup," I confirmed. "I'll let you get back to work."

"Okay babe. Love you."

"Me too," I smiled to myself and hung up.

Turning again to the trophy case, I stared at the picture. Losing Caleb, Lisa, and Timmy had been hard, but my mother and Evan were right. What happened to me was significant. The heaviness of that night I didn't just carry *in* my heart, but *on* my soul.

The memories of the dead may live on in the hearts of the living but escaping death could haunt one's soul. How could I have not considered that fact, all this time? Even more curious, I wondered, how long would that truth have stayed in the shadows, had I not been brave enough to confront it?

CHAPTER SEVEN

"HERE WE ARE," EVAN SAID AS WE PULLED INTO THE parking lot at *Fiero's* later that night. The pizza parlor was popular with the locals, and at this time, anyone inside would be a familiar face.

"I'm glad we're doing this," I hopped out of Evan's Jeep. I was looking forward to a night with Sam and Tony.

"Me too," Evan shoved the keys into the pocket of his jeans and stuck out a hand.

"Think they'll be surprised?" I asked, reaching for it with my uninjured one.

"Oh, I think so," Evan smiled and pulled the door open.

It'd been hard not to say anything to Sam when we exchanged texts earlier in the day to confirm plans for tonight, and I was anxious to tell her.

"And Tony doesn't know anything?" I asked as

we stepped inside.

"Nope," Evan smiled and looked around.

Thankfully, Tony and Sam had gotten there early to grab a place to sit. The Red Sox were playing the Yankees, and a crowd had gathered to watch the game on the big screen. It looked to be standing room only.

"Yo, guys," Tony called from a booth towards the back, waving both hands. Evan stuck a hand up in acknowledgement and steered me through the crowd with the other.

"Hey brother," Tony got up as we approached.

"What's the score?" Evan asked, shrugging out of his vest, and pushing up the sleeves of his shirt.

"Two to one, Sox."

"Alright," he gave Tony a high-five.

"Laney," Tony smiled, reaching to give me a hug. "How are you, doll?"

"I'm good. Where's your better half?"

"Aw, you wound me," he reached into the bucket of beer on the table and handed one to Evan. "She's grabbing another round. Want one?"

"Yes, please. Although you'll have help me," I held up my injured hand.

"What happened?"

"Accident."

"Does that mean I have a chance at beating you

tonight?" he removed the cap from the bottle and handed it to me.

I was famously good at darts. My father had a board in his study, and I'd play whenever he was in there working. Tony on the other hand, was horrible, and had been trying to beat me for the past year.

"Didn't hurt my throwing hand," I said cheekily as he removed the cap and handed me the bottle.

I grabbed it with my good hand and his eyes widened. "What's that?" he pointed to my finger.

"What's what?" Sam echoed as she approached the table, bucket in hand. Then she saw what Tony was pointing at and screamed. "Omigod!"

"Let me get that," Evan laughed and grabbed the bucket, setting it down on the table.

"You're engaged?" she asked excitedly.

"Yes!" I smiled wide.

"Really?" Tony looked at Evan.

"Yes, really," Evan laughed.

"Oh, man, this is huge!" Tony leaned in to give me a hug, and then grabbed Evan's shoulder, giving it a squeeze. "Congrats, brother!"

"Thanks man," Evan nodded and the two hit the necks of their beer bottles together.

"Let me see the ring," Sam motioned for me to stick out my hand.

I stuck it out and she grabbed it and pulled it closer to see. "Oh Laney," she swooned, "it's gorgeous!"

"Thank you," I blushed.

"It looks like it was made for you. Was it?" she asked Evan.

"It's been in my family for years."

"Can I dig around the family jewels sometime?" Tony joked.

"That's all there is my friend."

"Somehow, I doubt it," he laughed, lifting his beer to take a sip.

"Never know, brother," Evan clapped Tony on the back.

"Can't blame a guy for trying."

"That you can't," the two laughed.

"Oh, you two," Sam shushed them. "I want to hear everything, and don't leave out anything. I want every...detail."

"And...there they go," Tony shook his head, and he and Evan turned their attention to the TV to watch the game.

"Lanes," Sam gushed. "Seriously, that ring is gorgeous."

"I know," I admitted, looking at the ring for the hundredth time today.

"Did you know?"

"Not at all."

"Really?"

"I mean, sure, we've talked about the future, but honestly, I had no idea he was planning to propose."

"When did it happen?"

"Sunday, during our run."

"Sunday?" she smacked me on the arm. "You waited until today to tell me?"

"We wanted to tell you in person."

"Well," she eased, "that's true. Hearing on the phone would've sucked."

I laughed and nodded, picking at the bottle's label with my bandaged hand, absentmindedly.

"Omigod!" she shrieked again.

"What?" I jumped.

"Your hand...what happened?"

"Oh," I pulled it back down to my lap, smile fading. "A stupid accident."

"Are you okay?"

"Yeah, just a cut...keep forgetting about it, actually."

Sam took a sip of her beer, looking at me from over the bottle. "Well, maybe Tony will finally have a chance at beating you at darts tonight."

"I already told him it's not my throwing hand."

Sam laughed. "Did you pick a date yet?" she

asked, focusing her attention back on the engagement.

"You sound like our mothers."

"Oh, I bet they're going to have a field day."

"It's already begun," I reached for my own beer, taking a sip. "We'd only been engaged an hour and they wanted to know if I had picked out a dress."

"They're excited," she smiled. "Can't blame them."

"I don't. But this was right after he proposed. Can you imagine what they will be like in a month?"

Sam laughed again. "How did he do it? Was it romantic?" she asked, eyes dancing.

"It was," I blushed, remembering every word of his proposal.

"You're playing this cool, but you're over the moon, aren't you?" she nudged me with her arm.

"I'm anything but cool."

"I'd be jumping out of my skin," Sam grinned.

"Oh, I am." I looked over to Evan and feeling a tug on the invisible thread that connected us, he turned and winked.

"I knew it!" she pointed at me. "I could see how crazy you two were about each other in high school. Everybody could."

"Well, you and Tony are pretty adorable, too."

"Sure," she nodded. "But we're not you and Evan. No one is. You're...perfect."

"No one is perfect," I looked again at Evan; knowing well in the equation of us, he was the flawless factor.

"If you say so," she smiled, then looked at the bandage on my hand. "Okay. So, I need something for my column this week. What's the real story with that hand?"

Sam was a reporter at *The Current*. Her column was sharp and witty, and she had a talent for making small town news seem exciting.

"I dropped something at my mom's shop."

"That's it?"

"That's it."

"Darn," she pouted, then looked down at my ring, and brightened.

"No," I protested, knowing exactly what she was about to say.

"Oh, come on, a wedding announcement is just what I need!"

"Our mothers want to have an engagement party."

"So, let them."

"Wouldn't an announcement scoop a party?"

"Wedding announcements can be profiles of the couple...a story of how you met, your life together, pictures looking blissfully happy. A party is more about showing your ring off to everyone."

"I don't know…"

"Oh, come on! Everyone adores you two. You're Lake Haven's favorite couple. Your engagement is big news."

"Now you *really* sound like my mother," I rolled my eyes.

"Please?" she pressed her hands together.

"I'll think about it."

"Deal," she held her bottle out and we clinked them together. "Look," she pointed at Evan and Tony, changing the subject. "They look like twins from behind."

Sure enough, the two were standing exactly the same—one hand shoved in their front pocket, beer bottle in the other, and heads slightly tilted to the right.

"I'm glad Evan has Tony," I confessed.

"Are you kidding. Tony is lucky to have Evan. He adores the guy. And I, you."

"Aw, Sam," I pretended to wipe a tear from my eye.

"I mean it," she laughed.

"Okay, okay," I laughed back. "In all seriousness, I feel the same. I'm lucky to have you in my life. We're both, lucky to have you in our lives.

Which is why…" I paused, the idea coming to me suddenly. "I want you to be my maid of honor."

"What?" she slammed her bottle down, beer foam splattering across the table.

"Yes!" I nodded emphatically. "I want you to be part of our special day."

"Laney," she wiped the drops from the table with her hand. "Are you serious?"

"Do you even have to ask?"

Sam threw her arms around me and squealed with delight.

"Hey, what are we missing?" Tony and Evan turned around. A commercial was on, and a couple of heads had turned, hearing her scream.

"Laney asked me to be her maid of honor!"

"Oh yeah," Tony smiled. "Well, right on. I'll have the cutest arm candy, then."

"You didn't," I grinned at Evan.

"I did," he smiled back. "Tony's going to be my best man."

"Great minds think alike," I laughed.

"Hey everybody," Evan called out, and pointed at me. "This beautiful lady has agreed to be my wife!" The room erupted in a round of applause. "Drinks on me!"

Evan waved for the bartender to put the drinks on his tab, and I turned to Sam, apologetically.

"There goes your story."

"Oh," she waved her hand. "I'm going to be your maid of honor. That trumps a story, anytime."

"Our moms are going to be so angry," I smiled at Evan as he leaned down to give me a kiss.

"They'll get over it," he whispered. "It's our life, remember?"

"Our life," I nodded, then turned and shouted, "I'm getting married!"

The bar erupted into another round of applause and Evan looked at me, eyes dancing. "You and me...always."

"You and me," I agreed, and kissed him again.

"Alright, you two," Sam chided. "It's time for that one to show you how much he's improved since your last match."

"What about the game?" I asked.

"Sox have this in the bag," Tony smiled.

"Oh yeah?"

"Sure," he rubbed his hands together. "I've been waiting to show you how much I've improved."

"Alright then," I grabbed my beer in my good hand. "Twenty bucks. Best out of five?"

"I do believe the lady has thrown out the gauntlet, my friend," Evan laughed.

"You're on Thomas!" Tony turned his ballcap backwards.

"Good luck!" Evan called and he slid into the booth next to Sam, and Tony and I made our way through the crowd to the bar.

"You can get the next round," Tony said as he shoved a couple of dollars into an oversized glass and grabbed two cups of darts.

"Sounds good," we pushed through the back door and stepped onto the patio. With everyone inside watching the game, the space was ours and we had our pick of dartboards.

"Ladies first," Tony opened up one closest to the door, then set the cups down on one of the high tables nearby.

"I'm fine if you want to go first."

"No way," he rapped a knuckle on the tabletop. "You're up."

"Alright," I reached inside one of the cups and removed the darts, stepping up to the makeshift throw line taped on the floor.

It wasn't too hard to manage with my injured hand not being my throwing hand, but I was trying to move it as little as possible. I knew if I aggravated it again, I'd be looking at stitches, and didn't want that to happen. Holding it level at my waist, I took my first shot.

"Man, Evan really upped the game with that ring," Tony said casually, as the dart sailed through the air, hitting close to the bullseye.

"It's not going to work," I shook off his attempt to distract me.

"Guess not," he laughed. "Doesn't it weigh your hand down, though?"

"Nope," I grabbed my next dart.

"Anything I buy Sam will be small potatoes compared to that rock."

"What?" I turned around as it was leaving my hand.

"Oh, damn!" Tony put his hand over his mouth as it hit the bullseye. "Even with no eyes on the board the lady is a legend. I don't know how you do it, Thomas."

"Are you going to propose to Sam?" I asked excitedly.

"Sure," he nodded, taking a sip of his beer.

"When?"

"Sometime in the future."

"Do you have something planned?"

"Not yet."

"Why not?"

"This is your time to be in the spotlight...you and Ev."

"That's not necessary. Sweet, but if you want to propose to Sam, you should."

"Nah," he waved off the idea. "You two are the

best and deserve for it to be about you for a while. Now, enough with the niceties," he nodded to the board and winked. "Take your next shot."

"Okay," I laughed and turned, shooting my last dart. It hit in the same spot as the previous.

"Man," he looked at the board in disbelief. "You're hustling me."

"Maybe," I walked up to the board and removed my darts. "Alright, you're up."

Tony stepped up to the line and took his first shot. It landed near the outer ring. "Someone has been practicing," I nodded, impressed.

"You noticed."

"Well, you're hitting the board, not the wall. That had to take practice."

"Cheap shot, Lanes," Tony laughed, as he reached for his next dart.

"All is fair in love and darts," I blew him a kiss.

We continued to rib one another for the next couple of games, both of which I won.

"And to think I was planning to give you a sympathy round," he said as we began our next game.

"Come again?" I laughed.

He nodded to my injured hand. "What happened?"

"Dumb accident," I said as I stepped up to the

line to take my first shot.

"No, what *really* happened," he watched as my dart sailed straight into the bullseye.

"Nothing," I insisted.

"Nothing, huh," he eyed me curiously as I took my next shot, hitting another bullseye. "Well, whatever it was, you sure look to be taking it out on the board."

"What makes you say that?"

"You're concentrating. You never concentrate."

I shot my third dart, hitting the board, dead center. "Bam…that's three in a row, Spencer! How's that for concentrating?"

"Yeah, yeah," he waved me away as I went to remove my darts. "So, really…what's up?" he asked with a bit more seriousness when I returned.

Tony was right. Although, not about concentrating. Something had been sitting in the back of my mind all day, and I'd been trying hard to ignore it. And it wasn't the dart game, or even my mother's suggestion I consider counseling. It was Dean.

While I knew the person I ran into today, wasn't the same as the version of him I knew in that world I experienced when my heart stopped, I couldn't ignore the powerful wave of déjà vu that hit me the moment he walked into my mother's shop. Maybe if

I knew who Dean was now, I could separate fact from fiction and forget about him altogether.

I stared at the dart in my hand. "Do you remember Dean?" I asked finally.

"Danvers?" he asked. I nodded and looked up. "Sure," he put his foot behind the line and prepared to take his first shot. "Mom runs the gift shop and dad works on the docks."

"That's him," I watched his dart sail to the board. "Nice shot," I whistled when it hit close to the bullseye. "You really *have* been practicing."

"Thank you kindly," he bowed. "What about him?"

"I ran into him this morning."

Tony turned to me quickly. "With your car?"

"No," I rolled my eyes. "At my mother's shop."

"Oh," he laughed and turned again to the board. "Did he move back?"

"Don't know. He didn't say."

Tony steadied his hand for his next shot. "Well, sometimes people just want to be where everyone knows their name."

"Thanks for that earworm."

"You're welcome," he tipped an imaginary hat, then shot the dart in his hand.

"Did you know him well in school?"

"Not really. You?" Tony asked, his last dart

sailing to the board, landing in no score territory.

"Not really. I knew his sister a bit. She was on cheer with Lisa."

"Nellie," Tony nodded. "That's right. She had a thing for Tyler. Speaking of, did you hear his dad is selling the store?"

"No! Really?"

Garrity's had been the town's grocery store for 150 years, and the idea of it becoming a chain store made me sad.

"Yup. Tyler's moving to Florida so there's no one to take over when his old man retires next year."

"What's in Florida?"

"The sun," he laughed. "But yeah, it's a shame," Tony agreed, walking to the board to remove his darts. "Oldest shop aside from Hannaford's. Great ice cream in the summer. Wait…what were we talking about?"

"Oh," I cleared my throat. "Danvers."

"Right, Dean," he put his darts down on the table. "He's back you said?"

"He was at the shop when this happened," I held up my injured hand.

"Oh yeah?"

"He scared me, and—"

"What do you mean, he scared you?"

"Didn't see him standing there and it startled me." He pressed his lips together and looked at me. "What?" I asked.

"What?" he asked in return.

"What is that for?"

"Nothing," he knocked on the table. "Ready to go again?"

"Not yet," I held off on grabbing my darts. "What was that look you gave me for?" I asked again.

"Give me a second," he closed his eyes.

"For?"

"To think."

"About?"

"Give me a second," he laughed. "I'm getting older. It takes me awhile. Okay," he said finally, opening his eyes again.

"Okay, what?"

"It's nothing. Never mind."

"Never mind? Tony, have you lost your mind?"

"It's nothing," he insisted. "Really."

"Spill it, Spencer."

"We're not playing until I tell you, are we?"

"Nope."

"Okay," he exhaled. "I was just trying to remember if he was a member of your fan club back in high school."

"My *what*?" I laughed; not sure I'd heard him correctly.

"Guys that wanted to ask you out."

"I think you're confusing me with Lisa. She's the one who had guys lining up at her feet."

"Sure," he nodded. "Because they could."

"What?" I asked, his riddled response confusing me.

"Darts," he pointed to the board. "I'm getting better, right?"

"Tony..."

"It doesn't matter now, does it?"

"You brought it up."

"Yeah, but it was such a long time ago. And it's not what I was thinking."

"It was a long time ago," I agreed. "And I'm not sure if you remember or not, but I didn't have any kind of fan club. I didn't get asked out a lot...or well, ever."

"Yeah...and there's a reason."

"And that reason would be?" Tony looked inside and I followed his eyes. "Evan?"

"Bingo," he held up a dart in confirmation.

"I'm so confused."

"Look," he smiled. "There were plenty of guys that wanted to ask you out in high school, but they didn't, because they knew better."

"Because of Evan?"

"Yup."

"Well, he's always been overprotective."

"It was more than that. He didn't want you dating anyone. And I mean, anyone."

Tony wasn't telling me anything I didn't already know. Evan had always cared about me, and I him. But I had no clue the extent to which he'd let others know those feelings.

"He wanted to do everything with you.... including Homecoming."

"Homecoming?" I repeated, straightening.

"When the ballots for Senior Court were distributed and your name wasn't on it ...man, I'd never seen Evan angry before, and wow, was he pissed."

"Wait," I placed my hand on Tony's arm. "Why did he think my name would be on it?"

My name *had* been on the ballot, but I'd erased it before making copies for voting. I'd sworn Timmy to secrecy and assumed we were the only ones who ever knew.

"Because Evan made sure it was on there."

"What?" I asked in surprise.

"Yup," Tony nodded. "And it wasn't hard to get it on there, either. Everyone adored you."

"But he knew how badly Lisa wanted to be

Queen."

"Yeah, well," Tony shrugged. "Evan wanted *you* to be the one standing up there next to him."

My chest tightened with regret for that moment which never was. But I didn't know what that had to do with fan clubs or Dean Danvers?

"How is any of this related to Dean?" I asked. Did the possible answer to the long-unsolved question of why Dean had showed up in my near-death experience, hang in the air?

I'd read once, that our subconscious was its own world. Had Dean liked me in school and Evan knew? Maybe that small kernel of knowledge had imbedded itself into my mind and twisted itself into the version of Dean that pursued me in that world I went to when my heart stopped.

"No," Tony smiled. "That would've been me."

"You?" I exhaled, my shoulders easing like a balloon losing air.

It was a relief to hear there wasn't an unexplained connection between me and Dean that I wasn't aware of, and that his presence in my near-death experience was still nothing more than just, randomness.

"Evan was my boy and the two of you were endgame," Tony explained. "I knew it. We all knew it. I just, helped make sure nothing stood in your way. That's what I was trying to remember earlier...if I had ever spoken to him about you, and, I remembered I didn't. Like I said, everyone knew better."

"Because of you."

"It's what friends are for."

"Does Evan know about this so-called fan club?"

"Of course," he nodded.

"And does he know you threatened every guy in school on his behalf?"

"I didn't threaten, I merely talked. And no," he stepped up to the line, preparing for our next game. "He doesn't. Although, at the end of the day, none of it really matters anymore. It's ancient history. You two are getting married!"

Tony was right. Evan and I *were* endgame, and no version of Dean would ever get in the way of that truth.

"Man," I exhaled. "I wish I'd known all this."

"Why?" Tony laughed.

"High school would've been different."

"How so?"

"I wouldn't have been so naïve. Maybe asked a few guys out."

"One, that would have never happened," he laughed. "You were every bit as crazy about Evan, as he was you. And two, we *were* young and naïve.

Having an issue with a guy who liked the girl we liked," he laughed. "That's some high school level stuff right there. But that's what we're supposed to be at that age, right?"

Tony pulled his hand back and released the dart. It sailed fast to the board, landing close to the bullseye. "Did you see that?" he turned to me excitedly, pointing at the board.

"I did," I nodded approvingly. "Well done."

"The student has become the master."

"Well," I laughed. "Let's not push it."

"Loser buys next round," he challenged.

"You can't grab your wallet while shooting."

"Oh, come on," he laughed.

"Alright," I held up my hand. "Shoot."

"Just watch," he threw his dart. It sailed through the air, and while it looked as if may hit dead center, it shied to the left.

"Looks like you're buying."

"What kind of gentleman would I be if I let the lady buy anyways," he shrugged. "Alright, be right back."

I looked inside to the large crowd gathered at the bar. "You may be awhile."

"What's the point of these long arms if I can't get what I need."

"Hey Tony?" I called as he started to make his

way inside.

"Yeah?"

"Thanks."

"For?"

"Being a friend to me, even when I didn't know it."

"I got your back, Thomas," he gave me a thumbs up, then turned back around and headed to the bar.

CHAPTER EIGHT

THE SOUND OF LAUGHTER CARRIED ACROSS THE WATER, and into the night. The storm that threatened offshore had changed course, clearing the skies, leaving a beautiful night. Excited by the change, Evan suggested we order a pizza to go after the game ended and head to the boat. After grabbing a couple of six packs at the all-night liquor store down by the docks, we settled into the benches on deck and cracked open the pizza.

"Lanes," Sam held up the lid. "Another slice?"

"I'm good," I held up my hand; too drunk on the stars to care about food. The sky was bright, the light, endless.

"Now this, was a great idea," Tony sat back, stretching out his long legs.

Evan sat next to me, resting his hand gently on my thigh. "I'm glad the weather heard our plea," he looked up. "Nothing better than this."

"It's pretty perfect," I agreed.

"Ev, another beer?" Tony reached into the six pack and held out a bottle.

"Sure," Evan reached for it. "Thanks."

"Least I can do. Provide the brew, while you provide this view."

Evan laughed, shaking his head. "Think the Sox are going to do it?" he asked. "After tonight they're only a few games away from the playoffs."

"I think they may," Tony took a sip of beer. "Although, I hate to jinx it."

"I hear you," Evan popped the cap from his bottle. "About time, too. Their last few years have been disappointing."

"That they have my friend," Tony leaned back.

"I'm so glad that storm passed," Sam took a bite of the slice of pizza in her hand. "I was dreading it. I could another month or two before the newsroom turns into nothing but weather reports and snow conditions."

"We were just talking about that this afternoon," I sighed. "I think an early winter may be headed our way."

"You never know," Tony smiled. "We could be in for a heat wave. You know how weird the weather is around here."

"True," I looked out across the cove. The water

was like glass, the passing storm leaving no evidence of its existence.

"Did you do something different since the last time we were here?" Sam asked, looking around.

Evan called the boat's restoration a marathon, not a race, and had lovingly worked on it over the past seven years. He was always doing something here and there but hadn't spent time on it lately because of all the hours he was putting in at the hotel.

"Nope," Evan leaned back. "Same as the last time you were here."

"I could've sworn..." she pretended to look around and then turned her eyes to my hand. "Oh, my bad, it's the Rock of Gibraltar on Laney's hand," she laughed. "*That's* what's new."

"Man, you guys are getting married," Tony smiled. "That's wild."

"How is that wild?" Sam asked, brows pinched.

"Not wild bad," he clarified, and her face eased. "Wild as in...man, we're getting old. Soon, we will have kids, and then before you know it, we will be taking those kids to school, coaching their Little League teams..."

"That sounds great, right there," the heat of Evan's hand spread up my leg.

"Speaking of school," Tony lifted his bottle,

taking another sip. "How is it being back at Lake Haven High?"

"I love it."

"Yeah?"

"Yeah," I nodded. "The students are so young and excited about everything. Except this new student that just arrived."

"New family in town?" Sam asked, curious.

"Not sure," I admitted. "File says she's staying with a relative, but I don't have much more information than that."

"No one in Lake Haven has heard anything?"

"Nope."

"Strange," Sam pressed her lips together, and I could practically see her reporter wheels turning.

I too, felt it was odd. If there was a new person in town, everyone knew their backstory, before they even arrived.

"Not sure *what* the story is, but I just want to help her while she's here."

"That's why you were the perfect person for that job," Evan smiled at me lovingly. "You care about people."

"You're biased."

"No," Sam agreed. "You love to help people. Always have. Do you remember Founders Day, junior year, when Millie's oven broke?"

"Oh," Evan grimaced, and closed his eyes. "Don't remind me."

"Do I know this one?" Tony asked.

"When Laney found out," Sam continued, "she asked everyone in our class to bake two pies that night."

Millie owned the bakery in town. Her pies were award-winning, and a staple of the weekend that celebrated our town's founding.

"Um," I laughed. "Without pie, Founders Day would've been any old weekend."

"Oh, for sure," Sam agreed. "A festival without pie is just a gathering in the street. But not everyone in school could bake. When I showed up to *Millie's* for my shift the following afternoon, there were all these pies. Only, they weren't pies. More like, sheets of slop."

"I forgot you worked there in high school," Tony smiled in recollection.

"How could you forget? You got more than your fair share of free donuts."

"Sugar from my sugar," he winked.

"You...should...have...heard Millie," Sam continued. "She was about to close the shop and move."

"Oh, I know," Evan nodded. "My dad sent me to the hotel that night to open the kitchen for her.

When she arrived, she was frantic, rattling off what she needed; calculating the number of pies she could bake if she used every oven. I was there all night, while Millie commanded me to stir faster...add more spice...check the timer."

"You helped her?" I looked at Evan in disbelief.

"Yeah," he nodded.

"But...why?"

"It was important to you."

"You never told me this."

"I didn't?"

"No, you didn't," I smiled, recalling how tired Evan had looked at Founders Day that year. "Is that why you hate pumpkin pie now?"

"Guilty. The kitchen at the hotel smelled like it for months."

Just when I thought it wasn't possible to love Evan more than I did. "You're something else."

"Something, good?"

"Oh," I leaned down, and whispered in his ear. "Something very, very good." He gave my thigh another squeeze, and it shot electricity through me.

"That's your girl," Tony smiled. "Most generous heart on the planet."

"That it is," Evan locked his eyes on mine.

The laugher softened, as the boat swayed gently beneath us. "I took a look at what you sent over earlier," Tony said, breaking the silence.

" And?" Evan asked.

"I like it. I have a thought or two. I'll shoot them to you in the morning."

"Sounds good. Thanks."

"That's my job," Tony held up his beer.

I was proud of Evan for how hard he was working on the hotel's expansion. Especially his focus on making sure it helped the local community. I was most proud, however, on his choosing Tony to serve as project manager.

Tony had always dreamed of a career in baseball. When the Minor Leagues recruited him out of high school, it looked like that dream would come true. Unfortunately, a torn rotator cuff midway through his first season, cut it tragically short.

When Tony returned home, the boy's high school baseball coach was the first person to show up on his doorstep, with a handful of college applications in hand. He enrolled in school, just as Evan and I started our second year of college, and with the delay of our last year due to the accident, the three of us wound up graduating around the same time.

Tony had majored in business, like Evan, and had a knack for bringing people together.

Combined with Evan's vision, they were the perfect team to make the hotel expansion a success.

"Hey," Sam leaned her head back. "No talking business tonight. We're celebrating."

"That business," Tony smiled at Sam, "is going to change lives."

"I hope it will change a lot of lives," Evan added.

"Amen to that," Tony agreed.

"Like I said," I looked at Evan, filled with pride. "You are incredible."

"Oh, get a room," Sam joked.

"Don't tempt me," Evan laughed.

"I got something that will cool us off," I smiled slyly.

"What are you thinking?" Evan eyed me suspiciously

"You guys up for a little midnight swim?" I asked, standing up and kicking off my shoes.

"Are you kidding?" Evan straightened.

"Count me in!" Tony jumped up.

"It's not midnight," Sam looked from me to Tony as if we were crazy.

"Evan's got some swim trunks below deck if you want Tony. And Sam, you can borrow one of mine."

"Who needs suits," Tony laughed as he slipped out of his jeans.

"I don't think Laney wants to see what you've

got," Sam laughed.

"We'll turn the lights off," I suggested.

"Count me out," Sam shook her head.

"Ev?" I asked.

"What about your hand?"

"It's fine," I shrugged.

"You're crazy."

"Am not. Come on," I pulled my shirt overhead. "It'll be fun!"

Evan spit out his beer and jumped up quickly to switch off the starboard and port side lights, just in time for me to wriggle out of my pants and run excitedly to the front of the boat in my bra and underwear.

"Last one in buys the next round!" I shouted, before pushing off the deck and slicing through the icy water, and Tony followed.

"That's cold!" I heard him holler as I was coming up for air.

"You'll get used to it," I laughed, going back underwater. It skimmed over my body like silk, as I swam below the surface.

Evan and Sam looked down from the boat, shaking their heads as Tony and I laughed and splashed each other.

"She's right," Tony waved at Sam. "It feels great once you get used to it. Come on in!"

"I'm good," she lifted her bottle and took a sip.

"Aw, come on," I dared. "You don't know what you're missing."

"You, I've seen," she pointed to Tony. "And you," she laughed again, "I don't need to see."

"I'm not naked," I tugged on the strap of my bra.

"Oh yeah," Tony laughed and tossed his shorts up on deck.

"Tony!" Sam shrieked as they landed by her.

"Is that a challenge?" I asked, raising an eyebrow.

"You wouldn't?" Evan grinned.

"Wouldn't I?"

I slipped my underwear off under the water, then flicked them up towards the boat.

"Laney," he spit out his beer as he watched them land next to him on the deck.

"Atta girl!" Tony flashed me a thumbs up as I released the snap of my bra and tossed it up to the deck, as well.

"What's going on?" Sam turned to Evan, laughing.

"I have no idea," he looked down at me and Tony, shaking his head with laughter.

Tony splashed around, going under the water and back up. "Keep your eyes closed," Evan warned, jokingly.

"It's too dark to see anything," he laughed.

"The girl gets engaged and goes crazy," Sam laughed. "I hope you know what you're in for, Evan."

"Oh, I know," he looked down at me and flashed a brilliant smile.

"Sure, you don't want to join us?"

"I'm enjoying the view from here," he smiled.

"Party poopers."

"They really are," Tony agreed, treading water.

"So," Sam shot Tony a wry look. "How do you plan on getting out?"

"The ladder."

"No one wants to see that."

"Are you kidding?" he laughed. "Everyone wants a drink of this tall glass of water."

"Stop," I grinned. "It's hard to tread water while laughing."

"Well, to be honest," he held his hand next to his mouth so that only I could hear what he was saying. "I was wondering how I'd get out without flashing you."

"I'll close my eyes."

"Can I trust you? You're not a married woman yet."

"Never know. I have a lot to make up for, apparently."

We both laughed and he swam over closer to talk out of earshot from Evan and Sam. "I hope I didn't embarrass you earlier...about the whole high school fan club thing."

"Not at all. It makes me feel a bit better, actually."

"Yeah?"

"Sure. All those years I felt like I was invisible. It's nice to know I wasn't."

"Trust me," he smiled. "You weren't."

"Can I tell you something?"

"Shoot."

"I don't think it's sunk in, that Evan and I are engaged. I had to pinch myself earlier to make sure I wasn't dreaming."

"I know what you mean," Tony moved his arms back and forth to tread water. "I felt like that in the Minors. Those first weeks ...man," he smiled. "Every time I ran onto the field, I wanted to pinch myself."

"You must miss it."

"I do," he nodded. "But I try not to dwell on the past. Can't waste the present trying to change things that already happened."

"You're right," I looked over at Evan. How often had he told me the same thing?

"Best advice he ever gave me," Tony added. I

turned to him, surprised by the confession. "He was there for me when everything happened with my arm, and I will never forget it," Tony confessed. "When I said he was one hell of a guy earlier, I meant it. There isn't anything I wouldn't do for him."

"He is pretty great," I agreed.

"And soon, you will be Mrs. Great," he laughed. I looked down into the water, my ring shining back at me in the night. "It's real," he splashed my face. "No matter how many times you pinch yourself or stare at that rock."

"Hey buddy," Sam called to Tony. "Time to get out. I've got an early deadline in the morning."

"Aw, man," he swam up to the boat. I turned my head as he climbed the ladder, then wrapped the towel Sam handed him, around his waist.

"Go get warmed up," Evan nodded below deck. "I'll put some coffee on."

"Like I said," Tony clapped him on the back and pointed. "Best guy on the planet."

I swam to the ladder and once Tony and Sam were below deck, climbed up. "Now that's a view," Evan grinned.

"Give me that," I laughed, reaching for the towel he held out to me.

"Oh, not so bold now, are you?" he pulled it

from my reach, playfully.

"If you don't give me that towel, I'll go below deck, in my birthday suit, and grab one myself."

"You wouldn't dare."

"Try me."

The grin on his lips grew wider. "What am I going to do with you?"

I grabbed the towel from his hands and wrapped it around me. "Anything you want."

After Tony and I dried off and changed back into our clothes, the four of us had a cup of coffee, then said goodnight.

"Well, my friends," Sam gave me a hug after stepping off the boat and onto the dock. "This was a great night. Congratulations again, I'm so happy for the two of you."

"Thanks," I squeezed her tight. "You two be okay walking back?"

Instead of driving home, Evan suggested we stay the night on the boat, but it meant both our car and theirs, were back at Fiero's.

"We'll be fine. Go and take care of that hand."

I'd removed the wet bandage after getting out of the water and needed to clean and wrap it. But other than that, it felt fine. The chilly water had taken the soreness out.

"Will do."

"Ev, my man," Tony gave Evan a fist bump. "Excellent night as always."

The two followed with a hug and a pat on the back, then Sam and Tony made their way up the dock. Once they faded from view, Evan and I headed below deck to get ready for bed.

After Evan cleaned my hand and wrapped a fresh bandage around it, I slipped into a pair of pajamas I kept on the boat for nights like this.

"What's on your mind, Davies?" I asked, feeling Evan watching me from where he sat on the edge of the bed.

"Just thinking back to our first night here."

I stopped buttoning my shirt remembering it well. The first night we ever spent together—that magical night when the stars aligned, and our hearts met—had been just like tonight.

Being with Evan made me feel alive, unlike *anyone* I'd ever been before; the combination of confidence and fulfillment, giving me the idea to do something unlike *anything* I'd ever done before.

He'd watched me that night, just as he did tonight—shaking his head, with a smile on his face—as I dove head-first into the icy water, naked, in the middle of the night.

"It feels so long ago," he leaned his head down and rested it against my stomach.

I ran my unscathed hand through his hair, thinking too, how these past two years felt like a lifetime.

"You cold?" he looked up at me, eyes soft.

"Not at all. You?"

"Not at all," he smiled.

"Tired?" I asked.

"No," his lips pulled into a smile. "You?"

"Not at all."

"Want to practice for that future Tony was talking about?"

"Practice does makes perfect."

Evan grinned and pushed open the unbuttoned half of my shirt, gently running a finger along the scar on my abdomen. It had faded with time, but it would never disappear. Not completely. It would always be there, to remind me of the past, and haunt my future.

During a routine check-up last year, my doctor warned of the potential effect scarring from my internal injuries might have on being able to conceive. She'd advised me to see a specialist, but I figured I'd deal with it later. But for the first time since that day in the doctor's office, her words came crashing to mind, and I realized later was now.

I'd not thought much about having kids until Evan and I happened, and then once we did, the life he wanted became one I wanted, too.

Evan had always talked about having a family, someday, and I knew that meant me. But I also knew, no matter what happened with my ability to give him that family he wanted, that he would love me unconditionally.

Still, as he looked up at me, eyes filled with need, I realized suddenly, there was nothing I wanted more.

Hours later, as I lie in bed, mind racing with the thought of the obstacles that could lie ahead, I couldn't stop myself from thinking—no matter how scary nightmares can be, it's the dreams which never come true, that could be the darkest of all.

CHAPTER NINE

THE NEXT MORNING, THE RINGING OF MY CELL PHONE woke me. I patted around the bed, before finding it on the nightstand.

"Lo?" I answered.

"A little birdie told me the cat's out of the bag," the cheerful voice of my mother responded on the other end.

"What time is it?" I asked sleepily, my lids heavy and head groggy.

"Seven," she said casually.

"Grapevine's early this morning," I wiped the sleep from my eyes.

I wasn't surprised someone would tell my mother about Evan's announcement at *Fiero's* last night. It was a full house, and small towns liked to talk. I just didn't think they started this early.

"Small town. Good news travels fast."

"Right," I yawned and turned to Evan's side of the bed, finding it empty.

"So, now we have to get a move on with save the dates," she continued.

"Save the dates?" I looked around, wondering where he was.

"For the engagement party." I sat up and yawned, the sleep beginning to lift. "We didn't think you two would want to keep it a secret for long," she continued. "But now that folks know, we really should send out an announcement and let people know the date and time of the party."

"Okay," I yawned again, the words announcement and party clear, but the rest running together.

"You two have fun last night with Tony and Sam?" she asked, changing the subject.

"We did."

"Are they happy for you two?"

"They are," I licked my lips, needing water and a strong cup of coffee. "Hey, mom, can I call you later?"

"Of course," she replied in her sing song voice. "Oh, before you go...how's the hand?"

I lifted it up, almost forgetting about the injury. "It's fine."

"Good. Okay, honey, talk to you later. And don't

forget, ask Ev about—"

Before she could finish, I hung up. I knew what she was about to say, and it was frankly, too early for any more party talk.

"Rise and shine," Evan called as he came down below deck, with a paper bag in one hand, and tray of coffees in the other.

That's where he went, I stretched and pushed the covers off me, as the smell of coffee filled the cabin.

"We used the rest of the coffee last night," Evan set the tray and bag down on the counter in the galley. He sounded more awake than I was and wondered how that could be possible. "And... after talking about *Millie's,* I woke up with a craving for muffins."

"A night of drinking will do that," I smiled and swung my legs over the side of the bed, both of us knowing well, that's not why he'd woke up with an appetite.

"Right," he winked.

"Regret your little skinny dip?" he asked, watching with bemusement as I made my way slowly to the counter.

"What makes you say that?"

"You look tired."

"I am," I grabbed one of the coffees and took a sip. It was hot and strong, and Evan had prepared it exactly as I liked. "This is just what I needed, thank you."

"My pleasure" he smiled, then took the other one. "It was quite a night."

"It was," my cheeks burned with the memory of his touch. "But I stayed up for a bit after you fell asleep."

"Bad dream?"

"No..." I played with the coffee sleeve. "Overactive mind."

"Oh?" he lifted his coffee to take a sip.

"I was ...thinking."

"About?"

"Kids."

"What about them?"

"Well, we've not talked about it much, and..."

"And?" he nodded for me to continue, taking another sip.

"And I was wondering, what the future looks like to you...where kids are concerned."

"Well," he leaned back against the counter. "I want a family, and I want it with you."

"How many kids do you want?"

"How many can we order?"

"I'm serious," I rolled my eyes.

"Okay," he laughed, and reached into the bag, pulling out a muffin. "In our future," he paused to take a bite, then continued once he'd finished chewing. "We have a daughter, who has me wrapped around her finger. She can thank her mom for that. And we have a son. He's a spitfire," he smiled. "Loves his mom, and baseball, and brags about his Uncle Tony all the time."

"Do we have a dog?" I asked, feeling myself getting excited about Evan's vision of the future.

"Yes," he nodded emphatically. "You wanted something small and lovable. I wanted something big...to protect my girls."

"Where do we live?"

"We built a house on that abandoned lot across the way from where we are now. It took some time, but we love it."

"Wow...you've given this some real thought."

"Just a bit," he smiled. "Haven't you?"

"Yes," I admitted.

"And?"

"Well...there's you and me."

"That's a good start," he smiled.

"We have a son," I continued. "He's the sweetest little guy and he adores his dad." Even though it was just a fantasy, I felt strong adoration for the little boy I could see in my mind, with Evan's eyes. "And we live where we do now, only its ours—we bought it."

"Sounds good," Evan beamed.

"Yours sounds pretty good, too."

"Either will be perfect."

I turned my attention to the countertop, drawing a line between two speckles. "What if perfect isn't possible?"

"What do you mean?"

"What if," I looked back up, finding his eyes on mine, "neither one of those beautiful futures, are possible?"

Evan looked at me, puzzled, then his expression softened, as he understood what I was saying.

He set the muffin down and wiped the crumbs from his hands. "No matter what life throws at us, we'll get through it together. That's the deal, right?" I nodded, knowing that's what he'd say. "Besides, we've got plenty of time. That's down the line."

"Down the line?"

"Sure," he shrugged. "Did you think I wanted kids tomorrow?"

"Kind of got that impression last night."

"I guess," he smiled softly, "it's still hard for me to believe that you're mine. I get caught up in wanting everything I've always wanted with you, right now."

I understood this feeling. Hadn't I said something similar last night? "I just really want to give you that future you want."

"A future with you...*that's* what I want."

I thought about Evan's belief in us and the growing, visceral need in me, to give him everything he wanted. "What if I want it...now?"

"The future?" he asked, clearly puzzled again.

"What if I told you," I came around the counter to where he stood and leaned in, "that I can't stop thinking about it...and that the idea I might not be able to give you that future makes me sick to my stomach."

"Lane—," he started to respond, but I cut him off.

"What if I told you, that I don't want to waste any time...and that I want to try to give you that future you want as soon as possible."

"What are you saying?" he asked, eyes searching mine.

"I'm saying...that I wouldn't be opposed to trying to have a baby as soon as we are married. Or even...sooner."

"Like, how soon?" he swallowed.

"Like...now."

"Now?" he repeated, the pulse point in his neck visibly accelerating.

"Does that scare you?"

"No, it doesn't scare me," his lips pulled into a

grin. "Are you kidding?"

"No, I'm not kidding. And you're okay with the idea if it were to happen?"

"Of course," his smile grew wider.

"What about down the line?"

"I didn't want you to feel any pressure."

"So, that's yes?"

"Oh," he wrapped his arm around my waist, and pulled me close. "It's most definitely a yes."

"Good," I shoved my hand into the pocket of his jeans and pulled out his cell phone.

"Well, *that's* not what I was expecting," he laughed.

"Call my mom," I held it out to him.

"And I was definitely *not* expecting that."

"Do it," I ordered playfully.

"And?"

"When she answers," I leaned in, whispering in his ear, "say good morning." Evan dialed my mother's number and when she picked up, did as I asked. "Now," I continued, whispering so only he could hear me. "Tell her we can do two weeks from Saturday for the engagement party."

I knew my mother was about to ask about dates for the party when I hung up earlier, and also knew she and Evan's mom would be hounding us until we gave them one.

He relayed the information, and while my mother expressed concerned it didn't give her and Evelyn time to pull something together, she thanked him for letting her know—adding she was glad one of us had manners, given the way I'd abruptly hung up on her earlier.

"Tell her," I bit down on his earlobe gently, and he closed his eyes and clenched my shirt. "I was tired and needed coffee."

He repeated what I said, and I moved my mouth down to his neck; the pulse point beating more wildly under my lips. "Now," I ran my hand up his chest, "tell her, you need to get to work and that I'll call her later."

After telling her the last part, he muttered goodbye, then hung up—dropping his phone quickly, and lifting me up onto the counter, and kissing me. "Are you sure you have to go to work today?" he asked while moving his lips down to my neck.

"Yes," I wrapped my legs around him, and leaned my head back. "Don't you?"

"Yes...but I know the boss."

"Lucky," I whispered.

"Principal Edwards seems like he'd be okay if you took a sick day."

"He would...but can we not talk about him right

now?"

Evan laughed and pulled back, eyes searching mine. "Are you sure about this? I mean, are you *really* sure?"

"I am," I nodded, feeling the surety deep in my core.

"And what if it happens?"

"Then it happens," I smiled, the idea filling me with hope. If it happened, it meant I wasn't damaged. That I was capable of giving Evan everything he wanted.

"This is not how I imagined today would go," his eyes flickered.

"Well," I reached up, running my thumb along his lower lip. "How about we do something else unexpected?"

"Like?"

"Let's pick a wedding date. That way, if it *does* happen, we'll be ready."

"Being married won't make us ready for kids," he tucked a strand of hair behind my ear.

"I know. But at least it won't be *completely* scandalous."

"When are you thinking?" he laughed, knowing well, the wagging tongues of this town.

"Spring... after Easter?""

"Sounds perfect."

"I'd marry you tomorrow if I could. But..."

"Our mothers," he finished my thought.

"Not to mention, I love the idea of being able to go outside and pick anything I want for my bouquet. The hills are always so alive and colorful in the spring. And I was thinking... we have the ceremony here, on the boat...at sunset. Just family and friends. And then, we have the reception at the hotel. That way, we get what we want...and our mothers get what they want."

"You've really given this some thought," he smiled, eyes wide and full of light.

"Oh, I have." In the recess of my mind, I'd given us every thought imaginable, and it was those dreams...those forever musings of my heart...that brought our future to life.

"Will the timing work.... given all that is happening with the hotel?"

"Groundbreaking won't happen until the summer. That is, if City Council gives us the green light."

"They will."

"Even if they didn't, it wouldn't matter. I'd marry you any day."

"Well then, there's just one thing left."

"And that is?"

"When do we tell our mothers?"

"Let's wait a few days. Make them sweat a bit," he said mischievously.

"I love it. We have a date for the engagement party... a date for the wedding..."

"And now," he pulled me into his arms, "we start on the rest."

CHAPTER TEN

I PERKED UP AT THE SOUND OF EVAN'S CAR COMING down the drive, surprised to hear him home so early. He'd been late the last couple of nights, preparing for the City Council meeting later this week, and I expected him to be late tonight, too.

Two weeks had passed since that night on the boat, and life was good. My mother and Evelyn were working round the clock to pull off our engagement party, which was only days away, and also relieved Evan and I had settled on a date for the wedding. Surprisingly, they were okay with our plans for an intimate ceremony, if it meant they got to plan the reception, and were glad we'd given them more time to plan, than we had for the party.

I was also making progress with the new student at school. She seemed to be warming up a bit and our weekly meetings had become more two-way in conversation. I still didn't know much about how long she'd be in Lake Haven but tried to do what I could to get her to see this town for what it could offer to her, for however long she was here, and not view it as someplace she was stuck.

My hand had also healed. To my relief, no trace of the injury remained. And my nightmares, while not fully disappearing, had become less frequent. I was optimistic for what lie ahead, and wondered if in my decision to embrace the future, had I finally let go of the anxiety and naivety of the past?

"Don't you read your texts?" Tony asked coming into the kitchen, slightly out of breath.

"Tony," I said with surprise, looking up.

"I've got like, thirty seconds before Ev comes in."

"So, it *was* his car," I looked to the front door, slightly confused.

"We came here together."

"Ah," I nodded with understanding. Tony, too, had been working hard to prepare for the upcoming meeting, and I assumed, Evan had suggested they come here to work. "Do you want to stay for dinner?"

"Sure," he nodded. "But you better put on another plate."

"Is Sam joining you?"

"Listen," he leaned in.

"To?"

"Who's coming to dinner."

"Who?"

"Guess?"

"Guess who's coming to dinner?" I smirked at my own play on words.

"Lanes," Evan called as he made his way through the door.

"Too late," Tony turned and leaned against the counter.

"In here," I called. "What has gotten into you?" I smacked him on the arm.

"Hi," Evan greeted me with a kiss.

"Hey," I smiled.

"I brought home company for dinner. I hope that's okay."

"I don't mi—" I started then stopped cold.

"You remember Dean Danvers, right?" Evan smiled.

"Laney," Dean walked in behind Evan, smiling. "Good to see you again."

"Again?" Evan reached into the fridge and grabbed three beers, holding one out to Tony and the other to Dean. "You didn't tell me you two ran into each other?"

"Just in passing," Dean reached for the bottle appreciatively.

"Ah," Evan twisted the cap off his beer. "Well, welcome to our home."

I turned to Tony, now understanding what he'd been trying to tell me. "Dean came to the hotel earlier to submit a bid for the project," he explained. "Runs his own construction company."

"One minute you're doing one thing, and the next something else," Dean shoved a hand in his pocket and laughed softly. "Wild how fast life changes."

"Isn't that the truth," Evan held up his bottle, and Tony and Dean hit the necks of theirs against it. The sound of the glass connecting, banged loudly in my ears.

"I saw a flyer in town about the City Council meeting," Dean continued, "and it caught my eye. Jobs are hard to come by in my area right now, and my crew could use some work."

"Dean lives in Portland," Evan took a sip of his beer. "Submitted the best bid we've seen so far."

I looked at Dean, hating how his presence unnerved me. I straightened and pushed the nervousness that was trying to rear its head, aside.

"So, you're in construction," I said with confidence.

"That's right."

"Out of Portland."

"Right again," he smiled.

"Aren't you looking for a local crew?" I looked to Evan.

"Dean is from here," Evan shrugged. "It's practically the same thing."

"Isn't Portland kind of far?" I turned back to Dean. "I mean…that's quite a drive for your crew."

"It is," he agreed. "When the project starts, that is, if I'm lucky enough to get it, they'll stay here during the week and go home on weekends."

"Isn't that stressful?"

"Can be…but they're used to out-of-town projects."

"And you?"

"I'll move back to manage everything," he looked to Evan. "That is if we all feel this is a good fit."

"Thought we'd fill Dean in more on the project," Evan continued. "We haven't chosen a crew yet, and it would be great to have one locked in when we meet with City Council."

"But the meeting is in two days."

"That's why I'm here," Dean replied. "Bit of a crash course and hopefully, come to an agreement. Hope you don't mind another mouth to feed?"

"Maybe we can order takeout?" Evan suggested.

I wasn't sure what game Dean was playing, but

whatever it was, he would be playing alone. No one, especially him, would flip my world upside down ever again. This was my life, and I set the terms.

I painted the most pleasant smile on my face that I could and pushed my apprehension aside. "Takeout won't be necessary. Dinner is the least we can do to repay a favor."

"Favor?" Evan asked, curious of my choice of words.

"Dean was at my mother's shop when I hurt my hand."

"Oh?" he looked to Dean.

"That's where we ran into each other."

I knew Evan well-enough to know this bit of information had piqued his interest—both why I hadn't mentioned it, and Dean.

My omission wouldn't be of concern. I was always running into people in town. Not to mention, life had been a whirlwind since we got engaged, and whom I ran into, would easily slip my mind. Dean, on the other hand...

"I didn't do anything...I mean much," Dean corrected.

"Oh, sure you did," I countered, feeling like the hunter in this game of cat and mouse. "And because of that, I'd like to thank you."

"Thank me?" he repeated.

"We have some steaks in the fridge, and I can make a salad. No better way to say thank you than a home-cooked meal."

"You sure?" Evan looked at the stack of menus on top of the microwave.

Keep your friends close and enemies closer, I thought.

"Sure," I smiled sweetly. "Why don't you go out back and fire up the grill? Just let me know when it's time to put the steaks on."

"Alright guys," Evan walked over to the back door. "You heard the lady."

"Be right there," Tony motioned to the fridge. "I'm just going to grab a six pack."

"Alright," Evan pulled the door open. "Dean?"

"Coming," he nodded, and stepped outside with Evan.

Tony waited for the door to close before turning to me. "Weird, right?"

"How so?" I reached above the stove for a tray, set it down on the counter, and then opened the fridge and grabbed the package of steaks we'd planned to grill on the weekend.

"We were just talking about him at *Fiero's* like what, a week ago?"

"That was two weeks ago," I corrected,

unwrapping the paper, and removing the steaks.

"Right, two weeks ago," he continued, "and then poof, there he is."

"Well, like everyone always says…small town. Hand me the salt and pepper, would you," I pretended to brush off the comment, even though I was in silent agreement.

Tony handed me the shakers next to the stove and continued as I seasoned the steaks. "I'm curious why he didn't say anything about what happened with your hand."

"Maybe he forgot."

"Maybe," Tony considered.

I set the shakers down and looked out back. It was strange to see Evan and Dean talking easily with one another, considering the last time I'd seen them — well, versions of them — together. Those two versions of them couldn't be in the same space together. But the men outside looked like they were old friends. I didn't think I'd ever feel comfortable around Dean, however. Too much water under the bridge, even if that bridge were a fake world I'd experienced, and no one else.

"Or maybe he didn't say anything because of Ev," Tony continued.

"What do you mean?" I turned from the window.

"He's not going to risk this job. It sounds like he needs the work."

"And?"

"And… anyone can see *you* are what makes Evan tick. If he had even the *slightest* indication Dean had anything to do with you getting hurt, that'd be it. His bid would go right in the trash."

"Possibly."

"No," he looked back at me in seriousness. "Not possibly. I know."

I considered what Tony said. "Do me a favor?"

"Anything."

"Keep an eye on Ev, would you?"

"Are you kidding? That's my boy. You don't even have to ask."

"I know…just, make sure no one takes advantage of him."

"You can count on it. That's part of my job. Already had to talk with a few folks."

"Oh?"

"Yeah, people do funny things in business."

"Who?" I asked, curious to know who might be trying to pull anything on Evan, as they were about to lose me as a customer.

"No can do," he laughed. "Business is business. Besides, Dean doesn't seem that like kind of guy if I'm being honest. He seems a bit lost."

"I don't get that feeling."

"You never know the weight in someone else's backpack."

"Or in their arms."

"You saw the size of those guns, too?" Tony laughed, opening the fridge, and pulling out a six pack. "Just remember," he closed the door and tucked the beer under his arm. "You've got these guns behind you," he held up an arm and flexed.

I couldn't help but laugh. "Should I call Sam and have her join us?"

"She's working on story. Going to pick something up on the way home and take advantage of the quiet."

"Got it," I grabbed a bowl out of the cabinet, and opened the fridge, pulling out a bag of mixed greens, bin of strawberries, and container of feta cheese.

"You good?" he asked, reaching for the door.

"Yup," I nodded. "All good. Go on outside. Just tell Ev to come in to grab the steaks when the grill's ready."

"Aye aye," he saluted and went outside.

Once done making the salad, I poured myself a glass of wine and watched as the three men talked and laughed. From where I sat, it looked like any group of friends, having drinks, after work. And for them, that's all it was. For me, however, I felt like I was in *The Twilight Zone*.

I was in the middle of pouring myself a second glass of wine, when the backdoor opened. "Ready for the steaks, babe?"

"I um, came in to use the bathroom," Dean said apologetically.

I spun around to find him smiling at me, an embarrassed expression on his face. "That way," I swallowed, pointing down the hall.

He nodded and made his way to the bathroom, then returned a couple of minutes later, stopping just before the kitchen, to look at the pictures on the wall.

"Is this high school graduation?" he stared at one of Caleb, Timmy, Lisa, Evan, and me.

"Yes," I said simply.

"Great picture," he smiled.

"Thank you," I reached for my wine glass and took a sip.

All five of us had a copy of it once. Mine had moved from my room in the apartment Lisa and I shared in LA, to the one Evan and I shared in New York, to my office, where it sat now. The copy on the wall was Evan's.

"I meant what I said that day in your mom's shop," Dean said, looking from picture to picture. "I was really sorry...about what happened."

"Thank you," I held my glass tight, not sure what else to say.

"Do you wish you could go back and do it over?"

"Do ...what over?"

"Those years," he nodded to the picture.

The brazenness of his question made me freeze. Who did Dean think he was? He didn't know me well enough to ask such questions.

But I didn't say this. I simply answered with the truth, while shooting him daggers with my eyes, which bounced off his back. "I used to."

"Used to?" he repeated. "Why not now?"

"I learned to let go of the impossible."

"Letting go," he turned to me with a curious look in his eyes. "Sometimes easier said than done, right?" I stared at him saying nothing. "How's your hand?" he asked, changing the subject.

"It's fine."

"No problems?"

"Nope."

"Good," he smiled and then looked out the window to Evan and Tony. "Those two are great. They seem close."

"They are."

"It's a shame about Tony's arm. He was a good

ballplayer."

"He was," I agreed.

"And you and Evan...you seem good."

"We are great." I took another sip of my wine, thinking about Tony's earlier comment. Dean didn't seem lost at all. He seemed, curious. "May I ask you something?"

"Sure," he smiled, appearing pleased by the ask.

"Why are you here?"

"In Lake Haven?"

"No," I shot back. "My house."

"It was Evan's idea."

"And how long will you be here?"

"At your house?"

"In Lake Haven."

"Well, that depends on a few things."

"Like?"

"Whether I win."

"The bid?"

"Right," he nodded and the space between us again grew quiet. "Can I take anything out for you?" he asked finally.

"These," I pushed the tray of steaks towards him.

"Got it," he reached for it happily. "Anything else?"

"Just that."

Dean grabbed the tray and looked at me as if he wanted to say something else. Then, as if changing his mind, he turned back around, and walked outside, leaving me in silence.

***

Later that night, after saying goodbye to Tony and Dean, Evan came out to the deck with a blanket. I'd come outside after dinner, curling up in one of the chairs, and stayed out here while the guys wrapped up.

"Thought you could use this."

"Thanks," I smiled up at him, and pulled it onto my legs.

"Thank you for dinner," he sat down in the chair next to me. "It was great."

"My pleasure."

"I'm sorry I didn't call and let you know I was bringing them home."

"Tony is always welcome," I leaned my head back.

"What did you think of Dean? He's changed since school, right?"

"I didn't really know him in school," I stared out across the water.

"Me either. But he seems like he's a good guy,

and his bid is really solid."

"And his past?" I turned to Evan. "I mean… past work. Did you check it out?"

"He showed me some pictures. Looks good from what I can tell. Tony is going to call his references tomorrow."

"That would be smart."

"Still, you're concerned," he said matter of fact.

"What makes you say that?"

"Don't get me wrong…you were a gracious, lovely host," he reached for my hand and kissed it. "But I could tell something was wrong."

If Evan could tell I was wary of Dean, I wondered if it was time to tell him why? It'd been surprisingly easy to tell him about the bad dreams that'd been plaguing me.

"I guess," I began after weighing the pros and cons of telling the truth. "I'm protective of you. This project is going to be huge, and we don't know him well. It's been a long time since high school, and we didn't exactly know him well then, either."

"Well," Evan thought about what I said. "It sounds like things haven't been great for him the last few years. I'd like to help him out if I can. Do me a favor…trust me?"

The sincerity in Evan's voice, matched that of his eyes. This incredible human…the love of my life, who trusted me without fail, was asking me to trust him, and give Dean a chance. Couldn't I do that, even if the ask were to trust someone I could barely look at?

I placed my hand on Evan's cheek and smiled. "What I wouldn't do for you, Evan Davies."

He grabbed my hand and gave it a kiss. "But I am curious...why didn't you tell me he was there the day you hurt your hand?"

"My mind was probably in the clouds," I smiled, the memory of his proposal making me forget all about Dean.

Evan kissed my hand again, then held it in his as we turned our attention to the water, enjoying the early fall night. It was beautiful out, but winter could come at a moment's notice, chilling everything to the bone — and all signs were pointing to an early winter.

CHAPTER ELEVEN

EVAN PADDED INTO THE KITCHEN THE NEXT MORNING; eyes sleepy, hair tousled. Even half-awake he was beautiful and flipped my stomach.

"Why are you up so early?" he asked, yawning.

"I signed up for a class."

"And it starts this early?" he opened the cabinet and removed a cup.

"It's not early."

"Oh wow," he yawned again, looking at the time. "Didn't realize the time."

"What time did you go to bed?"

"Late," he reached for the French press on a cutting board next to the stove and poured a cup.

"You might want to heat that."

"Thanks," he opened the microwave and placed his cup inside and set the timer. "Did you sleep well?"

"Not really."

"Nightmare?"

"Yeah," I exhaled with frustration, although, not entirely surprised. I could only imagine what Dean's presence had done to my already struggling subconscious; my innate distrust for him, burrowing into my mind, deeper.

"Same as always?" Evan asked.

"Mostly. It was a bit different. Changed some."

"How so?"

After the dream had shaken me awake, I realized through the remnants that lingered, that the darkness was no longer around me; cold shadows instead, threatening me from behind. And in front of me now stood a wall that stretched up and out, infinitely.

"Why don't you have your coffee first," I nodded to the microwave, the beep of the timer indicating his coffee had finished reheating.

"I can listen and drink," he removed his cup and blew on the steam that was rising.

"It can wait," I shrugged. The nightmare wasn't going anywhere. "How are *you* feeling? You've been working hard."

"Yeah," he ran a hand back and forth over his head.

I looked to his coffee, noting the lack of cream and sugar. "Need the octane?"

"I need all the fuel I can get. We're in the home stretch."

"Is your dad pleased with the way things are going?"

"I think he is," he nodded, taking a sip.

"I'm sure he's as proud of you as am I."

Evan was humble, sometimes to a fault. He wasn't one to brag or seek attention. But he deserved recognition for an idea that would help the town.

"Thanks," he smiled, the sleep beginning to lift from his eyes. "Now," he took another sip. "Tell me about the nightmare. Is it better or worse than before?"

"Neither. Just…different."

"So, what's changed?"

"Well," I leaned against the counter. "The darkness isn't oppressive or all around me, and there's a wall."

"A wall?" he repeated.

"Yeah," I chewed my cheek. "I don't know…it's just annoying because I thought they'd gone away. It'd been a few days."

"Do you have any thoughts about why it came back, or changed?"

Yeah, Dean…he is the harbinger of all things dark I thought. "No clue," I said instead.

"Well," he yawned a third time. "I'm no expert but it sounds like your mind might be trying to tell you something."

"My thought, too. Which is why…I started looking around online earlier, and well, one link led to another, and I found some interesting stuff."

"About?"

"Sole survivors," I replied carefully, waiting for Evan's reaction. To my surprise he simply waited for me to continue. "As much as it pains me to admit, my mother may have been right. Apparently, those groups she told me about *have* been helpful."

"Tell me more," he lifted his coffee and took a sip.

"How about, I tell you more tonight when you get home?"

"Why?"

"You had a late night…and you don't really need to worry about this before work."

"Laney…"

"I can tell you later. It's not that important right now."

"You are important, always."

"But—" I eyed the clock.

"But…nothing," he insisted. "Tell me more."

I crossed my arms considering how much I should tell him. I'd read so much while he was sleeping, and I was still digesting it all. "From what I read," I tried to paraphrase what I'd learned, as best as possible. "Sole survivors tend to possess a deep-seated guilt at having lived through something others did not. It's called survivor syndrome and quite common."

"Are nightmares associated with survivor's syndrome?"

"They are," I nodded. "Dreams are the mind's way of processing trauma. And nightmares, the body's response when it fails to do so. And another thing...it can manifest months after a traumatic event, or even, years."

"So, being back here, may have nothing to do with your dreams?"

"Exactly. Interesting, right?"

"Very," he agreed. "So, is the session you found for those with survivors' syndrome?"

"Not exactly."

"What do you mean, not exactly?"

"Well...in researching all of this, I stumbled upon a paper written by a doctor who has made a connection between nightmares and near-death experiences."

"Your mother still doesn't know about what you

experienced, right?" Evan asked, setting his cup down.

"No," I shook my head. "You're the only person. But Ev... this doctor is amazing. She's published research and has books on the topic, too. And...she hosts sessions all the time for near-death survivors."

"And *that's* what you signed up for?"

"Yes," I said excitedly.

"So, you *don't* think these nightmares are some kind of side-effect of survivors guilt?"

"I think a part of me will always carry some kind of guilt about that night. The fact that I lived, while they didn't. But..." I continued when it looked like he was about to cut me off. "I'm thankful I *did* survive, because I get to be here and have this amazing life with you."

"But you said your mother was right?" he asked, and I could see the confusion in his eyes.

"About groups for survivors. They do appear to help. But after looking into this doctor's work, I don't think that's what's happening with me. I think the nightmares might be related to what happened when my heart stopped." Evan looked down, growing quiet. "What do you think?"

"What do *you* think?" he tossed the question back to me.

"This doctor has a lot of experience and I think

she could help me. Help…us."

"I wasn't aware we needed help."

I walked over to Evan and wrapped my arms around his waist and looked up. "We don't. We're perfect. But if we are going to bring a child into this world, they shouldn't have to worry about the weight of the past."

"The past isn't all bad," he ran a hand up and down my arm.

"No," I smiled. "It's not. There is so much that is good. But that child will be part you and part me. And the part they get from me… I want it to be free from the weight of that night. I want that little person we create, to get only the best of me."

"Lanes," he exhaled. "You are the best of you."

"You're biased."

"I may be," he smiled. "But I mean it. You are strong, and loving, and smart, and loyal. But…" he continued when he saw I was about to protest. "I understand."

"You do?"

"I do," he tipped my chin up. "I support your decision. Whatever it may be. I'm behind you, one hundred percent."

"Yeah?" I brightened.

"Of course," he nodded. "I will always support you."

"Thank you," I leaned in and hugged him tight.

"So, this session," he asked when I pulled back. "Where is it?"

"Bangor."

"Bangor?" he scrunched up his nose.

I laughed, knowing how strange it was to find something in a city as small as Bangor, for a group of people that was likely, even smaller. "This doctor is part of some kind of expansion program to give rural communities access to mental health services," I explained.

"That's a long drive for a session."

"I thought about that. But…" I paused to take a breath. "The session is next week, on a Friday, so I thought about asking Sam and making a girls weekend out of it."

"Now that sounds like a great idea," Evan smiled. "If the Sox do well this week that will be playoffs weekend."

"See," I gave him a squeeze. "It's like it was meant to happen. You do whatever it is you do when you have a whole weekend together, and Sam and I can do all the things we do. Maybe, we could look at some wedding dresses."

"Oh yeah?" he smiled.

"I've been getting some ideas."

"Anything you'd like to show me?" he asked

coyly.

"You'll have to wait until our wedding day. For now, it's time for work."

"Yeah," he looked at the clock and reached for his coffee, taking one last sip, then put the cup in the dishwasher. "I should probably get going, too."

"Race you to the shower?"

"You're on," he laughed.

We sprinted down the hall and up the stairs to the bedroom; Evan scooping me up as I reached the door to our room. "I win," he laughed, dropping me onto the bed.

"That depends on the way you look at it."

"Oh, I am," he hovered over me.

I reached up and pushed a lock of hair off his forehead. "How did I get so lucky?"

"How did *we* get so lucky?"

"Who knows," I smiled. "But let's bottle it and save it for the meeting."

"Baby," he smiled. "With you by my side, I don't need luck."

***

That afternoon, I met up with Sam for lunch at Shangri-La, an Asian Fusion restaurant that opened over the summer.

159

"What would you say to a girl's weekend in Bangor?" I asked as we sat down at our table.

"I'd say when do we leave?"

"Friday after next."

"Nice," she clapped. "Where are we going?"

"Bangor."

"Bangor?" she said with less enthusiasm. "Not Paris or Rome?"

"I have to go there for a work thing and thought it might be fun for you to come along. We can do a spa day, maybe even shop for wedding dresses…"

"Now that sounds fun," she grabbed one of the menus the server placed at the end of the table. "Do you have some ideas on what you want? Dress…not food."

"I do," I smiled.

To say looking for dresses was overwhelming would be an understatement. My mother had brought over a stack of wedding magazines, and with being an inch or two thick, there were hundreds of pages to look through.

I'd only made it through two so far and there had been hundreds of pages of dresses. Long dresses, short dresses, silk, and lace. The options were endless. However, it had only taken those two, to get a sense of what I liked and didn't.

"What are you thinking?" she asked as the

server approached to take our order.

"Hold that thought," I whispered and nodded for Sam to go first. When she finished, I gave the server my order, then waited for them to leave to continue. "Nothing too fancy. Bare shoulders, but not necessarily strapless. Definitely not a princess dress."

"No?" Sam asked.

"Not my style," I laughed. "You know that."

"I know," she smiled. "But sometimes, weddings do weird things to people."

"True," I agreed. "But not me. I'm thinking simple, but elegant. Because wow," I laughed, "you should see some of the dresses that are out there."

"Oh, I have," Sam rolled her eyes.

"Yeah?" I asked, reaching for the iced tea I'd ordered when we first arrived.

"Of course," she lifted her own drink, taking a sip. "You're not the only one marrying her Prince Charming someday."

"Any ideas when you and Tony may tie the knot?" I asked, curious how her response may differ from what Tony said at *Fiero's*.

"In time," she smiled. "This town can only take one wedding a year."

As suspected, she and Tony aligned on shining the spotlight on me and Evan. "Well," I set my glass back down. "I fully expect you will be trying on dresses with me."

"Oh," she nodded in seriousness. "You can count on it."

"Including, the truly awful bridesmaids' dresses."

"Oh no," she groaned. "Do I have to?"

"Yup," I laughed. "I want you to try on the most ridiculous, most poufy, most vibrant colored-dress possible."

Sam started laughing. "Only if you try on the biggest, laciest, most princess-like wedding dress we can find."

"Oh no," I laughed back.

When the server arrived with our meals we were laughing hysterically. "Oh man," Sam dabbed at her eyes with a napkin. "This is going to be fun."

"It is," I nodded.

"Where are we staying by the way?"

"There's a cute boutique hotel that just opened. I thought we could give it a try."

"Sounds good. And why Bangor again?" she asked, digging into her food.

"I signed up for a class."

"A class?" she asked while chewing.

"For school," I dug into my food as well.

Saying the class was for school, seemed

harmless. I was the guidance counselor, and any kind of training or class that would enable me to better support students, seemed logical.

"Well, I'd do anything for a weekend away," Sam said. "Except, listening to some kind of info session where I walk away owning a timeshare."

"Aren't those a thing of the past?" I asked, taking another bite of my food.

"Seems they're on the rise again."

"Timeshares?"

"Yup. Up and down the Eastern Seaboard. What's old is new again. Oh man, this is so good."

"It is," I nodded, taking another bite.

We continued with our meals, talking throughout, and by the time the server had cleared our plates, it was time to go.

"Well, I'm pleasantly stuffed."

"Me too."

"I'll be coming back."

"Same," I agreed.

"I'm excited for the trip," Sam smiled.

"I thought a weekend for the guys to do beer and baseball would a perfect time for us to do some spa time and shopping."

"That's all Tony can talk about," Sam laughed. "The Sox and the playoffs. I know the boy loves baseball, obviously, but it couldn't be a more perfect time for a weekend getaway. Between that and work."

"Things busy?"

"With City Council tomorrow and your engagement party on the weekend, I have stories lined up for the next couple of weeks," she smiled. "And, who knows, whatever trouble we get into could work its way into a future column."

"Ha!" I laughed. "You wouldn't."

"I wouldn't," she laughed. "But I do envy you. Don't get me wrong...Tony is a dream, and I adore him to bits, but everyone wants to be looked at the way Evan looks at you."

"You don't see the way Tony looks at you," I countered.

"I'm serious," she said dreamily. "What you two have...I tell you. It's the closest thing to magic I've ever seen."

"Can I tell you something?"

"Shoot."

"Magic scares me," I said with flat honesty.

"Why is that?"

"We can't control it."

"Did you look that up online?"

"I'm serious," I laughed gently. "Sometimes, I feel like no matter how hard I try, there is something greater at work, pulling the strings."

"Can I tell you something?"

"Please," I nodded.

"We all feel that way," she confessed.

"Really?"

"Sure," she shrugged. "But it's not as scary as you might think."

"What do you mean?"

"Don't you think it is weird I moved away, only to be drawn back here at the same Tony returned home from the Minors? I didn't plan that, but *something* did. And I'm glad it did. He's the best thing to ever happen to me. But I don't know if we would have wound up together had something not given us that push. If that's not forces beyond our control at work, I don't know what is."

I hadn't thought of it that way before. Forces out of our control can be for good, as well. "You're right."

"But you and Evan," she shook her head. "That's not just something at work. That's lifetimes at play."

"Lifetimes?"

"You two have this deep connection that goes way beyond the time you've been on this planet."

"You think?"

"Oh yeah," she nodded. "You can see it when you're together. It doesn't matter where you are, you and Evan are your own universe."

Sam was right. He was my center of gravity.

"Hey," I protested when she grabbed the bill as the server placed it on the table. "I invited you to lunch."

"You get dinner in Bangor."

"You sure?"

"Absolutely," she reached for her wallet. "By the way, when do you want to leave that Friday?"

"Session starts at five, so probably morning?"

"Perfect. I'll take the day off. I'll tell Bill I'm following up on a story."

"Are you sure he'll be cool with that?"

Bill Reid had been the editor of the paper for the last few years. My dad had called him a stickler once, adding, that was why he was the best editor the paper had ever seen.

"Sure," she placed a handful of cash down on top of the check. "Verifying sources is all in a day's work. Besides, why do you think I became a reporter?"

"You love to write stories?"

"Gosh, no. I like the flexibility," she winked and got up from the table. "Shall we?"

"Lead the way," I grabbed my bag and followed her out of the restaurant.

"Let the countdown to Bangor begin," she swung an arm over my shoulder. "Man, Lanes, we're going to paint that town red!"

CHAPTER TWELVE

THE NEXT EVENING, SAM AND I MET UP AFTER WORK SO we could go to the City Council meeting together. Evan and Tony had been at the hotel all day preparing, and we planned to spend a couple of minutes with them before the meeting began.

"Look at those two," I nudged her with my arm as they approached. Evan was in a black suit and grey tie, and Tony navy one, with a red tie. Both suits fit perfectly, and I guessed Anna, the hotel's tailor, had adjusted each suit, to make sure they looked perfect for tonight.

"Hey," Evan reached for my hand, leaning in to give me a kiss.

"You ready?"

"Yup," he nodded, exuding a confident countenance.

"Tony, you look terrific."

"Thank you kindly," he adjusted his tie, as greeted Sam him with a kiss.

"You two are going to knock 'em dead," she said excitedly, wrapping her arm around his waist.

"That's the plan. And when that fails, we've got Mr. Charm here," he laughed.

"No way," Evan adjusted his shirt cuff. "You're my pinch hitter."

"Man," Tony shook his head. "Did you ever think coach would be right?"

"I know," Evan nodded.

"Right about, what?" I asked.

"Coach used to always tell us...go to college and get a degree. If you're lucky enough to play ball professionally, you'll need it, because it's not if your career will end, but when. Old man was right," Tony said softly with a melancholic smile.

"He's proud of you," Evan clapped Tony on the shoulder.

Lake Haven High's beloved coach passed away last summer, and not once had I seen more grown men cry, than I did the day of his memorial — including my father, and Evan's, who also played under the coach, decades earlier. He'd been a mentor to so many, including Tony.

"For you, Coach," Tony looked up.

"For Coach," Evan agreed, and they hit their

fists together.

"So," I cleared my throat. "What time will our parents be here?"

"They should be here any minute. Actually," he nodded across the street, "there they are now."

Sam whistled as Evan's parents got out the car first, followed by mine. "Man, your parents are no joke."

Our parents traveled like a pack. Like wolves, but with less bite. At least, where our dads were concerned. Our mothers, however, were another story. Together, they were fierce, especially when it came to their children.

"That's a power squad, right there," Tony straightened as our parents crossed the street. "Mr. Davies," he stuck out a hand and greeted Evan's father as he approached.

"Tony," Jonathan shook his hand and clapped him on the back. "You ready?"

"Just another day at the park sir," Tony said confidently.

"That it is," he nodded, then looked to his son. "Ev, you ready?"

"Ready as ever," he smiled.

"Remember, Mayor Cartwright may have let you slide down the banister in Haven House as a kid, but he's no joke in these City Council meetings.

He can be tough."

Caleb's family had lived in the Mayor's Mansion for generations—every male Cartwright a mayor of this town—and we grew up there alongside him.

The historic residence had been the home of Captain Laurence Haven, our town's founder, and added on to over the years. The new portions of the house were spacious, with long, wide halls that we'd run down. We used to ride our bikes down those halls, racing around and around the house, until Tony slammed into a table one day, breaking a hundreds year old vase, and his dad forbade it.

"Noted pops," Evan nodded at his father.

"And…" Evelyn, ever the doting mother, leaned over and straightened Evan's tie. "Mrs. Chambers from the Parks Division will be eating out of your hand if you mention your conservation efforts."

"Got it mom."

"The list of businesses in support of the expansion? They all planning to be here?" Jonathan asked Tony.

"Everyone is confirmed and scheduled to be here," Tony confirmed.

"And those planning to vote in opposition?"

"There are people that oppose the expansion?" I asked, surprised.

"Always is," Jonathan smiled.

"But the expansion will benefit the town. Who would oppose?"

"You'd be surprised. But nothing to worry about," Evan gave my hand a squeeze. "We're good there, too."

"Laney," Evelyn gave me a hug, surrounding me in a heady cloud of perfume. "How's my favorite daughter-in-law?"

"Future and only, daughter-in-law," I laughed while hugging her back.

"I've always considered you my daughter," she winked when we pulled back.

"I'm good," I smiled. "Do you know who is opposed to the expansion?"

"No one that matters," she waved off the idea.

"Is it many?"

"Just the old and new."

"Meaning?"

"I think you're more nervous than Ev," she laughed. "Don't worry about it, hon. Everything will be fine."

"I'm not nervous, I'm just curious who'd be in opposition to financial security and prosperity."

"There's always a few," she shrugged.

Once my mother and father finished saying hello to Sam and Tony, they turned their attention to me and Evan. "Well kids…I knew this day would come and I couldn't be prouder. The torch is now officially, passed. You're the next generation of this town."

"I shall not waste my days in trying to prolong them, I shall use my time," Evan said with sincerity.

"Jack London," my father pointed at Evan with a smile.

"I learned from the best," Evan stuck out his hand and my dad gave it a shake.

"Don't let that one get away," my father looked at me and smiled.

"I don't plan on it," I gripped Evan's hand tighter.

"Alright, alright," my mother waved her hands. "Let's go grab our seats. The meeting is about to begin."

"Okay, Marina," my father smiled, and she weaved her arm through his. "Evelyn, shall we?" he held out his other one and Evan's mother took hold of it. "I promised these two beautiful ladies I would escort them inside while Jonathan talks with the boys. Can I offer you two ladies an escort as well?"

"Go on," Evan nodded.

"You sure?"

"Yup."

"Okay," I leaned in to give him a kiss. "Good

luck."

"Ready?" Jonathan looked from his son to Tony, placing a hand on both of their backs, then turning to form a huddle.

Watching them together reminded me of a moment from that baseball game in high school, where the boys played for the state title.

It was bottom of the ninth, two outs, and there was a runner on third. Lake Haven was up by one, and the batter stepping up to the plate was all that stood between our team and the win. Tony and Evan stood like they did now — coach in the middle, and each of a side.

The setting sun cast a magical glow over the field as everyone in the stands watched nervously; the opposing team hollering and cheering, waiting while the upcoming batter took a couple of aggressive practice swings.

When Tony, Evan, and their coach, broke from the huddle, you could cut the tension with a knife. I remember holding my breath as Tony wound up for his pitch, and when the ball cracked off the bat, you could hear a collective gasp of everyone in the stands.

The hit had been a hard ground ball, straight up the middle, but Evan, as if expecting this play all his life, shifted left, and scooped it up, throwing it home in one graceful move. Tyler Garrity stood protectively over home plate, eyes on the runner sprinting home, and when he caught Evan's throw and bent his knees, tagging the runner out, pandemonium broke out. The players in the dugout ran into the field, jumping into the arms of their teammates, shouting out in victory as they tossed their gloves into the air.

I hoped tonight they guys would be celebrating a win again.

"Why don't you four go on ahead," I smiled at my father. "I'll be there in a minute."

"You, okay?" my mother asked.

"Just need a moment."

"Okay, honey," she reached out for my arm and gave it a squeeze, then turned and headed in with my father, Evelyn, and Sam.

Once the door closed behind them, I turned and looked out. City Hall sat on top of a hill, providing a view of the whole town. Boats rocked gently in the cove, as cars traveled up and down Main Street. It was picturesque, and tranquil, and no place like it in the world. It was home, and always would be. And my father was right. We were this town's future, and everything Evan was doing to make life better for everyone else who called Lake Haven home, made my heart swell with pride.

After taking one last look, I turned around, and headed inside. *Time to play ball,* I thought as I slid into the seat my father saved for me, just as the council members called the meeting to order.

***

An hour later, I sat anxiously inside with dozens of others, hands wrenching in my lap as we awaited City Council's vote.

The meeting I thought would be a slam dunk, had surprisingly, turned out to be complicated. While Jonathan was a pillar of calm, having been through countless meetings like this before, Tony and Evan looked like they were back on that baseball field, playing for the state title—anxious, and ready for the win.

Most locals had pledged support and backed the plans, as expected, but a handful had expressed concern and voiced them, openly.

The first, were the owners of the small tree farm outside town. They believed it was going to take acreage earmarked for wildlife preservation and wanted assurances the expansion would not displace the animals that called the area home.

Another voice of opposition was a couple that moved to Lake Haven a year earlier. They'd hit it big on tech stocks and built a bed and breakfast on the waterfront. They believed the hotel's expansion would take away from their business, by keeping tourists on the property, and away from town.

The biggest surprise, however, was resistance from Mr. Hardy, a beloved Lake Haven octogenarian, who was irritated, more than anything, that the town seemed to be growing and forgetting its history.

Evan and Tony were prepared for each point of concern, with well thought out responses. Jonathan even made a personal promise to Mr. Hardy, that he would collaborate with him on a Historical Center in the hotel. But when City Council called for a vote, I could see Evan and Tony were confident, but eager for the meeting to be over.

Then, the unexpected happen.

When Councilmember Evers asked for the last time, if anyone was in opposition to the project, the door opened, and in walked Dean. Whispers filled the room as he approached the podium, and Evan and Tony watched with curious expressions on their faces.

"My name is Dean Danvers," he addressed the Council, grabbing the sides of the podium and clearing his throat, before continuing. "I've been listening from outside because I don't do well in crowded spaces." He paused to take a breath and looked around. "I left Lake Haven right out of high school. I was a shy kid, which was a surprise to many of you given I'm Katherine Danvers son." A person in the row closest to the podium laughed. "I left because I enlisted in the military. It seemed the best option to whip a kid like me into shape, and as you can see it worked," he turned around to those seated, and smiled. Another round of laughter broke out, including Tony and Evan, who nodded.

"What is he doing?" I mouthed to Sam.

"I have no clue," she mouthed back.

"I've come home over the years," Dean continued, turning his attention back to the Council. "Not much, because well, when you're in the service that's your home, and those you serve with are your family. In a way, the service felt right, because I felt like I belonged. I never really felt like I did, here. It's hard to be lonely in a small town, but when you feel like an outsider, believe me, it can be."

Dean again paused and looked over at Evan and Tony. "Those two weren't really my friends in high school, but if I could go back and do those years over, I'd like to think they would be. You see," he removed the mic and walked over to address each Councilmember, directly. "I came home recently and these two welcomed me with open arms. They said, when you're from Lake Haven, you are family. Evan Davies invited me into his home...a classmate he hadn't seen for years...and cooked me dinner, because *that's* the kind of person he is."

Jonathan looked to his son with pride, and I shifted with the remembrance of that awkward dinner.

"This project is going to be big," Dean continued. "Not only will I be able to help my guys put food on their tables, but they have worked hard to find opportunities for all of you, to put food on your tables, too. There aren't too many people out there willing to do that. Despite all the ugly in the world, there is still good out there. There are still people willing to look out for one another."

Dean looked across the room, as a few folks nodded, while a handful of others, wiped their eyes. I stared at him in disbelief. If this were an act, it was one of the best I'd ever seen.

"I served with some incredible men and women from small towns, just like ours, with big dreams and plans for the future. But they will never have the chance to see those dreams come true because they never came home." Dean paused and looked down. To some, it may have appeared to be an awkward place to stop. But I knew why he had. I'd done it myself, more times than I could count. He was filling the space between loss and grief, so that it could not join forces, and pull him under. "We support their dreams," he continued, lifting his eyes back up. "The dreams of those who are no longer with us, so that they too, live on. That's...all I wanted to say. Thank you."

The room was silent as he replaced the mic to the stand on the podium. Then slowly, one by one, people began to stand, and then clap, and in minutes, the entire room was on its feet. Dean Danvers had saved the day. My villain had become their hero, and there wasn't anything I could do about it but stand, and clap, as well.

CHAPTER THIRTEEN

On Saturday morning, an invitation arrived by carrier, instructing us to be at the hotel by five o-clock. There was nothing else written on the card, only that the dress code was casual.

It'd been twenty-four hours since the City Council meeting, and with the hotel project approved and our engagement party hours away, there was excitement in the air. Our mothers had shared little with us about the party, but I knew they'd worked hard on it, and I was looking forward to tonight.

"Is this a typo?" I asked, handing Evan the invitation. I'd assumed, knowing my mother and Evelyn, it would be semi-formal.

"Don't think so," he smiled.

"What do you mean, don't think so?"

"I mean," he smiled, dropping it down to the

entryway table, "it isn't a typo."

"You know something," I narrowed my eyes, detecting the calmness of his response.

"Maybe."

"What aren't you telling me?"

"Nothing," he smiled, making his way into the kitchen to rifle through a stack of papers on the edge of the counter.

"Nothing, huh? Then why are you looking at mail you've already looked through?"

"I'm not," he continued digging until he pulled out a manila folder from the bottom of the pile. "I was looking...for this."

"And that is?"

"Paperwork from City Council."

"Mm-hmm," I eyed him suspiciously.

"Don't believe me," he laughed, opening the folder to show me its contents. Sure enough, it was paperwork for the expansion, with a giant PASSED stamped in red ink.

I was still in shock about what happened. Dean's speech had all but sealed the deal for the project, and Evan and Tony couldn't help but make a toast in his honor when we all went out after the meeting to celebrate. I, however, couldn't bring myself to say the words, 'to Dean.' Lifting my glass in his honor had been hard enough.

"Why do you know if something is up, and I don't?" I asked, thinking about the cryptic invite.

"They needed an accomplice."

"By they, I assume you mean our mothers?"

"Correct."

"Well, what does casual even mean?"

"Casual, is casual. I can't say anything more."

"What?" I laughed. "Are you serious?"

"Very," he nodded.

"So, no black dress?"

"The one hanging on the door in the bedroom?"

"That's the one."

"Darn it," he snapped. "I was looking forward to seeing you in that."

"What kind of casual party would our mothers throw?"

"If you keep asking me questions, I will give in and that will ruin the surprise."

"Surprise?" I asked, intrigued by his word choice.

"Yes," he looked back down at the folder, avoiding my eyes.

"What if I try really hard to get it out of you."

"Don't," he laughed.

"Don't, what?" I took a step towards him.

"They've worked night and day to make this happen for us."

183

"And…" I smiled sweetly, placing my hand on his chest.

"I am impervious to your charms."

"Since when?" I laughed.

"Since now," he backed up.

"Evan…" I coaxed.

"Laney…please? I don't want to ruin it. And if you keep looking at me that way…"

"You'll what?"

"You know what."

"But I need to know."

"And you will, when we get there."

"That's hours away."

"So, you'll know then."

"I just don't understand why you know what's going on, and I don't?"

"I'm better at keeping secrets."

"How so?"

"That ring on your finger," he winked and then headed down the hall.

"Do you know what you're wearing?" I called after him.

"Yup."

"What?"

"Clothes."

"Funny," I muttered, making my way upstairs, curious what the night had in store.

When we arrived at the hotel later that day, it was quiet. Absent was the sound of music and laughter that normally greeted me when entering the lobby. Aside from the elevator chime and sound of typing behind the registration desk, it was still.

"What's going on?" I looked around, expecting to see guests, or, at least, our parents. But it was still, which was highly unusual for a Saturday, engagement party aside.

"This way," Evan grabbed my hand.

Instead of heading up the stairs to the dining room, we walked past the main staircase and exited through a back door.

"What's out here?" I asked as we continued through the garden.

"You'll see," he smiled.

"The party is outdoors?" Even our mothers' outdoor parties had a dress code beyond my skinny jeans and sweater.

"Trust me," he smiled as we followed the pebble path that ran along the edge of the property. It was just before twilight and the sky looked like it was on fire. A blanket of violet, red, and orange, stretched out infinitely.

I stopped and tugged on Evan's hand. "Have you ever seen anything more beautiful?" I asked, looking up.

I loved this time of day, when the world basked in neither darkness, nor light, but a kaleidoscope of ethereal beauty. It was if a painter had swept their brush across the sky.

"No," he agreed.

"There's nothing like it."

"You can say that again."

I looked down, finding his eyes on me. "I meant the sky."

"I was too," he smiled.

"It's gorgeous," I warmed, feeling the heat surge between our palms.

"They said the weather would be beautiful tonight."

"Mother Nature on the event staff, too?"

"You have no idea who helped with this one," he smiled. "Speaking of...shall we?"

"Where are we going?"

Evan looked at me, revealing nothing but a grin, and then we made our way over to the steps that connected to the beach, and walked down them, hand in hand.

As we descended, a heady blend of floral and spice tickled my nose and filled my lungs, and the light around us changed. The combination of sight and smell evoked the feeling we'd left one world and stepped into another. And as we reached the last step and looked down the stretch of beach belonging to the hotel, I realized that we had.

The hotel's beach cabanas had transformed into comfortable gathering spaces of bright, bold colors—all outdoor furniture replaced with textured carpets, bold jewel-colored sofas, ottomans, and hanging lanterns—while tables covered in fabric of corresponding color, were set up, and adorned with decorative lanterns.

"So?" Evan looked at me, smiling excitedly. "What do you think?"

Incense burned from a series of tall metal lantern stands, filling the air with a blend of cardamon, saffron, jasmine, and orange, while dozens of fire columns, which replaced the torches that normally served as the beach's source of light, burned bright.

It was exotic and lavish, and I'd never seen anything like it. "I think we're under-dressed," I said, looking around in disbelief.

"Anna is there," he pointed to a cabana at the far end of the beach with its panels closed. "She has some dresses waiting for you."

"Is that why we were told to dress casual?"

"To throw you off," he touched my nose.

"Well, it threw me off," I laughed.

"The party doesn't start until six, so you'll have plenty of time to find something you like."

"That's why it's so quiet."

"Well, that, and my parents closed the hotel for the night."

"I can't believe this," I looked around again, amazed by everything.

"I was hoping that's what you'd say," Evelyn said, coming up behind us.

I turned around and found Evan's mother smiling at me. "I can't believe you did all of this."

"Why wouldn't we?"

I shook my head, trying to find the right words to convey what I was feeling. "It's... incredible."

"Well," Evelyn clasped her hands together, obviously pleased. "You two didn't give us much time. But..." she surveyed the beach. "I like to think Marina and I pulled it off."

"Oh, you did," I nodded, meeting her smile with my own. "This is incredible."

"Speaking of your mother," she pressed her lips together in a playful scowl. "You can blame her and Ev if you don't like the choices that they picked out for you. I had some ideas, but they insisted on picking out your selections."

Evelyn knew fashion better than anyone, and

had she had picked out something for me, it would've been stunning, and over the top—like her own outfit. As usual, she looked stunning. The cream caftan she wore, paired well with her golden skin, and her short dark hair, slicked back, showed off large gold statement earrings and necklace.

"You look amazing."

"Well, thank you," she placed a hand on my cheek. "But this night is about you. Anything you want or need...Anna has it covered. And you," she looked to Evan, "your father needs you in his office."

"Work?" Evan asked.

"He's having trouble putting himself together and your clothes are up there. Can you go and help him, and get yourself changed as well? Laney needs to get dressed."

"Alright, alright," he nodded then turned to me. "You good?"

"She'll be fine," Evelyn insisted.

"I'm good," I smiled.

"I'll be back in a bit," he leaned down to give me a kiss, then turned for the stairs.

"Go," she shooed him away and watched as he climbed the stairs.

"That boy," she waited until he'd reached the top, then turned back to me. "Everything he does is for you."

"I'm a lucky girl," my chest tightened knowing well, his feelings for me.

"This was all his idea, you know. He had the kernel and we simply, helped him bring it to life."

"Really?" I asked and she nodded, smiling wide. "But how on Earth…"

"Interesting word choice," her eyes glistened.

"What do you mean?"

"When you two were kids, that's what I called you…the Earth and Moon. A connected existence, neither possible, without the other."

I thought about the first time I realized I loved Evan Davies. I was six and had kissed him on a dare. The moment my lips touched his cheek, the world shifted; he was the Earth, and I never wanted to be out of his orbit.

"You are his world," she smiled. "Everything he does is for you."

"I am so proud of the human he is, and man he's become. He is everything to me."

"I know," she wiped her eyes. "And that is all a mother wants for her child. To love and be loved."

"I love him more than I can ever put into words."

"I know," she reached for my hand and put hers on top of it, holding it tight. "Oh, look at me."

"I'm sorry," I laughed, my own eyes tearing up.

"Oh, heavens," she waved off my apology, and we laughed; the two of us fanning our eyes as we made our way to the cabana where Anna was waiting. "Have fun," she hugged me goodbye before I stepped inside, and left.

There was a broad selection of dresses, and it was easy to see which my mother had picked, and those Evan had. But after trying on at least half a dozen, I settled on a sky-blue organza dress with gold leaves, lantern sleeves and a plunging neckline. It was flowy and dream-like and I loved it.

After helping me pull my long hair back into a bun, Anna gave me a pair gold chandelier drop earrings and a wrap for when it got colder.

"So, which one did you choose?" Evan asked as he pushed through the panels of the cabana an hour later, eyes closed.

I turned from the mirror and found myself speechless for the second time tonight. Evan had changed into a dark grey linen suit, with a white button-down cotton shirt, left untucked. He looked beautiful and sexy, and my heart skipped a beat.

"Take a look," I swallowed, anxious for him to see.

He opened his eyes slowly and placed a hand on his heart. "You look stunning."

"I was going to say the same thing about you."

"Can I tell you a secret?"

"Of course," I smiled.

"I knew you'd choose that one."

"How?"

"Because I know how much you love the fall, and the pattern looks like leaves."

Evan was right. The dress reminded me of falling autumn leaves and was exactly why I preferred it over the others.

"So, you chose what you were wearing on chance?" I lifted an eyebrow, seeing how well his outfit, complimented my dress.

"I chose on knowledge," he countered. "I know you better than anyone, Alaina Thomas, which is how I was able to pick out this." Evan reached into the inside pocket of his jacket and removed a black velvet box.

"What's that?"

"You'll have to open it and see," he grinned, holding it out to me.

"You already got me the best gift in the world," I held up my hand.

"Open it," he encouraged.

"Evan, you need to stop spoiling me."

"Never," he smiled wider.

Sighing with mock exasperation, I reached for

the box and lifted the lid; delicate hinges creaking as it opened, revealing a gold locket, in the shape of the moon.

"May I?" he asked. I nodded and turned, watching in the mirror as he removed it from the box and lifted it over my head. "This is something new," he lowered it down to my neck, then fastened the clasp. "If I know what love is, it is because of you."

"Are you getting sentimental on me, Davies?" I reached up, touching the chain gingerly.

"That's what's inscribed…in the locket."

I reached for the locket and opened it, and sure enough, Hermann Hesse's famous words greeted me in elegant script.

"I love it," I turned around. "And you."

"We're going to have an amazing life," he looked at me, eyes shining.

"I know," I smiled back at him, butterflies fluttering in my stomach.

"But first," he held out an arm. "There's tonight. Are you ready?"

"Lead the way," I wrapped my arm through his and together we stepped into the night.

CHAPTER FOURTEEN

EVAN AND I STROLLED THE BEACH, MARVELING AT every detail. We were anxious to see it all before the guests arrived.

In addition to the cabanas, outdoor sitting areas had been set up along the beach, with large ornate carpets, and bright, oversized pillows. While two full-service bars anchored each end of the party, and served a mixture of beer, wine, and signature cocktails, created especially for the night.

A dining area had also been set up, with tables heaped with a variety of decadent dishes including mezes, pita, hummus, tzatziki, tabbouleh, and couscous. As well as dozens of cheeses, roasted nuts, and fruits, including oranges with cinnamon, pears, apricots, and figs, and hot plates made to order, including chicken tagine and pomegranate salmon.

I was admiring the desert table, piled high with almond cookies, Turkish delight, and baklava, when my mother found us.

"Oh honey," she clapped her hands together. "You look beautiful."

"Thank you," I greeted her with an enormous hug. "And you..." I took a step back, admiring her in turn. "You look wonderful."

My mother wore a red caftan with long, bell sleeves, and a gold belt cinched tight at the waist. Her hair, pulled low into a ponytail, showed off her jewelry, which she'd kept simple to a pair of gold hoop earrings and large gold bracelet.

"Well, thank you," she smiled at the compliment. "And, as usual, Evan was right," she looked me up and down. "That dress, is gorgeous on you."

"Well, it was hard not to pass up. It's incredible. In fact, all of this... is incredible. You and Evelyn have really outdone yourself."

"It was fun, that's for sure," she looked around, nodding. "A little hectic to get things here on time, but it all worked out, thankfully."

From the carpets to the hanging lanterns to the ornate gold bowls, I could only imagine the care and detail that went in to selecting each item. And as my mother shared stories of the places, she and

Evelyn went to, in order to find a specific plate, or lantern, I understood just how extraordinary of an effort it was between her business and the hotel's resources, to find everything.

"I can't believe you did all of this in two weeks."

"We are pretty impressed, ourselves," she laughed. But, well...it was worth it. It *is* a special night," she winked at Evan.

"Do you want to fill me in on where the inspiration for all this came from?"

"You'll see," she pressed her lips together in a knowing smile.

"That's it?"

"That's it," she nodded.

"And everyone invited. Were they told of this...theme?"

"It was on the invite, as well as strict instructions not to say a word to you."

"I'm surprised no one said anything the last few weeks, especially at the City Council meeting."

"I may have reminded them," Evan said casually.

"And those who opposed the expansion?"

"What about them?"

"Did you remind them," I laughed.

"Of course.

"Wait...I was joking. They'll be here?"

"Everyone was invited," my mother confirmed.

"And you're okay with that?" I asked Evan.

"Why wouldn't I be?"

"They opposed your project."

"But they don't oppose me," he smiled. "I've talked with each of them, since."

"You have?"

"Sure."

"Why?"

"Because your fiancé understands business is business," my mother said simply, as if the answer were obvious.

"Well, you're a bigger person than I am."

"Are you really going to hold a grudge against Mr. Hardy?" he laughed.

I thought about the dear old man whose family had been these parts as long as my own. "I guess not," I exhaled, understanding his point. "But that couple from California, maybe."

To this my mother and Evan both laughed, and I could tell by the look in their eyes, they may have agreed.

"What are we talking about?" Sam asked as she and Tony arrived.

"I'll see you later," my mother leaned in and gave me a hug. "Congratulations again," she whispered, then winked at Evan and left to find

Evelyn.

"Hi!" I greeted Sam excitedly as my mother walked away. "You look amazing," I stepped back to admire her outfit.

She was wearing a green dress, which hugged her waist, and ended just above the ankles, so as to not swallow her petite frame; her brown pulled into a braid on each side, and wrapped into a small bun, bound by a gold ribbon.

"Thank you," she looked me up and down. "And you... and this...it's like something out of a movie."

"It really is," I agreed.

"And you didn't find out?" she asked, turning back to me.

"I knew absolutely nothing until we arrived. Although, I can't believe you didn't tell me."

"I'm a reporter. I know how to protect my sources."

"Okay, fair enough. But what about you, Tony? How could you not have told me?"

"All I can say is, wow," he nodded and looked around. "We're in for some night."

"That we are," Evan clapped his friend on the back.

I wrapped my arm around Evan's waist and leaned into him. "You clean up well, Spencer."

"Why thank you," he stuck his chest out proudly.

Tony looked great, wearing an olive-green linen suit and cream button-down shirt, which complimented Sam's outfit brilliantly. "I picked this out, all on my own."

"Right," Sam laughed. "With help from Evelyn's look book."

"Your mom created a look book for tonight?" I laughed and looked to Evan.

"You know how she is," he shook his head gently.

If my mother and Evan's were able to pull this off in three weeks, I could only imagine what was in store for our wedding. Not to mention, any kind of look book Evelyn would create for that event.

"Well," Evan wrapped his hand around my lower back, pulling me close. "Let's get this party started, shall we?"

"Yes!" Tony clapped, and the four of us made our way over to the bar, excitement in the air as the night extended before us.

***

My mother was right—practically the whole town had showed up, including the couple from

199

California, who walked around mingling, nodding at everything with approval.

"These Moroccan mojitos are delicious," I reached for the glass Evan handed to me, my second drink of the night.

"I know," Sam swirled a stick skewered with lime in her own glass. "I could drink these all night."

"I think you already have," Tony laughed. "What's that, your third?"

"Who's counting?" she swatted his arm playfully.

"No one," Evan replied. "We all have rooms waiting for us, so drink up."

"We do?" I asked, unaware we'd be staying the night at the hotel.

"Yup," he took a sip of his own drink. "Tonight, the hotel is ours."

"Isn't it always?" Tony asked, good naturedly.

"I mean," Evan laughed. "I reserved rooms for the four of us. So, drink as much as you want. Stay out as long as you want. Whenever you're ready to turn in for the night, the room is there."

"No way," Sam moved along to the music streaming from the speakers concealed among the rocks. A rhythmic mix of guitar, lute and percussion filled the air, and I too, swayed along. "I'm staying here until the sun comes up. This is probably as close to Casablanca as I'll ever get."

We laughed and clicked our glasses together, as the night continued.

For the next few hours, Evan and I said thank you to hundreds of guests offering their congratulations—mingling separately and together, effortlessly—but when Mayor Cartwright arrived, we set our drinks down, found one another, and greeted him together. He may have been our town's Mayor, but he was also Caleb's dad, and we'd always considered him another parent.

"Mayor Cartwright," I reached out to give him a hug. He'd put on weight since Caleb's passing, and the wrinkles around his eyes had increased, noticeably. "We're so glad you could make it."

"I wouldn't miss this for the world," he said jovially.

"We appreciate you being here," Evan stuck out his hand.

"That was some City Council meeting," the mayor shook it, then patted Evan on the back.

"It was," Evan nodded.

"Did you sweat a bit?"

"Not at all, sir."

"I always said Caleb could learn a lot from you."

"Well," Evan smiled in remembrance of our

friends. "He taught me a thing or two as well."

I'd felt Caleb's spirit throughout the night. He was the life of every party, and would have been of this one, too.

"I suspect he would have been in rare form tonight," Mayor Cartwright mused.

Sensing the sarcasm in his response, Evan nodded gently, but didn't say anything.

Caleb had started drinking in high school, and it only escalated in college. We'd all noticed, including his father, and Evan had even talked to Caleb about it a couple of times.

We knew Caleb's father didn't approve of his partying, and it had been a source of contention between the two. Still, we didn't like to hear his father's inferred criticism. Especially, since Caleb was no longer here.

"Well kids," Mayor Cartwright smiled. "Congratulations on your engagement. I wish you nothing but the best. Don't be strangers, okay?"

"We won't," Evan shook his hand again, and we watched him walk away.

"Was that weird, or was it just me?" I asked, waiting until he was out of earshot.

"You felt it too?"

"Makes me sad to hear him talk about Caleb like that."

"Me too," he nodded as we watched the Mayor make his way to the bar.

"Are you having a good time?" Evan asked as we turned back to one another.

"I am," I smiled, buoyant with happiness. It was the first time we'd been alone since the party began and I was anxious to know what my mother and Evelyn were referring to when I asked about the theme. "Care to tell me now, what this is all about?"

"Our engagement?" he pushed an errant hair from my eyes.

"No," I tipped my head. "The food, the cabanas, the music…"

"You'll see," he smiled mysteriously.

"When?"

"Soon," he leaned down and kissed me, the taste of mint on his lips mixing with that of lime on mine.

My head swam, both of us lost in the magic of the night, that we didn't realize anyone was there until the sound of someone clearing their throat grabbed our attention.

"Hey," Evan pulled back, greeting Dean with a sheepish grin.

"This is something," Dean greeted us, and looked out across the party.

"I'm glad you could make it," Evan shook his hand.

I wasn't aware Dean was planning to be here. But, seeing the way he more or less saved the day at the City Council meeting, Evan had no doubt invited him.

"Surprisingly, it smells just like this."

Evan closed his eyes in response to the comment. "Oh man…I'm sorry. I didn't think—"

"Don't apologize," Dean held up his hand, cutting off Evan's apology. "It's your party."

Seeing Evan and Dean together on this beach, jolted me back to that night in my near-death experience when the two fought.

"Beaches bother you?" I swallowed, trying to ignore the recollection.

"Dean spent time in the Middle East," Evan explained.

"But it's okay," Dean insisted.

"Are you sure?" Evan asked.

"It's fine," he nodded. "I'm glad to be here."

"Good," Evan exhaled. "In that case, why don't you go on and mingle. You made quite the impression at the meeting the other night, and I suspect there some people here that would like to talk to you."

"It was nothing," Dean smiled. "I only spoke the truth."

"Well," Evan said good-naturedly, "all the same.

Go grab yourself a drink and have fun."

Dean started to walk towards the party, then stopped. "Wait," he said abruptly, and turned, extending his hand in our direction. The moment sent a wave of déjà vu crashing into me and I swayed; my arm twinging with the phantom pain of Dean's vice-like hold.

"Woah," Evan laughed, placing a hand on my lower back to steady me. "Too many mojitos?"

It didn't matter that night in my near-death experience — where Dean grabbed me, and he and Evan nearly fought — hadn't really happened. That world had been real to me, and apparently still haunted me, in this one.

I closed my eyes, pushing the memory of that night from my mind, and when I opened them again, and looked down, saw Dean holding a bottle in his outstretched hand.

"I just wanted to give you this. To say thank you... and congratulations."

Evan grabbed the bottle and read the label. "Bodegas Vega."

"A friend suggested it. I don't drink wine, but it's supposed to be good."

"Good," Evan shook his head. "It's one of the best. The hotel sommelier has been talking about this forever," Evan looked from the bottle to Dean.

"This is really thoughtful, Dean. Thank you."

"Why don't we go uncork it and have a drink?" Dean suggested, obviously happy with Evan's response. "Maybe today is the day I become a wine drinker after all."

"How about later? There's some more people we have to get to."

"Of course," Dean waved his hand, dismissing his ask. "This is a big night for you two."

Evan smiled and reached for my hand. "Go on, and we'll meet up later. And grab something to eat. There's plenty of food and well...everything."

"Sounds good," Dean looked from Evan to me. "Congratulations again. I'm...really happy for you both."

"Thank you," Evan gripped my hand tighter, and Dean walked away.

"That was...nice," I said after he'd left, looking at the bottle in Evan's hands.

"It was extremely generous," Evan agreed. "This wine is *really* expensive."

"Oh yeah?"

"Yeah," Evan smiled.

"Wonder why he decided to gift us something so extravagant?"

"I don't know," Evan looked to the beach, watching as a couple of guests walked up to Dean and began talking. "But what I *do* want to know," he held the bottle down at his side and reached for me with his other hand. "Is where were we?"

I inhaled as he leaned in and pressed his lips to mine, forgetting all about Dean.

"There you are," Evelyn cleared her throat.

Evan and I laughed and pulled apart, sheepish grins on our faces for the second time in minutes.

"Ev, why do you have a four-hundred-dollar bottle of wine?"

"It was a gift."

"A good one," she eyed the label with approval. "But everyone was instructed no gifts. Give it to me, you're almost up."

"Almost up?" I looked at Evan, puzzled, as he handed his mother the bottle.

"You ready?" she asked slyly.

"You have no idea," he smiled wide.

"What's going on?" I watched as Evelyn called out to a hotel staff member and asked them to bring the wine up to the lobby.

Once the staff member left, the three of us made our way to the center of the beach, where another team member stood, holding a mic. They handed it to Evelyn and the music stopped.

"Hello, everyone," she tapped it and a sea of faces turned towards her and it grew quiet. "Thank you so much for being here with us tonight. I hope you're having a wonderful time." Guests whistled and cheered, and Evelyn smiled. "Excellent," she waited until it was silent again to continue. "We are so glad you could be here tonight and help us celebrate the engagement of our beloved Evan and Laney."

Guests again cheered; a couple even tapped their glasses. Evan leaned down and kissed me, as was the custom, and I blushed at the weight of everyone's eyes on us as he pressed his lips to mine.

"Marina and I hoped for this day, longer than probably, anyone," Evelyn continued, looking to my mother for a moment with a knowing smile. "And while there were times, we didn't think it would ever happen," she smiled softly and looked at me and winked. "We are thrilled it has. Laney, we love you so much and couldn't be happier to have as a member of our family."

Evelyn blew me a kiss and my eyes teared up. "Part of what makes this night so special is that we are able to share it will all of you," Evelyn turned back around to the party, oozing charm and grace. "We are so lucky for your support and friendship and want to thank you all for being here on this magical night. And... speaking of magic," she turned to Evan, "I think this is where I turn it over to you."

Evelyn held the mic out to Evan, and he kissed my hand before letting it go to grab it. Fire from a nearby column crackled in the background as he cleared his throat and began.

"Thanks mom, and dad," he smiled at his parents with gratitude, then turned his attention forward. "And all of you, thank you so much for being here tonight. It looks like everyone is enjoying themselves." Tony called out, as did Sam, in addition to a couple of whistles and cheers from other classmates. "Good," he laughed, "that's what I wanted tonight to be about. Family, friends, and a little bit of magic. Which, speaking of…I've gotten more than a few questions about all of this. And…" he held his hand up when one guest called out and then another. "I am finally going to tell you. It starts, with this beautiful lady right here."

"Me?" I whispered as Evan turned to look at me.

"For as long as I can remember, I've been crazy about this girl," he winked. "In fact, when I was six years old, I told her father I'd marry her one day."

I widened my eyes and looked over to my father, who laughed and nodded. "True story!" he called out.

"Do you know what he said?" Evan continued, and I turned back to him. "Well, to be honest, nothing," he laughed. "Instead, he walked over to the bookshelf in his study, pulled out the biggest book I'd ever seen, handed it to me, and said, 'Son, when you've read this, come to me, and we'll talk.'"

A handful of guests called out my father's name and laughed. "That sounds like Denver," my mother nodded emphatically.

"The book," Evan paused, "was *Arabian Nights*."

I looked from Evan to the beach, and everything began to make sense. And as I realized it, so too, did the guests. They smiled and nodded with excitement and Evan continued.

"But what I didn't know, is that book he handed me is one of three. A collection of two hundred stories, across a thousand and one nights, that are, let me tell you, not the easiest to read when you're seven."

"Or, when your head is on baseball!" Tony called out.

"That, too, brother!" Evan pointed to him and everyone around us erupted in laughter. "But I accepted that challenge from Mr. Thomas, and I read every story in every volume, because there was nothing that was going to stop me."

I'd remembered hearing my father over the years, ask Evan every now and then, 'How are you coming along on that book I recommended, Ev?' To which Evan would smile, and respond, 'Good, Mr. Thomas, good.' I was always curious how many books Evan had borrowed from my father over the years. I never would've imagined it was one he'd been reading all that time — and the reason.

"The day I finished that incredible series," Evan continued, turning to me again. "Your dad and I finally had that talk, and when we were done, I felt like the luckiest guy in the world."

I didn't know when Evan finished the book, or even when he and my father had spoken, but I felt the weight of that moment, and knew no matter when it had been, no matter how well the conversation went, it would've been too late. Evan wouldn't confess his feelings, let alone ask me out on a date, because of 'the rule.'

We'd created the agreement in middle school, when all our friends were beginning to have crushes, passing notes to classmates that asked the daring question, 'Will you out with me?' And it seemed like the best way to protect our friendship.

The simple pact, however, made as children, had laid the path Evan, and I, would walk, for the next ten years. And even though Evan had spent years preparing for the day he could confess his feelings to me — reading a book, more dauntless than time itself to do so — he never did because of that promise.

He didn't say any of this, however. He didn't have to. I knew our story, and as he looked at me, his heart speaking to mine, I knew just how great the lengths, Evan would go for me. He'd kept his feelings a secret, for me. He hid his heart from everyone, for me. And this party, his toast, and my beautiful locked, reflected the love he'd carried all of those years, for me.

"I read every one of those stories for you," Evan smiled at me, eyes luminous. "And ever since that day when I spoke with your father, I've waited for this moment. Every challenge we've faced…every turn life has thrown at us…I'm reminded of the lessons I learned in those stories. Lessons of fate and destiny and how the impossible is worth fighting for, no matter how long it takes. But the biggest thing I learned," he paused and swallowed, "and also, the most relevant…is that in all of the universe, there is only one moon. And you, Alaina Elizabeth Thomas, are my moon. You are my destiny. You are, my *Arabian Nights*."

My eyes teared up. A lump, the size of the moon itself, stopped me from saying anything, as I stared at Evan, speechless, feeling more love than I'd ever felt in my life.

A server appeared, holding a tray of champagne

flutes, and Evan grabbed one, handed it to me, then grabbed one for himself. "So please join me," he held up his glass, and waited as dozens of servers passed out flutes to every guest, then turned again to look at me with the biggest smile I'd ever seen. "In toasting this remarkable woman that I have loved for as long as I can remember. I am so thankful that in all the stories of the world, you chose to be mine."

Everything blurred around me. The lights, the guests, the night...it all faded away, except for one thing. Evan. I may be his moon, but he was my story. And would be...for a thousand and one lives, and longer.

CHAPTER FIFTEEN

THE PARTY CONTINUED INTO THE NIGHT, OUR PARENTS and their friends retiring to their rooms shortly after midnight, while me, Evan, Tony, Sam, and a handful of friends from school, continued celebrating long afterwards. But eventually, guests began to leave, until it was just the four of us, and Tyler Garrity.

"I'm so glad you came tonight," I smiled at Tyler.

"Well, thank you for inviting me," he smiled back. "I wouldn't miss the party of the century before leaving."

Tony lifted the glass in his hand, tall frame swaying. "I think, and I may be going out on a limb here, but our boy here is right. This very well may be the best party I have ever been to."

"It was pretty incredible," Tyler looked across

the beach. "I can't believe your moms pulled all this off."

"Me either," I smiled, still buoyant from the beautiful words of Evan's toast.

"You know, if I remember correctly," Tyler added, "we've had some fun events in this town over the years. And, if memory serves me correctly, your moms were responsible for planning many of them."

"Probably," Evan smiled.

"I can't believe your dad is selling the store," Tony said to Tyler, shaking his head. "You're going to miss those epic parties...and this place."

"I know," he nodded. "But no more cold winters for the old man. And no more for me! My bones can't take it."

I knew he was trying to sound excited but couldn't help but hear a hint of sadness in his voice.

"Squatting behind home plate will do that," Tony laughed. "Most catchers can't walk after thirty-five."

"You know, I thought of that the other day," I piped in.

"Garrity's squatting behind home plate?" Tony lifted an eyebrow.

"No," I rolled my eyes. "That game in high school...where you guys took state."

"Oh, Laney," Sam let out an exaggerated sigh, evidence of way too much to drink. "You don't know what you've done."

"What?" I asked innocently.

Sam looked from Tony to Tyler and then Evan. "You do realize, the three guys, involved in the that historic play are *right here*."

"I know," I laughed. "That's why I said it."

"But you also know, they're at that age where they're not just about talking about their glory days, but still foolish enough to think they can re-enact them."

Tyler looked to Tony who looked to Evan who, without missing a beat, slipped out of his jacket, tossed it over a nearby chair, then walked over to a table not completely picked clean, and reached for an orange.

"You wouldn't," I eyed the piece of fruit in his hand, then watched as he tossed it to Tony, who set his glass down, just before catching it.

"Look what you started!" Sam laughed.

"Me?" I laughed back. "You put the idea into their heads."

Tyler, seeing the orange in Tony's hand, sprinted down the beach, then turned, getting into a deep squat, as if he were awaiting Tony's pitch.

Tony hurled the fruit down to Tyler, who,

pretending to also be the batter, caught it, then got up and threw the orange over Tony's head, just like the line drive ball, years earlier.

Evan sprinted and reached out, surprisingly catching it, then threw it back to Tyler, who caught it and kneeled, tagging Tony, who had sprinted home as if he were the runner.

"You're out!" Sam called and Tyler and Evan ran to each other, yelling and cheering.

I watched in bemusement as Tony made his way over to where Evan and Tyler jumped up and down, clapping each other on the back, yelling as if they were eighteen again.

"You guys are something else," I laughed.

Tyler reached for his lower back and twisted from one side to the other. "Oh man, I should've stretched."

"You looked like a pro my friend," Tony gave him a high-five.

"Coming from a pro, I appreciate that man, thank you."

Tony slung his arm around Tyler and pulled him in for a squeeze. "Don't mention it."

"Man," Tyler laughed. "Are we really this old?"

"We are not old," Sam laughed.

"The best years are yet to come," Tony agreed.

I looked over at Evan, warming at the thought of

what could be in store for us not too far in the future. As if having the same thought, Evan looked at me and winked.

"You can't leave this, Tyler. You just can't," Tony chided.

"Agree," Evan twisted from side to side. He was still in great shape, but even that reach seconds earlier ago, harkened back to a kind of athleticism that is only possible when you're a teenager. "We need Garrity's. What's Florida got that Lake Haven doesn't?"

"Um," Tyler looked down considering the question, then answered simply. "Chris."

"Ahh," Tony eyed his friend. "A girl? Well, no wonder."

"Not exactly," he cleared his throat.

"A little honey on the side is nothing to be ashamed of my friend."

"No," he looked up. "I mean, it's not a girl. It's...Chris*topher*," he said, emphasizing the second part of the name.

"Christopher," Sam repeated.

Tyler nodded slowly, looking at her with uncertainty.

"Well, that's smart," Tony shrugged. "Save some money by getting a roommate."

"Hey," Sam called to Tony and motioned for

him to stop talking.

"What?" he asked.

Sam widened her eyes, as if with the change in diameter, Tony would understand what she was trying to say. And, as if communicating in their own secret language, Tony's eyes widened. "Oh," he said slowly, and then again. "Ohhhh!"

Tyler watched as Tony's expression changed from surprise to understanding, and when Tony smiled and stuck his hand up to high five Tyler, the relief on his face was evident.

"Hey man, that's rad! Can I say that ...is it rad? Or cool? Or...what?"

"Congratulations, babe," Sam looked at Tony. "Just say, congratulations."

"Well yes," Tony stuck out his hand. "Obviously. Congratulations! Tell us more. Like when...and how...and when..."

"Tyler," I smiled encouragingly. "Tell us more."

Tyler looked from Tony to me, and seeing nothing but acceptance, visibly eased, and proceeded to tell us about the guy he met two years earlier, on a trip to Miami.

"He sounds amazing," Sam gushed once Tyler had finished.

Tyler's boyfriend, Chris, was a bartender, and had been asking him to move to Miami for the past year.

"It's been tough to have to choose between him or my dad's store. But…I talked to my dad, and he thought it might be easier."

"For whom?" I asked.

"Me…this town," he shrugged. "He was concerned about how it may be for me…being here."

"Why?" Tony laughed.

Tyler looked at Tony. "You know how people are around these parts."

"Um, I'm pretty sure I don't," Tony laughed.

"They're not fond of outsiders."

"You're not an outsider."

"My mother is not from here and the town loves her like she is," I added.

"Okay," Tyler crossed his arms. "Let me say it this way. You know how folks here can be narrowminded. He was concerned it may be difficult for us."

"The only concern I have is that ice cream your dad has every summer, disappearing forever. To heck with the rest," Tony waved his hand. "You belong here, and so does this love of yours. He's with you, he's with us. End of story."

"You don't know what it means to me for you to say that. But not everyone thinks that way."

"Love is love," I shrugged.

"For you all, maybe. But there are more single-minded people in this town than you might think."

"There are a lot of single-minded people in every town," Tony countered. "Don't change your life out of fear."

"My dad is getting older," Tyler crossed his arms. "He doesn't need the stress. And Chris' job is there. There's no work for him here."

"He tends bar?" Evan asked. Tyler nodded. "Does he like it?"

"He does," Tyer smiled. "Makes good drinks, too."

"Better than these?" Sam looked into the glass in her hand.

"You have no idea," Tyler grinned.

"Bring him up here, then," Evan suggested. "We could use a bartender at the hotel."

"What?" Tyler looked at Evan, slightly puzzled.

"I'm serious. There are plans for another bar in the expansion. Have him come up and see what we're doing, and if he likes it, the job is his."

"Are you serious?" Tyler asked, clearly surprised by the offer.

"Yes," Evan nodded. "There's going to be a lot of jobs when it's done, and it would be nice to have one less position to worry about filling."

"Great idea," Tony agreed.

Just when I didn't think Evan could surprise me anymore, he upped the ante.

"This expansion is supposed to help the people of this town," Evan continued. "If that means making it possible for those who belong here, to stay here, then it has served its purpose."

"And what about...the rest?" Tyler asked skeptically.

"Let me ask you this," Tony cut in. "Do you want your dad's store to stay in the family?"

"Yeah," he nodded. "The idea of that place no longer being around kills me."

"Does your dad want you to stay?"

"He does," Tyler nodded. "He just doesn't want anyone to give us any problems."

"So, he's met your fella?"

"The two went deep sea fishing when we went to Miami last year and I swear, my dad may like him more than me."

"Then, what's the problem?"

"You've read what happens in small towns when someone is different."

"Old man Closter... that's different," Tony laughed. "You my friend, are no different than anyone else."

"He's got a point there," I held up my hand,

thinking about the man who dressed like a pirate and liked to tell stories to anyone that would listen, of the years he spent on the whaling ship of Laurence Haven, our town's namesake. "Last I checked, you don't think you're over two hundred years old and finish every sentence with 'Aye, Matey.'"

I didn't know if it were the night, the nostalgia, or the alcohol, but as we all laughed and I looked around and saw the love in everyone's eyes, I could feel the love and believed it had the power to do anything.

"You're no different than me or Evan," Tony said once we'd stopped laughing. "Who you love, doesn't matter."

"Agree, one thousand percent," Evan nodded.

"Give it some thought," Tony encouraged. "Talk to your dad. See what he thinks."

"I know he'd love to keep the store in the family," Tyler considered Tony's advice.

"Then the offer stands," Evan stuck his hand out. "Talk to Chris, have him come up here and check out the plans. If he likes the idea, let's talk."

"And hey, maybe we can ask Evan and Laney's moms to throw you two a coming out party?" Tony added.

"That may be a bit too much, too soon," Tyler

laughed.

"I'm sure she would love nothing more. You say the word," Evan smiled. "But after the wedding, of course. Something tells me her hands are going to be full after tonight."

"You two picked a date?" Tyler brightened.

"We did," I said happily. "Weekend after Easter. And bring Chris. I'd love to meet him."

"Really?"

"Of course. He's your plus one. He's always welcome."

"Guys," Tyler looked around…I don't know what to say."

"Say…" Tony bent down and picked up the orange. "Let's play a little ball!"

I laughed, watching as the guys tossed the piece of fruit back and forth. This is how life should be. As long there was love, what else mattered?

"Where are you going?" Evan called out as I headed to the cabana.

"I'll be back," I pointed at the guys. "Go on, they need another player."

Despite the beautiful weather earlier in the evening, it had grown cold as the night went on. After finding the wrap Anna had given me in the cabana, I stopped to look in the mirror, reaching up to touch the locket Evan had given me. The words inscribed, and his toast, wrapped around my heart and squeezed tight.

"My moon, my heart," Evan said softly, coming up behind me, and wrapping his arms around my waist.

I leaned my head back against his chest. "Tonight, was perfect," I said dreamily, filled with happiness.

"Were you surprised?"

I nodded and turned, placing my hand on his cheek. "Your toast was so beautiful. And all of this," I looked around, drinking in the last moments of the night. "I am the luckiest person in the world."

"I am," he leaned down and kissed me, sending a wave of fire down my spine. "You are my world, Alaina Thomas."

"Don't start something you can't finish," I whispered through his kiss.

"Who said I can't finish it?" he pulled back, lifting an eyebrow.

"Everyone is outside."

"Actually," he leaned in. "They're not."

"What?"

"They've gone up to their rooms."

"But I've only been gone a few minutes."

"Take a look for yourself."

I walked over to the panels, pulling them back to

peek outside, and sure enough, Tony, Sam and Tyler were making their way up the stairs, arms slung around one another. The beach was quiet, and we were alone.

"I didn't get to say goodnight," I let go of the panels and turned back around.

"You'll see them at brunch tomorrow and say good morning."

"There's a brunch?"

"Not formally. We just planned it."

"Why do you never cease to amaze me?"

"Probably the same reason you never cease to amaze me," he wrapped his arm around my waist.

"Can you believe Tyler's news?"

"Sure," he smiled softly, pulling me closer.

"Did you know?"

"No, but I'm glad he found someone. And truth be told, there's a few folks in town, I think he'd be surprised to learn, have a few secrets of their own."

"Really?" I asked, eyes wide. "Like whom?"

"Not my secrets to tell. But perhaps if he shares his life in the open, others will feel comfortable to do the same."

I hoped for Tyler, that Evan was right, wanting anyone that was lucky enough to have the kind of love that we did, be able to share it.

"Want to know another secret?" he asked.

"Go for it," I smiled.

"If I don't get to be alone with you right now, I'm going to lose my mind."

"Evan," my cheeks burned.

"What do you say?" he nodded to the oversize sofa in the corner.

"We can't."

"We can do whatever we want."

"You planned this."

"I hoped," he smiled playfully.

"You wanted the night to end like this."

"Laney," he laughed. "Since we were in high school, I wanted every night to end like this."

We both laughed.

"I love you, Evan Davies."

"And I you."

"I will remember this night, always."

"Make it one to remember?" he winked.

I considered the idea of a night with Evan under the stars. Nothing but us and the smell of spice in the air.

"It's just you..." he leaned in and kissed me. "And me..." his lips trailed down to my neck. "And this amazing cabana."

"This is crazy," I grinned as he scooped me up.

"No crazier than I am of you."

"Or I, of you."

"A couple of fools," he agreed, carrying me to the sofa, and we ended the night just like the Earth and the Moon — in our own universe.

CHAPTER SIXTEEN

THE FOLLOWING MONDAY, I SAT AT MY DESK, STARING out the window. I couldn't stop myself from smiling. The weekend had been magical, and I was floating.

"Ms. Thomas," the school secretary Janie, knocked on my door. "There's a student here to see you."

"Right," I shook the dream-like haze clouding my mind and turned around, facing forward at my desk.

"Everything okay?"

"Yeah," I nodded, then thought, why not get her advice. "What would *you* give someone as a thank you gift?"

"Depends," she shrugged as she stood with her hand on the doorknob.

"On?"

"What I was thanking them for."

"A party."

"You wouldn't by any chance, be talking about that amazing party on the beach this past weekend, would you?" she asked.

"Maybe," I smiled.

"I'm not sure *how* you can thank someone for throwing you *that* party," she laughed. "But thank *you* for inviting *me*. I can now cross that Nile cruise off my bucket list."

"That's Egypt," I laughed.

"Oh," she waved me off and laughed. "You know what I mean."

I looked through the door to where Niña sat quietly in the waiting area, book open on her lap. "How is she today?" I asked, looking back at Janie.

"Seems a bit down," she whispered. "Who knows, though. She's hard to read."

Niña *was* hard to read. But the last few weeks, I could see her letting her guard down. She still loved to ask me questions, but also now appeared to be more comfortable talking about herself. As a result, I'd gotten to know her better by what she *did* share.

The first, was that she was a voracious reader and understood literature in a way that would make my father proud. The second, was that she was enthusiastic about culture and history and was extremely proficient in Latin-based languages. Third, and most important, I'd discovered that underneath her tough exterior, was a bright student with a wry sense of humor. I felt a connection to her and wanted to help her as much as I could.

"Should I send her in?" Janie asked.

"Please," I nodded.

"Ms. Thomas will see you now," Janie stood with her back to the door, motioning for Niña to make her way to my office.

I stood up and waited for Niña to close the door. Once she had, I sat down and folded my hands gently, and placed them on the desk.

"So...how are you today?"

"Looks like someone had a good weekend," she answered my question in the way in which I'd become accustomed — with one of her own.

While another adult might find it nosey, I knew it was a defense mechanism, and took it as a compliment she was interested in talking, period.

"It was good," I smiled. "And you...did you have a good weekend?"

"It was okay," she exhaled and sat down.

"Did you do anything fun?"

"Not really," she shrugged.

"How are classes?"

"They're fine."

"And AP Spanish...you still enjoying that class?"

"Mr. Cervantes is cool. At least I can speak Spanish with him."

"I'm sure he loves it."

"He does," she nodded. "So, you had a good weekend," she said again.

"I did," I nodded. "My family threw an engagement party for my fiancé and I."

"Oh yeah?" her eyes brightened, the word party appearing to grab her attention. "How was it?"

"It was incredible."

"Looks like it. You're glowing." I placed a hand on my cheek, and it did feel warm. "Was there a theme?"

"Yes."

"And?"

"And...what," I laughed.

"What was it?"

"Aren't we supposed to be talking about you?" I smiled.

"Please?" she pleaded; brown eyes wide. "Can we not talk about me right now?"

I sat back and looked at her, wondering if I shared with her, would she share with me?

"It was an *Arabian Nights* theme," I said finally.

"Oh, yeah?" she sat up, face brightening. "Did

you know, there is heavy Spanish influence in Morocco?"

"There is?"

"Yes," she said excitedly. "From the food to the language to the architecture. And...there is also influences from the Arabian Peninsula in Spain. Andalusia is beautiful. The Alhambra is stunning. Do you want to see some pictures?"

"You've been?"

"Of course," she dug into her backpack.

"Recently?"

"I've been there many times. We lived in Spain when I was younger."

"Really?"

"Until I was nine," she nodded. "Before we lived in Mexico."

"Wow. You lived in Mexico, too?"

"We did," she nodded, removing a cell phone from her backpack. "Before Los Angeles."

"Seems like you've had some great adventures," I watched as she scrolled through her photos. Although, what I really wanted to say was it sounded like she moved quite a bit for a girl her age, and that it must be hard being the perennial new kid.

"Europe is amazing," Niña continued. "More freedom, less rules. And the history...it's just incredible. Here," she held out her phone. "Take a look."

I reached for the phone and looked down—the building in the photo breathtaking.

"It's a palace," she said dreamily. "And a fortress, and it has the most incredible gardens," she tapped on the phone and showed me a couple of pictures, explaining more about its origins and architecture.

"What's this?" I pointed at the phone. It was a photo of a fountain in the middle of a courtyard.

"That's the Court of the Lions. It's more than five hundred years old."

"And this?" I asked when she flipped to another.

"That's Room of the Beds."

"The tiles are so bright."

"The whole place is rich in color. Everywhere you walk, there are reds, and golds, and blues."

"It reminds me of our engagement party," I said softly.

"Yeah?" she sat back.

"My mother and her best friend really went out of their way to make it feel like a page right out of *Arabian Nights*."

"Do you have any pictures?"

"Of course," I smiled.

"Can I see?"

I looked out my door, and seeing the office empty, reached for my cell phone, and showed Niña my pictures from the party.

"Wow," she gushed, obviously impressed. "This is here?"

"Yes," I nodded. "On the property of the hotel my fiancé's family owns."

"Aqua Luna?"

"Yes," I smiled. "How did you know?"

"Small town, everyone knows everything."

"True," I laughed. "Have you been?"

"I drove by it on my way into town. That's some place."

"It is lovely," I agreed.

"You two look happy."

"We are."

"Did you meet here?"

"We grew up together. Our parents are close."

"That's cool," she sat back. "And you two were part of that group you told me about, right?"

"Right," I nodded and sat back.

I'd told Niña about Caleb, Timmy, Lisa, Evan, and me in a previous meeting, when I was trying to make a point about school and friends. I was surprised she'd remembered.

"Thank you for sharing those pictures with me."

"Oh," she grabbed her phone and shoved it back

into her bag. "It's no problem."

"And everything else...are things well?" I asked.

"Things are fine," Niña sat back and crossed her arms.

"Are you sure?" I asked, studying her body language.

She considered my question and then reached back into her bag and removed a crumpled piece of paper.

"What's that?" I asked, curious.

"You'll see."

"Can you unfold it for me?"

Niña made a fist and used the flat side to straighten the paper, then turned it towards me, so the words were right side up.

"Thank you," I smiled and after looking at it closer, saw it was a flyer for an upcoming dance at school.

"Can you believe it?" she asked, incredulous.

"You don't like dances?"

"It's not the dance. It's the theme. Look," she pressed her finger on the paper.

I looked down at the paper again, reading the title. "Día de los Muertos."

"Day of the Dead," she said.

"Yes," I nodded and smiled, "I know."

"Did you know not one person planning this

dance knows anything about Day of the Dead? How can kids that know *nothing* about the day, plan a dance that is *all about* it?"

"Well," I considered her question. "Why don't you teach them?"

"They wouldn't care. No one in this town even speaks Spanish."

"That's not true," I pushed back gently.

"Mr. Cervantes, doesn't count."

"There are lots of people in this town that speak different languages. And I don't see how speaking Spanish, has anything to do with whether one should plan a dance, or not."

"What I meant," she sat up, taking a deep breath. "Is that one should understand Día...its history, and the heritage of the people who honor and observe it, to plan a dance around it."

"So," I said for a second time. "Why don't you teach them?"

"Because no one at this school cares. They see it as a way to wear cool make up. They don't care about the deeper meaning."

"I'm sure that's not true."

"It is," she said, clearly frustrated. "I heard it with my own ears!"

"Look," I tried a different approach. "The Spanish Club is for students interested in the language. Why don't you start there...get *those* students involved?"

Niña considered the suggestion. "You might be on to something. Even those of non-Latin ancestry have lit a cancel to Santa Muerte."

"Santa, who?" I asked.

"Nuestra Señora de la Santa Muerte," she said dramatically with a wave of her hand. "She who safely delivers one to the afterlife. You said that you knew what Day of the Dead was," she sat back when it became obvious, I wasn't following.

"I know of it, tangentially. Do you celebrate her on Day of the Dead?"

"She *is* Día de los Muertos," Niña said, eyes wide. "It is she you see in parades, and on candles," she added, and reached for her phone again, and scrolled through her photos, handing it to me when she found what she was looking for.

"That's her?" I asked, looking down to a painting of a woman in white lace.

"Isn't she fabulous?"

"The one in the robe, holding a scythe?"

"That's her," she smiled. "You have a dance to honor Día, then you *must* bring her into it. Día doesn't exist, without Santa Muerte."

"So, is it like Halloween?"

"No," Niña rolled her eyes. "Día is not a day of

costumes."

"See," I nodded. "That's why, you're the perfect person to help the committee with the dance. You know so much." She listened to me, with a dubious expression on her face. "I mean it. You can help them do it right."

"You're asking me to join the committee planning the dance?" Niña pressed her lips together with disdain, and despite our age difference, I understood why.

When I was in school, only the most popular students were on the Social Committee. They could be difficult, even to kids they knew their whole life.

Lisa was on the committee all throughout high school, to make sure she had her say on every social event. The group was gossipy and from what I'd heard, nothing had changed.

"Can I keep this?" I asked, reaching for the paper.

"I guess. Why?"

"You'll find out the next time we meet," I said with a hint of mischief, then looked up at the clock overhead. Another minute and the bell would ring, and it would be time for Niña to head to her next class. "Anything else on your mind?"

"No," she exhaled.

"Well then, you'd better get a move on."

Niña stared at me, and for a moment, it looked as if she were about to say something. But then she got up from her seat, saying nothing.

"See you next week," I said cheerfully as she started to leave, wondering why she had gotten quiet there at the end.

"See ya," she waved stiffly and walked out the door.

After Niña left, I picked up the flyer. I may not speak Spanish fluently, but even *I* knew Santa Muerte translated meant holy death. Before recommending her to the Social Committee, I decided to talk with the only teacher likely to have any information about this Santa Muerte—just to see if there was anything I needed to know, as far as Niña's fascination was concerned.

After school ended, I made my way to Mr. Cervantes' class. "Ms. Thomas," he looked up when I knocked on the door. "Hola, cómo estás?"

"Hola," I replied. The greeting was the extent of my Spanish. "Am I bothering you?"

"Not at all," he pushed back from the desk and stood to greet me. "What brings you by?"

"I was hoping I could talk with you about a student," I stepped into the classroom and looked around.

"Oh?" he straightened.

"The transfer," I nodded. "Niña De León."

"Ah yes," he nodded, "Ms. De León."

"How is she doing?" I asked, studying the walls. They were vibrant and rich—a blend of travel posters matted against bright construction paper.

"She is doing well. Could teach this class, I suspect."

"That's good to hear," I smiled.

"She is quite enthusiastic about the language," he added.

"I'm aware," I nodded, making my way down the wall of the class, stopping to look at a framed etching on aged parchment. "What is this?" I asked, pointing up at the picture.

"Ah," he smiled and walked over to where I stood. "That is Quetzalcoatl."

"Is that a kind of god?"

"Hmm," he nodded.

"It's beautiful."

"It has been in my family for many, many years."

"What does he, or it, do?" I asked, studying the drawing, noting its various shapes and colors.

"He is an important god in Aztecan culture. Some may argue, the *most* important."

"How so?"

"Like other early civilizations, the Aztecs and

241

other natives of the region worshipped many gods and deities. Each played role in how they viewed life and death."

"Are these deities still important today?" I asked, looking back to the picture on the wall?

"Very," he crossed his arms and sat on the edge of a student's desk. "My abuela told me stories of Quetzalcoatl as a boy."

"And God?" I asked, feeling out of my depth.

"Despite the spread of Christianity in Mexico and Central Mexico, there is still profound respect and honoring of the old deities."

"Like Santa Muerte?"

"Ah," he nodded and smiled. "Nuestra Señora de la Santa Muerte." I noted the similarity of his enunciation to Niña's. "The protector."

"Protector?"

"Si," he smiled. "Those who follow Santa Muerte believe she is a protector of life."

"Even though her name implies death?"

Mr. Cervantes held up his hand to excuse himself, making his way over to a low bookshelf on the opposite wall.

"Celebrations of death go back thousands of years," he ran his finger down the row of books. When he found what he was looking for he removed it from the shelf and then walked back over to where I was standing. "The Aztecs viewed the universe as a circle. Death and life celebrated equally." He opened a book covered in brown leather and began flipping through the pages. "Santa Muerte, was *the* deity of this celebration."

"How do the two…God and deities, co-exist?"

"These deities have been around for thousands of years before Christianity. They are cultural. And culture is an important part of one's heritage."

"Can you believe in both?"

"The two are not mutually exclusive. To believe in one, does not mean you cannot believe in the other. In fact, those who believe in God, often believe in Santa Muerte." I raised an eyebrow. "It is curious, no?"

"You can say that."

"Santa Muerte protects. And when you ask, she will provide. Here," he held the book out to me. "Take a look."

I looked down at the page, finding a sketch of a skeleton. It wore a cloak, with bright blue eyes, encircled in black; bones, appearing delicate, like porcelain.

"The afterlife is not to be feared," he explained. "It is where those we love, live on. And it is she," he nodded down to the book, "Santa Muerte, who deliver the dead safely to the afterlife."

I noticed the colorful flowers adorning her head, like a crown, and in a strange way, I could see her beauty.

"Ms. Thomas," he asked as I handed the book back. "Why do you ask about Santa Muerte?"

"Oh," I nodded, remembering why I'd stopped by his class. I reached into my pocket and removed the folded-up flyer Niña had left with me, holding it out to him. "The Social Committee is planning a dance and I think it might be good for Niña to help make sure it's represented correctly."

"Ah," he looked at the flyer. "I'm sure other students for whom Día is of importance, would appreciate her knowledge."

I was relieved to hear Niña's interest in Santa Muerte wasn't an obsession, but rather, a genuine passion, one of interest, and heritage.

"It will be good for Ms. De Leon to be involved in the dance. Young minds can always benefit from learning about other cultures."

"You're right," I nodded. "Well," I looked over his desk, covered in assignments. "I'd better let you go."

"Very well," he nodded politely.

"Thank you for your feedback, and the history lesson."

"Any time," he smiled as I made my way to the

door.

"Ms. Thomas," he called as I stepped into the hall. I stopped and turned around. "She is lucky to have you looking out for her."

"Can you remind her of that when she is knee-deep in streamers and balloons?"

"I will," he smiled. "Ve con gracia...go with grace," he translated for me, and smiled.

Go with grace I thought, as I left Mr. Cervantes' class and walked back down the hall to my office.

CHAPTER SEVENTEEN

AFTER MY TALK WITH MR. CERVANTES, I WENT TO SEE Shelley, the girl's gym teacher and Social Committee faculty advisor. As suspected, she was glad to have Niña's help on the dance.

Shelley, too, had gone to school at Lake Haven High, and while she wasn't on the committee when she was a student, she was the perfect adult to supervise the one group in school that wielded power.

Members of the committee were both feared and adored. One wrong move, and you could become a social pariah. But one right move, and you'd run the school. As such, committee members were a handful and Shelley the best, and only person, who could keep them in line.

An incredible athlete in her day, everyone liked and respected Shelley — then and now. She could be fun when she wanted to be, and tough when needed, and the committee stayed in line when she was around.

She'd kept me apprised on how Niña was doing, and it sounded like things were going well. And the following week, when Niña stopped by for our weekly check-in, the smile on her face reinforced as much.

"Well," I sat back in my chair as she took a seat, sitting straight, instead of slumping, as had been the norm. "Looks like you're in good spirits."

"I am," she smiled, dropping her backpack to the floor.

She looked different. Was it her hair? Or makeup? Yes, make up. That was it. She was wearing less, and I felt as if I were seeing her for the first time. I hadn't noticed before how pretty Niña was, but now that I could, it was disarming.

"Thanks for changing our meeting to today."

Normally, Niña and I met on Fridays, but since I was heading to Bangor tomorrow with Sam, I moved all my appointments up a day.

"No prob," she waved her hand.

"So, things with the dance are good I hear?"

"Yes," she nodded. "A lot of work though because there were changes that needed to be made."

"And the others…they were okay with these changes?"

"They're all for them. They think Santa Muerte is just as cool as I do."

"That's great. And Día de los Muertos?"

Niña smiled, taking note of my enunciation. "Nicely done."

"Thank you," I accepted her compliment.

"They didn't know there was more to it than sugar skulls and face paint."

"Well, that must make you happy."

"It does," she nodded. "There's a girl from Spanish Club on the Social Committee. She roped me into going to a meeting and that was cool. It's more than just speaking the language. Mr. Cervantes has incredible knowledge about the old ways."

Of course, I knew this, given the conversation he and I had. But didn't let on that I did. "Oh?" I asked, eyebrows raised.

"Yeah…but don't read into it."

"Read into what?" I laughed.

"Clubs and stuff."

"I'm not," I laughed.

We sat there smiling at each other, and then she grabbed a picture on my desk. It was one of Lisa and me that we'd taken in a photo booth on Venice

Beach.

"She hated that picture."

"Why," Niña set it down.

"She didn't like her hair," I smiled ironically, remembering how perfect she looked; rejecting every picture, and ordering me to throw those we'd taken away. She never knew I'd ripped the one in the frame off, because I loved how we both looked in it.

"It looked fine," Niña laughed.

"Ah, well, fine, wasn't good enough, even though she looked perfect then, as always."

"So, she was pretty."

"No," I shook my head gently. "She was beautiful."

"Has age not been kind?"

I wondered what Lisa would have looked like now. Would she have been even prettier...if that were even possible?

"She's... no longer here," I said simply.

"She stayed in LA?"

"No. She...passed away...two years ago."

"I'm...sorry," Niña sat back, quiet.

"It's fine," I held up my hand.

"Do you miss her?"

"All the time."

"Do you wish she was still here?"

"Yes," I nodded, adjusting the band of my engagement ring with my thumb.

I always thought we'd be there for each other when we got married. I'd be her maid of honor, and she'd be mine. Although, something told me I would've played that role more than once.

"So, you five were like, The Breakfast Club?"

"What was that?" I asked, lingering in a future that would never be.

"A brain, a beauty, a jock…"

"Oh," I nodded, understanding Niña's reference. "It wasn't quite like that."

"Sounds to me like you were quite the power squad. I mean, I've seen the pictures in the trophy case."

"Well," I inhaled. "Caleb was a great basketball player. And Evan," I exhaled, "my fiancé…he was on the baseball team and Homecoming King."

"I've definitely seen her," Niña stared at the picture again.

"You would," I exhaled. "She was a legend. Captain of the cheer squad, Homecoming Queen…head of Social Committee. Her pictures are everywhere around here."

"And you?"

"What about me?"

"Which were you?"

"I was the one that loved them all."

"What are the other two up to?"

"They're gone, too," I said sadly. "Four of us were in a car accident the summer before our senior year of college and we lost them, too."

It was never easy to talk about them, but I knew I might have to during the session in Bangor and was trying to get more comfortable with the idea of talking about our friendship with strangers.

Niña was a student however, and our time together should focus on her. "So," I cleared my throat. "How are things with the dance?"

Niña bent down and rummaged through her backpack. "Here's the new flyer I made," she said proudly, placing a colored piece of paper on the desk. It looked a thousand times better than the one she'd brought to my office last week, with elaborate, black script, and bold, beautiful flowers.

"It's gorgeous," I nodded with approval.

"You think?" she asked, perking up.

"I do."

"I did it."

"Obviously," I smiled.

"What makes you say that?"

"Only one with knowledge of Santa Muerte, could've illustrated her duality of strength and beauty."

"Have you been reading up on her?" Niña asked, lips curling into a curious smile.

"I might have looked into her a bit."

"Well," she grabbed the flyer. "I'm glad. And... I'm glad you like it. We're making copies today and putting them up all over campus. Just wait. If we can pull off what I envisioned, it's going to be incredible."

"I'm sure anything that transforms the gym into your vision will be fantastic."

"Oh, well, you're in for a surprise because we're not having it in the gym."

"You're not?"

"No," she said mischievously, a sly smile pulling at her lips.

"Where are you having it?"

"The Boneyard."

"What?" I asked, surprised by her response.

"I came across it one day while exploring. It's the coolest thing here!" she said excitedly.

Cool wasn't exactly the word I'd use to describe The Boneyard. Eerie was more like it. "They can't possibly let you have a dance there. It's condemned."

The Boneyard was the nickname given to the old cannery and shipyard at the edge of town. The series of dilapidated buildings held together by an aging pier, was at one time, the center of Lake Haven's bustling seaport. But when the town experienced a boom in the 1930's and a new cannery built in the center of town, the old structure was abandoned and had remained empty all these years.

It'd been a popular place to go when we were kids. I'd heard stories of classmates dared to spend the night among the old rocking ships. While others had used it as a place to make-out and party. The creepy place, however, had always terrified me.

But not Lisa. She loved it. From her house the decaying structures looked like a different world, and she considered it her kingdom. I never understood how she could feel so at peace in a place of so little beauty, but she did, and she'd sit among the rusting buckets of steel for hours, staring across the sea — every bit its queen.

"Well," Niña continued. "You're right. They aren't letting us have it at The Boneyard. Not exactly."

"What does that mean, not exactly?"

"We're having it at The Conservatory."

"The Conservatory?" I repeated, equally as shocked as I had been when she'd said The Boneyard.

While the town ignored The Boneyard, The

Conservatory in the park across the street was a beloved piece of Lake Haven's history, and many efforts made over the years, to ensure its protection.

Once upon a time, the beautiful building of iron and glass, was where the ladies in town met for tea and strolled among the exotic plants and flowers from far-away places. Now, it was the jewel in Lake Haven's Historical Society's crown, and the place of countless social gatherings over the years.

I was surprised the Historical Society had granted the school permission to have the dance there. The greenhouse manager was particular about the grounds, and no high school class had ever held an event there—regardless of who asked—including children whose parents were on the board of the Historical Society, like my own.

"It's going to be perfect," Niña continued. "It's exactly what Día is about—life and death, in harmony."

"So, the dance *won't* be at The Boneyard?"

"We will be close enough to see its shadow, which is perfect."

As long as no students found their way out there, I imagined it would be safe. Although, I'm sure more than a fair share had been there before, most likely. "One question?" I asked.

"What's that?"

"How'd you manage to get the Historical Society's approval to use it?"

"We asked," she said simply.

"That's it?"

"Well, we promised to donate a percentage of the proceeds from the dance to their fund and they agreed."

"Ah," I pressed my lips together, knowing money talked in any town. Still, I was sure we'd had the same idea when I was a student and the Society had turned us down.

"And I'm glad we did," she added, eyes dancing. "Because it's going to be perfect. We're going to fill the space with marigolds and candles and the most beautiful garlands."

"Marigolds?"

"They lure souls back from the dead to living with their color and scent," she explained, crossing one leg over the other. "But...we really need some help with the altar."

"Altar?"

"It's the most important part of the holiday. You build them in honor of your loved ones and fill them with pictures and flowers and their favorite foods."

"Well, I'm sure Shelley can help you find someone."

"She hasn't been able to," Niña bit her lip. "And it's stressing me out. It's the most important part of the night. Do you know anyone?"

"A carpenter?"

"Yes," she nodded. "To build the altar."

"I can't think of anyone."

"You don't know *one* person that is good with wood in this town?" I started to shake my head in response, and then I thought of someone...Dean. "You know someone, don't you," she smiled.

"He's probably *really* busy," I tried to dissuade her, annoyed to have even thought of him.

"Please?" she put her hands together, pretending to beg.

In the brief time I'd known Niña, I'd never see her so excited. So animated. So...alive. Seeing her now, wide eyes reflecting the light, she oozed charisma and beauty, in a way I'd only ever seen in one other person at that age. And I could never deny her, either.

Not to mention, did I in a way, owe Dean...for all he did for Evan the night of the City Council meeting? He had come to our engagement party and not made a scene. He'd even left early, and simply waved when he left. I'd trusted Evan and he'd been right. Dean had turned out to be an *okay* guy.

"I can't believe I'm doing this," I grabbed my cell phone and text Evan. Niña watched excitedly as I scribbled down the number he replied with on a sticky note. "Give this to Shelley. Tell her to let him know I sent you."

Niña practically leaped across the desk and grabbed the paper from my hand. "Thank you so much!"

"My pleasure," I watched as she got up and slung her backpack over her shoulder — flipping her hair the same way Lisa used to do. The innocuous act nearly knocked the wind out of me, leaving me to wave numbly after her as she bounced out of my office, and into her day.

After she left, I found myself wondering if the spirits of those we loved came back without candles, without flowers...without any warning whatsoever, in those who possessed the spirit they once did. Or was the world forever missing their light, and we found it when we needed it most.

***

Later that day, as I packed up to leave and head home, Shelley knocked on my office door.

"Hey," I smiled, looking up.

"Hi," she leaned against the frame of the door.

"Thanks for the recommendation."

"Recommendation?" I asked, slightly puzzled.

"Dean...Danvers."

"Oh," I nodded. "Right. Niña gave you the message?"

"She did. I called him a bit ago."

"Did you remember him from school?"

"Of course," she nodded. "He was my year...sat next to me at graduation. Dwight, remember," she smiled, reminding me of her last name.

"Right," I nodded.

"He's changed," she smiled.

"Oh...you met with him already?" I asked, surprised.

"He was in the area and offered to swing by to take a look and see if he could help. Said it sounded like an easy job but needed to see for himself."

"Oh," I smiled politely. "That's...good."

"Oh, and the best part, he offered to do it for free."

"Free?"

"Didn't ask for a cent."

"Really? That's...generous."

"It was," she agreed. "Didn't surprise me, though. He was always a cool guy."

"Was he?"

"Yeah," she smiled. "We hung out a few times in

school. Did you two not know each other?

"Not really."

"Well, he's changed, that's for sure."

"That's what I hear."

"Maybe I should take him out for a drink. You know, say thank you." I shook my head at the playfulness in her voice. "Hey," she laughed, "he's not bad to look at. In fact, he's quite the looker, now. Besides, all the good ones are taken." She smiled at me and winked. I looked down at the ring on my finger, knowing well my good luck. "Anyways," she pushed up from the door. "Thanks again, Thomas. See you tomorrow."

"See ya," I waved, wondering as she bounced away, how could Dean have such an effect on anyone, when he had such an adverse one on me?

CHAPTER EIGHTEEN

On my way home, I stopped by Garrity's to pick up groceries for the weekend. The Red Sox had made the playoffs, and Evan was planning to have Tony and Tyler over to watch the game.

Evan looked forward to a weekend of beer and baseball, and I was both looking forward to, and nervous about, the session. On one hand, I was eager to see if it would help me find out if the accident were having a larger impact on me than I'd realized. On the other, I was looking forward to spending time with Sam and just having fun.

"Hey," I greeted Tyler as I bumped into him steering my cart through the produce department.

"Stocking up for the winter?" he asked with a smile, eyeing the load of groceries in my basket.

"Just the weekend," I laughed. "You're still coming, right?"

"Of course," Tyler nodded. "Wouldn't miss it."

"Good," I smiled. "Evan's looking forward to it."

Since the engagement party, we'd gotten together with Sam, Tony, and Tyler, and he fit right in with our group.

"Can I bring anything?" he asked, shoving a hand in his pocket.

"Just yourself."

"You sure?"

"Well, unless Chris is coming, then bring him, obviously."

"I think he may come up soon," Tyler smiled.

"Yeah?" I smiled back. I couldn't wait to meet Tyler's boyfriend. Every time Tyler said his name he smiled.

"I've been talking with him about Evan's idea, and he's really interested."

"That's great!"

"There's *a lot* to talk about, but you may meet him sooner than you think."

"I can't wait."

"I'm a little nervous, obviously," he spoke low so that only I could hear.

I was glad Tyler had found someone special, but it saddened me he felt he had to keep it a secret.

I never could wrap my mind around why anyone cared whom another loved. Hearts beat, and broke, all the same. Whom we loved, did not change this.

"Well, we've got your back," I said softly in response.

"So," he cleared his throat and leaned back. "What's on the menu this weekend?"

"Guess?"

Tyler looked down into my basket again—taking in the sausage, corn, baguette, onions, and parsley—then back up, eyes wide. "Aw, man," he clenched his fist with excitement. "Really?"

Any Mainer knew crab season was September to November, and with October well underway, it was the perfect conditions for a crab boil. The shells were hard, and meat full.

"The weather has been unseasonably warm, and the guys down at the docks keep talking about how this season's crab is the best they've seen in twenty years. Ev figured, why not throw a boil and take advantage of the weather."

"It has been beautiful the last few weeks," Tyler nodded. "Remember that year we didn't get any snow until like, January?"

"I do," I nodded with the recollection. "Were we in middle school, right?"

"I think so," he crossed his arms. "Man, Maine weather..." he laughed, shaking his head.

"Unpredictable, and ridiculous."

"It is," I agreed.

"Where is Ev getting the crab?" Tyler asked.

"At the dock. He's going to pick it up tomorrow morning."

"And the mussels, shrimp and clams?"

"I'm headed to seafood department now."

"Say no more," he held up a hand. "I got it."

"Tyler…" I started to protest but he wouldn't hear it.

"We got a fresh delivery this afternoon and I can have them wrapped up and ready to go in a few minutes."

"You don't have to do that."

"I know," he smiled and grabbed the end of my cart, leading me to the seafood counter.

As promised, it only took a couple of minutes, and when done, Tyler grabbed the end of my cart and steered us to a register with a CLOSED sign on the conveyor belt.

"When was the last time you checked out a customer?" I asked, as he removed the sign, turned on the register, and flipped the switch of the belt, on.

"Probably high school," he laughed as he punched in a code on the register, and I unloaded the basket onto the now moving belt.

As Tyler began scanning each item, I looked around the store; nostalgia greeting me everywhere. There was a carousel horse that gave rides to kids for a quarter in one front window, and an old-fashioned soda fountain, in another. I remembered Tony's comment about its ice cream being the best in town. He was right. I couldn't imagine a summer without a double scoop of mint chip from *Garrity's*.

Mary, who worked in the post office, was kneeling in front of her daughter at the register next to me, talking to her at eye-level as she pulled a candy bar from her hands. While Mr. Hardy made his way down the aisle slowly, as his granddaughter held a piece of paper in one hand, and pen in the other, checking off items as he put them into his cart.

The store had been an important part of the community for generations, and the idea of *Garrity's* not being here for my own kids, was heartbreaking.

I turned back to Tyler, an image of his dad scanning groceries for my own, flashing in my mind as other moments from years past, rolled by like a movie; generations of families imprinted on this town like a film strip.

"I hope you stay," I said quiet enough so only he could hear.

"Fingers crossed," he looked up and winked.

Once Tyler had scanned and bagged the groceries, he loaded them into the cart, and helped me to my car. "I need to talk to your manager about this incredible service," I nudged him with my shoulder.

"Just doing my job," he replied with a kind of humility that seemed to only exist now in small towns.

"I'll make sure Evan has extra beer on hand."

"You won't be there?" he asked as we stopped at my car, and I opened the trunk.

"Sam and I are going to Bangor for the weekend."

"Oh yeah?"

"Yup. Girl's weekend."

"Well," he began loading the bags into my car. "It's going to be a great game."

"I'm sure Evan will give me the play by play when I get home."

Tyler laughed and nodded. "Well," he said after loading the last bag into the trunk, "I think that does it. Tell Ev to call me if he needs anything and I'll bring it when I come over tomorrow."

"Sounds goo—"

"Hey," Dean strolled up behind us, cutting my response short.

"Danvers," Tyler stuck out his hand. "How are

you man?"

"I'm good," Dean gave it a shake. "And you?"

"Can't complain. Didn't get a chance to say hi at Evan and Laney's engagement party."

"It's okay," Dean jingled his car keys. "There were a lot of people."

"There sure were," Tyler nodded. "Did you have fun?"

"Yeah," he nodded. "It was good. Still bagging groceries?" he asked, eying the cart.

"Well," Tyler laughed. "You know what they say. No job is too big or too small for a business owner."

"I understand that all too well," Dean nodded, then looked over at me. "Laney, good to see you."

"You too," I replied politely.

Tyler looked over his shoulder to a flock of customers entering the store. "Well, I better get back inside. Tell Ev if he needs anything tomorrow, to give me a call and I'll bring it when I head over."

Dean looked at Tyler with curiosity. I debated whether to invite him; asking myself, *what would Evan do?*

"Tony and Tyler are coming over to watch the game," I explained lamely.

"Nice," he smiled.

"Did you...want to come over?" I asked,

knowing well what Evan would have done.

"Oh," he looked from me to Tyler, obviously surprised by my invite. "I'd love to...but I'm headed home for a few days."

"You're leaving?" I asked, wondering if he could detect the hope in my voice.

I'd grown used to bumping into Dean by this point. I'd seen him around town and even at the hotel with Tony and Evan. Still, if I had to choose between him being here or gone, I knew my preference.

"I just agreed to help with a project at the high school and need some of my tools back home."

"Ah, right. They're having a dance," I nodded, feigning to have slight knowledge of an event I actually knew a fair amount about.

"Sounds like they're going all out," Dean nodded.

"I'm sure they appreciate your help."

"It's a tight timeframe, with the dance only a couple weeks away. But Shelley was always cool in school and figured...why not help, for old time's sake. Besides, it might be good to stick around, should the guys need anything with the project."

After the City Council meeting, Evan and Tyler didn't have a choice *but* to choose Dean's bid for the expansion, and it was this reason, which made me think of suggesting him to Shelley. I wanted to make sure the good guy routine wasn't an act.

It wasn't that I didn't trust him. But it wasn't that I *did* trust him either. There was something about him I couldn't put my finger on. Instead of wracking my brain, trying to figure it out, I chose to instead, employ an out of sight, out of mind mentality when it came to him.

"Well," I crossed my arms, remembering how important the dance was to Niña. "The dance means a lot to a student I'm working with, so thank you."

"Are you planning to go?" he asked, curious.

"Don't think so."

"Aw, no trip down memory lane?" Tyler asked.

"I take that trip every day," I laughed dryly.

"I understand," Dean nodded. "Sometimes it can be hard to go back to the past."

No truer words had ever been said, I thought. Tyler seemed to agree, nodding his head gently.

The three of us stared at one another, an awkward silence growing, until Dean cleared his throat. "Well, I've got to get going. Tyler," he stuck his hand out, giving Tyler's a shake. "See you later. Laney, always a pleasure."

"Later," Tyler called out. "Man, it's crazy how much he's changed," he said to me once Dean had disappeared inside.

"I heard the service can do that to a person."

"Guess so," he nodded. "You know...I saw him a while back."

"Oh yeah?" I asked, holding my keys.

"I was in Bangor...on a date."

"That's a long way to go for a date."

"Not when you're looking for anonymity. I mean...I definitely got the feeling he wasn't expecting to see anyone. Seemed as surprised to see me, as I was him. In fact, I think it might have spooked him because I'd stepped away for a couple of minutes, and when I came back to the bar, he was gone."

"Maybe he wasn't up for company?"

"Maybe," he considered the suggestion. "I can't put my finger on it, but it seems like he's carrying a kind of...weight."

"Tony said something similar. Actually, he used the word lost."

"Yes!" Tyler snapped his fingers. "That's it. He looks lost." I considered the word again, and like the first time Tony suggested it, couldn't see it.

"When did you see him?" I asked.

"Few years ago. Early Spring, I think?"

"At a bar?"

"Yeah," he nodded.

Drinks with a stranger, might have been easier

than a conversation with someone from home. I understood this logic. After the accident, I did whatever I could to avoid talking with anyone from school. It's why New York had been the perfect escape. I knew no one, and no one knew me.

"Maybe he just wanted to be alone," I shrugged.

"Maybe," Tyler thought about my comment.

Not knowing what else to say, and honestly, not all that interested, I nodded to the car. "Well, my friend," I leaned in to give him a hug, "thank you for the groceries and helping me to the car. I'm going to get these home."

"Right," he waved me off. "Sorry, didn't mean to hold you up."

"All good," I smiled and walked around to the driver's side door, pulling it open. "Thank you again."

"Of course. Have fun this weekend!"

"We will. Have fun with the guys."

"Oh, we will," he waved, then headed back inside.

***

Evan greeted me when I arrived home, taking a bag from my hands. "There are more in the trunk," I nodded towards the door.

"I'll go get them," he jogged out to the car and returned with an armful of bags. "You got a lot of stuff," he laughed.

"Didn't want you to run out of anything while I was gone."

"You're amazing," he leaned in to give me a kiss after setting the bags down.

"Ran into Tyler," I grabbed the door of the fridge and pulled it open, putting away the cold items first. "He's looking forward to tomorrow."

"It will be fun," Evan said excitedly, putting away the non-perishables in the cabinet.

"Ready for the game?" I asked, eyeing the baseball cap he wore backwards on his head.

"Can't wait," he nodded.

"If I forgot anything or if you need something tomorrow, let Tyler know. He said he'd bring it over. And by the way, the seafood was on him."

Evan looked at the packages in the fridge, and those still in the bags. "There's like five pounds here?"

"I told him no, but he wouldn't think of it."

"I owe him."

"Yes, you do," I nodded. "So, you'd better make it a good boil."

You didn't have to be a good cook to know how to do a proper crab boil. But you did have to be a

Maine native. Both Evan's mother and mine, knew how to cook crab at least a dozen ways, and they'd passed their recipes on to us—including how to make the perfect crab boil.

"He even rang me up...*and*, helped me to the car," I continued.

"Probably because you're so charming."

"Hardly," I rolled my eyes.

"Hey, that's my fiancée you're talking about," he laughed.

"You know, this will be our first weekend apart in a long time?"

"I know," he nodded. "How long has it been?"

"Since last winter."

Evan and I had spent weekends apart while living in New York. He'd go home to work on the boat, and me, for check-ups with my doctor or to study for finals. But those weekends always dragged by, and I anxiously counted down the hours until I saw him again.

But surprisingly, I wasn't feeling anxious about being away from Evan this weekend. When we got engaged, everything shifted. And with our wedding date confirmed, I felt a kind of security that was irrevocable, no matter the distance that separated us.

"That's right," Evan nodded. "You came home

to sign the lease for this place, and I stayed in the city to study for finals."

"You remember that?"

"You have no idea what I keep track of up here," he pointed to his head.

"I'm going to miss you this weekend," I laughed, shaking my head.

"How about we make up for it, now?" he suggested, wrapping his arm around my waist.

"Don't you have groceries to put away?" I asked, feeling his breath, warm in my ear.

"I'm all done."

"How about tonight?"

"How about...now?"

"Ev," I whispered as I turned, and he leaned in to kiss me.

"Yes?" he asked softly, lips inches from mine.

"You forgot something," I leaned in and reached for a packet of seasoning.

"Right," he locked his eyes on mine, grinning from ear to ear. "That's exactly what I was thinking."

I swatted at his arm, and he laughed, reaching for the packet. "Are you anxious about tomorrow?" he opened a drawer next to the stove and tossed it in.

"Not really," I folded the bags and stored them

under the kitchen sink. "Maybe...I don't know."

"Having second thoughts?" he asked, hearing the indecision in my response.

"No," I paused and leaned against the counter. "But I am worried about rocking the boat."

"How so?"

"Things are going so well right now. The expansion is going according to plan, and I'm making progress with that student I told you about. We just had an amazing engagement party, and about to plan a wedding."

"Things are good," Evan agreed, smiling.

"It is," I smiled back. "Which is why I worry going deep into what happened that night might rock the boat."

"Ah," he raised an eyebrow, nodding with understanding. "You're worried if revisiting the accident will do more harm than good."

"Exactly. I mean, what if the nightmares get worse?"

"Well," he crossed his arms. "Maybe think of it another way."

"Like how?"

"Well," he leaned against the counter, mirroring my stance. "That night is about as heavy as life can get. If the nightmares you're having are about the accident, then they couldn't get any worse. After the dark comes the light, right?"

"You think?"

"Maybe," he shrugged. "Something I do know, however, is you researched the session, booked it, and you and I have talked about the accident more now than ever before, and from what you've said, the nightmares haven't gotten worse. That's got to mean something."

"That's true," I admitted. "But they have changed, again."

"Really?"

"Yeah."

"How so?"

"Well, for starters, the darkness is different. It's more of a green now."

"Green?" he asked.

"Yeah. And I get the feeling there is something behind the wall."

"Like, what?"

"I don't know, and its...frustrating."

"Hey," he reached for my hand, giving it a squeeze for encouragement. "You can do this. You are the strongest person I know."

"I'm not so sure about that."

"No," he insisted. "You are. Given what you went through and to be standing here now...I'd say you're stronger than you even know."

"Why do you have such faith in me?"

"I've always believed in you. You just have to believe in yourself. If there is something in your mind that you've forgotten and need to remember, you're going to find it."

"What makes you so sure?"

"Because you," he smiled. "Us. We are the light. There is nothing brighter."

I laced my fingers through his hand and leaned into him.

"Trust yourself," he whispered in my ear as he held me tight. "And…if you decide you aren't ready, and just want to shop all weekend, then send me pictures from the dressing room."

"That'd be just my luck to send a picture meant only for you, to my entire address book."

"You're right," he pulled back and laughed. "Don't do that. But you can do me one favor?"

"Anything."

"Don't worry about me or the hotel or anything else. Just focus on you…and have fun."

"Is that an order?"

"It is. And also…" I reached into his pocket for his cell phone and shut it off, then did the same with mine. "We start making up for lost time, now."

"Now you're talking," Evan winked and opened the wine cabinet, grabbing the bottle Dean had gifted us, along with a couple of glasses.

"Isn't that expensive?"

"And?" Evan set them down and reached into the drawer with the corkscrew.

"Isn't a wine like that supposed to be reserved for a special occasion?"

"What's more special than you and me?"

Evan removed the cork and filled each of the glasses. "You've got a good point."

"What should we toast to?" he asked, holding one out to me.

"The future," I smiled.

"To the future," he nodded, and tapped his glass gently against mine.

I was more committed than ever to my future with Evan and was hopeful for the weekend ahead. Nothing would stand in the way of my happiness, ever again. Not old fears, or hidden unknowns. Not even my nightmares. Whatever was causing them, was about to run out of hiding places.

CHAPTER NINETEEN

THE NEXT MORNING, AFTER PICKING UP SAM AND grabbing coffee to go, we made our way to Bangor. The drive was easy—the two of us talking and laughing the whole way—and by one o'clock we had checked in to our room, with hours to spare before I had to leave for the session.

"This place is amazing," Sam looked around our hotel room, approvingly.

"It is," I agreed, taking it all in.

As soon as we arrived, I knew we were in for a treat. The discount rate I'd found online was part of the attraction, but the property had been another. With its green hedges, potted rose bushes, and lush gardens, it was even more spectacular in person, and when we walked into the lobby, I felt as if we'd stepped into a fantasy land.

The hotel décor was what the front desk called

industrial whimsy, designed to pay homage to the classic tale, *Alice in Wonderland*, and everything emphasized the aesthetic. From the black and white checkered marble floor in the lobby and gold light fixtures and geometric shaped metal tables throughout the property, to the oversized furniture covered in bold colors, hookah parlor, and tearoom, you really did feel as if you were in Wonderland.

The guest rooms were also incredible. Ours was plush and spacious, with two queen beds, adorned with black and white striped bedding and decorative pillows, and a sitting area that included a loveseat and two chairs in corresponding fabric. There was also a spacious balcony that overlooked a rose garden, and unique details, including a deck of cards and glass rabbit lamp on a set of round nesting tables in the sitting area, and apothecary vases, filled with candy, which sat on top of an entertainment center underneath a flat-screen TV.

"Omigod!" Sam called from the bathroom. "Laney, come and check this out."

I wasn't sure how it was possible the bathroom could be as equally amazing as the room, but it was. A jetted bathtub lined the wall on one side, while a glass shower with half a dozen spray nozzles, was on the other. And the checkered marble pattern from the floor in the lobby, repeated on that in the bath, along with comfort amenities including fluffy towels and a bowl full of travel sized toiletries, which sat between the double sinks. Everything smelled new and fresh, and I couldn't wait to take a soak in the tub.

"This is pretty cool," I smiled.

"What shall we do first?" Sam asked excitedly.

"How about we freshen up and then explore the hotel."

"Perfect. And when it's time, I can walk you to the car so you can head to your class."

"Great," I swallowed, still feeling bad for lying to Sam. "I should be back in time for dinner, and then tomorrow…paint the town red."

"Spa in the morning, followed by shopping in the afternoon?" she suggested as we left the bath and walked back into the room.

"Sounds perfect."

"Great. I'll make reservations when you're in class. What sounds good?" Sam asked, lifting her suitcase onto the bench at the foot of the bed she'd claimed.

"Massage," I lay down on mine, and stretched.

"Oh, that sounds good. And a facial."

"That too," I snapped and pointed.

"What about mani pedis?"

"Why not," I laughed. "Let's do it all!"

"I think I am going to like traveling with you, Ms. Thomas," she smiled.

"Make sure that boutique I want to go to is on the list."

"You mean *Forevermore*?" she laughed.

While I knew my mother and Evelyn were dying to go shopping in New York and drag me to every boutique from SoHo to Fifth Avenue, I'd already found a dress in one of the impossibly thick wedding magazines my mother had given me. It was the only dress out of hundreds that had caught my eye, and I felt like it could be the one.

I was surprised to find, that of the limited number of stores that carried it, *Forevermore*, a boutique in Bangor, was one of them. And even more surprised when I called last week, to learn they had a sample in the store that I could try on.

"That's the one," I cringed at the name, while also thinking of all the fun I was going to have, making Sam try on the most colorful, bow-laden bridesmaids' gowns in the boutique.

"I wouldn't dream of skipping it," she unzipped her suitcase, removed a makeup bag, and then headed to the bathroom.

While Sam was getting ready, I got up from the bed and walked over to balcony and stepped outside. A light breeze stirred, carrying the smell of roses. I inhaled and filled my lungs, thinking about the session.

While I'd managed to not think about the possibility that in a couple of hours, I might be opening up to a room full of strangers about what happened to me two years ago, now that it was quiet with just me and my thoughts, I couldn't ignore it any longer.

How would it feel to reveal such an intimate part of my life to people I didn't know? I'd tried before, and one pair of disbelieving eyes had been hard. How would it feel to have more than one, listening and judging? Then again, couldn't they be just as afraid as I was? Feeling the same fear, or even asking themselves the same questions, now.

I knew if I gave these questions any more power, they'd overrun my mind. Instead of giving them anymore thought, I pushed them aside, determined to not think about them until it was time, and walked back into the room to get ready for my afternoon with Sam.

***

For the next few hours, we played tourist. Like two kids in a candy store, we fawned over everything from the adorable stores in the lobby to the photo spots scattered throughout the hotel, which included an oversized mushroom, and bottle that said 'Drink Me.' We each took pictures, and sent them to Evan and Tony, to which they responded with an LOL, and then we grabbed lunch at the hotel restaurant.

Like the weather at home had been the past few weeks, it was pleasant, so we opted for a table outside next to a koi pond, and when done, played a game of croquet on the lawn in the garden. There was also a life-size chess board, which we had fun playing, until a couple tapping their foot anxiously motivated us to wrap up our game and grab a drink. I'd almost forgotten about the session entirely, until Sam mentioned it was time for me to leave.

"Well, my friend," she gave me a hug after we made our way back to the lobby. "You know where you're going?"

"Yup. I'm good."

"Alright," she smiled. "I'm off to enjoy that tub."

"Knock yourself out," I laughed.

"How long is your class again?"

"Um...couple of hours?"

"Perfect," she smiled. "Plenty of time for me be lazy."

"Go on," I nodded to the elevator, envious she would be spending the next few hours relaxing, while I would be spending it, taxing my mind. "I'll see you later."

"Have fun!" she waved over her shoulder as she went one way, and I the other.

Fun, I thought, as Sam disappeared, and I went to the valet. I wasn't sure what to expect but knew fun was not the word. Then again, whatever word I *could* use didn't really matter. I had come all this way, after all this time, and the simple fact was, I needed to do this, fun or not.

After getting into my car, I made my way to the hospital where the session was taking place, and not more than ten minutes after leaving the hotel, I'd pulled into the parking lot.

A strange battle of nerves coursed through me as I turned off the engine and checked my reflection in the rear-view mirror. I knew I didn't *have* to go inside. I'd taken the first step. That would be enough if it were all I could do. But I knew I could do more because I needed to.

After getting out of my car, I followed the instructions on my registration paperwork, and headed to the building marked Learning Annex — entering the building through a set of double red doors. Pulling open the one marked ENTER I stepped inside and made my way down the hall; the sound of my shoes clicking against the blue linoleum, echoing along the wall. I felt just like Alice before she tumbled down the rabbit hole and wondered what awaited me at the end.

"Hello," a young woman sitting behind a table greeted me as a table came into view.

"Hi," I cleared my throat. "I'm here for the session?"

"Great," she reached for a clipboard. "What's your name?"

"Laney. I mean Alaina…Thomas."

"Nice to meet you, Alaina. I'm Dinah."

Of course, it is I thought to myself, remembering the name of Alice's cat, which stayed behind, looking after her as she disappeared into that land she did not know.

"Hi," I said politely.

Looking down at the clipboard in front of her, Dinah ran a finger down the list of names, then reached for a yellow highlighter when she found mine and drew a line through it.

"There we go," she looked up. "You're all checked in. Go ahead and take one of these," she handed me a name tag sticker and pen.

I leaned down to print my name on the tag, then straightened when done and looked into an open room to my right. "I assume we'll be in there?"

"You are correct," she smiled. "There is coffee and tea inside, and of course, cookies."

"Has everyone arrived?" I asked, flicking the name tag back and forth against the opposite hand, eyeing the handful of people inside.

"We're expecting a few more."

"Oh?" I'd counted eleven and wondered how many more there may be.

"There's a lot more of us than you think," she smiled.

"Us?" I tucked a strand of hair behind my ear.

"Heart attack," she pointed to her chest.

"So, you've participated?"

"I have," she nodded. "This group saved my life."

"It did?" I was surprised by the admission and felt bad for thinking she was one who watched while people like me disappeared into an unknown world.

"That's why I help run the program," she pulled the clipboard towards her. "I'm in grad school and help moderate the sessions. I also do the marketing and sign-in. Whatever I can do to pay Dr. Forester back for all she has done to help me."

"I can't wait to meet her. She is the reason I'm here."

"She's amazing," Dinah smiled. "I think you'll like her, and the session."

"What's it like?" I asked, wondering if there was anything she could tell me that would ease my nerves.

"I was really scared my first time," Dinah admitted. "My heart felt like it was going to beat right out of my chest. Which, given everything, was frightening in itself. But she really made me feel comfortable and understood."

"Do we have to say anything?" I wondered what would happen if I got inside and lost my nerve.

"Not at all," she smiled. "Some talk, while others listen. My suggestion...just be open to whatever you're feeling."

I peeled the backing off the name tag and pressed it down onto my shirt. "Be open," I repeated, then crumbled and dropped it into a waste bin by the door.

"We'll start shortly," she smiled. "Why don't you go in and meet some of the others?"

I nodded, made my way inside, and headed over to the refreshments table. Thankful to see plastic cups and not Styrofoam, the patron cup of therapy, I poured myself a glass of water and turned around.

The room wasn't cold and clinical as I'd expected. Instead, it had been set up to be a warm and comfortable space. Gone were the typical steel folding chairs one might expect to find, and in their place, couches and armchairs arranged in a living room setting. And soft music played in the background, as white candles on coffee tables flickered delicately, filling the room with the smell of vanilla.

"Those are extra," said a voice from behind as I reached for a cookie. I swiveled my head around, finding a tall girl with brown hair and glasses.

"Oh," I pulled my hand back.

"Kidding," she pushed her glasses up and smiled. "I'm Mary."

"Hi," I turned to face her properly, and reached out for the hand she'd extended. "I'm Alaina."

"Nice to meet you, Alaina. My grandma always said, you should repeat a person's name when you meet them. It helps you commit it to memory. So, Alaina, I'm doing that."

"It's nice to meet you, Mary," I smiled, doing the same. "Is this your first time?"

"Yes," she nodded. "You?"

"Yes."

"Do you live around here?"

"No. I mean, yes, I'm from Maine, but not Bangor. You?"

"I'm from Vermont, but it was either this or New

York."

"I didn't see New York on the list," I said, surprised. I would have gone there if I had.

I was comfortable in New York. I never felt as if I would run into the same person twice. But in Bangor, there was always the possibility I could bump into someone I knew. Not to mention, New York would have made for a better destination for a girl's weekend, that's for sure.

"It was open for like a day and then it closed," Mary explained. "Too many people."

"Wow, really?"

"I know. Surprised me, too."

We stood in silence, watching as another attendee entered the room and looked around with nervous anticipation.

"So, Alaina," she said my name again. "What brought you here? Well...besides the obvious."

I wasn't sure I was ready to spill my story yet, so how could I answer such a loaded question? "Thought it was time," I said simply.

"Can only run so long, right?" she asked wryly.

Something like that I nodded, taking another sip of water. "And you?"

"I guess, I was tired of people looking at me like I'm some kind of freak."

"I'm sorry," I smiled apologetically.

I knew how it felt—being greeting by eyes, which said what words could not—but people at home had moved on. It was just as well. I preferred silence to whispers. Silence was heavy, but you could hear whispers anywhere in a small town.

"I'm sure you understand what I'm talking about," she said as if reading my mind.

"Honestly…I haven't really told anyone. Except my fiancé."

"Oh yeah?" she asked, lifting an eyebrow. "Not a parent, or a friend?"

"Not a one."

"Wow," she whistled. "That's impressive. It was such a bizarre experience for me I *had* to tell someone. How did they take it…your fiancé?"

"He's supportive."

"Does he believe you?"

"He does."

"My girlfriend is like that…super supportive. She's the one that encouraged me to come to this, actually. She knew I was getting to the point where the next time someone stared at me weird, I'd probably punch them."

"My fiancé is like that. Not the punching," I smiled. "Just that he knows me better than anyone."

"Cool," she smiled and then leaned in slightly. "If I can be honest with you, I'm a little nervous."

"Me too," I exhaled, relieved to hear I wasn't the only one. "I just don't know what to expect."

"Me either. Once thing's for sure though...it beats seeing a therapist."

"Oh," I nodded emphatically. "I agree with you, completely."

"They don't get it," Mary said with disdain. "They think we're..." she held an index finger up on either side of her head and moved them around in circles.

"Because they don't know," I said matter of fact. "Unless you've experienced it, you just...don't get it."

"Exactly," she agreed and poured herself a glass of water. "Wow," she said after taking a sip. "My girlfriend was right. I already feel better."

"Me too." Being with another who experienced something like I had *was* cathartic.

"Should we send Dr. Forester our bill?" I asked.

"You're funny," she pointed at me. "I like you, Alaina."

"Thanks," I smiled. "I like you, too, Mary."

We talked until Dinah entered the room and clapped her hands, then stopped and turned our attention her way.

"Okay, everyone," she said, offering a bright, welcoming smile. "If you wouldn't mind finding your way to a seat, we're about to get started."

"Ready?" Mary asked quietly.

"Ready as I'll ever be."

"How about those two?" Mary pointed at a pair of armchairs with light blue pillows.

"Sounds good," I finished my water, then followed her to the chairs and took a seat.

I looked around and counted the people in the room. Sixteen, including myself, who experienced what I did, had come here for answers. And while I didn't know them, didn't know their story, I felt our likeness, and it eased my fear.

I sat back, eager for the session to start, and while it took a couple of minutes for everyone to find their seats, once they did, and Dinah began, I listened with an open mind, ready for whatever was to come.

CHAPTER TWENTY

DESPITE HER SMALL FRAME, DINAH WAS A GIANT. HER radiance broke through the collective apprehension of the room, batting aside every nervous cough and throat clearing. Her confidence amazed me, and I wondered what she had been like when she sat where I did now?

"Each of you is here today, because you experienced something only a handful of people have," she smiled. "An experience that has been documented throughout history... showing up in artifacts from some of the world's earliest civilizations. Yet, despite this, and the fact five percent of the population report having had one, much skepticism remains about what they are, and why they happen."

A hand in the back shot up, and Dinah pointed at its owner. "Yes," she smiled.

An older man, with wire glasses and a comb over, looked around the room nervously before speaking. "I read somewhere that scientists believe near-death experiences can be biologically explained. Is this true?"

Dinah considered the question, then asked him one in return. "Do *you* think what you experienced can be explained by simple physics?"

"I don't think it's hard to consider things happen in the body when we die. It would explain how so many people have seen a bright light," he said, using air-quotes on the last two words.

My hand shot up, as if it had a mind of its own. "Yes," Dinah pointed at me and smiled.

"I didn't see a light. Not even close." The surety of my voice surprised me, and I gave myself a motivational pat on the back.

"Or me," Mary spoke up in a display of solidarity.

The man with the glasses, looked at us with curious eyes. "What did you see?"

"It's not what I saw, but what I experienced," I said carefully.

"We all experienced, something," he shot back.

"No...I don't mean it that way. I mean, I didn't see something. I lived something."

The man watched me, skeptical, and I

understood his suspicion. I too, might have reacted that way, had I not experienced it myself.

"Sir," Dinah asked, and I sat back, relieved she'd intervened. "What is your name?"

"Um, Tom," he sat up and cleared his throat.

"Tom," she held out her hand. "Tell me, have you ever had an alien encounter?" The room laughed in response. "No, no," she looked around. "I'm serious."

"No," he said crisply once the laughter stopped.

"But if you *were* to have one, how might you describe what an alien looks like?"

"I'd say they have big black eyes, skinny bodies, and large heads."

"Exactly," she nodded.

"Exactly, *what*?" he asked, confused.

"Many of us, if asked, would think of aliens as beings with big heads and large, black eyes. Just as anyone asked to describe a near-death experience, would say something about a bright light."

"The point?" he asked, clearly irritated by her response.

"Within commonality, does not lie explanation," Dinah replied. "It is merely, a tactic to define that which cannot be, by those who need reason. A way to rationalize, if you will, that which defies what is possible." Dinah paused and turned her attention from the man back to the room. "There are many doctors who like to explain near-death experiences, by the commonalities in the recounts of those who have had them. These doctors, wish to define these experiences as nothing more than our brain's chemical reaction to trauma. But there are those who believe where explanations rooted in science end, the potential of something greater, begins."

Goosebumps pricked the skin on my arms and back of my neck. *This* was why I had come. To listen to one who believed near-death experiences were something greater...something beyond definition.

"Well, I'd like to meet those people," the man called out and the person sitting next to him laughed nervously.

"I can't think of a better way to introduce our host," Dinah stretched a hand towards the door. "Everyone, without further ado, it is my pleasure to introduce you to the incredible, Dr. Lilian Forester."

An older woman wearing a blue sweater, brown slacks, and platinum blonde hair, fashioned into a bob, entered. She stood tall, and confident, despite her limited height, and when she reached Dinah the two embraced and then she turned and opened her arms. One person clapped, and then another, until everyone in the room, was standing and clapping, united in a warm, enthusiastic welcome.

"Thank you," Dr. Forester smiled and put her hands together, bowing gently. "Thank you so much. I am thrilled to be here with all of you."

The clapping began to die down as we again took our seats, and when it stopped, she continued. "Thank you for that lovely introduction, Dinah," she turned and smiled, then faced forward again. "You are right. How can the ordinary define the extraordinary? How can an experience which defies science, be defined by it?" With the question, she paused and looked around the room, focusing her attention on each of us for a moment. When her eyes met mine, a rush of energy shoot through me, and I sat up straighter, hanging on her every word.

"It can't," she continued. "What each of you experienced, is real. The profound impact it had on you, is real. It is why others do not understand and cannot relate to what you have gone through. But that's okay," she smiled. "They aren't supposed to. It is *you* who must understand. No one else. And in time, I hope you will come to see them as I do."

"As a one-way ticket to the loony bin," a young boy called out. He sat away from the group, sweatshirt zipped all the way up to his neck, shaggy hair sticking out from under the hood he'd pulled over his head.

"No," she smiled humbly. "As the incredible gift

they are."

"Gift?" he grumbled and sat back, crossing his arms tightly. "Does it come with a return receipt? Because I'd like to exchange it for something else."

One person laughed, and another one coughed, and then Dr. Forester looked to Dinah and nodded, and she stepped forward.

"Five years ago, my heart stopped," Dinah began, and the room fell silent. If a pin dropped, it'd have been louder than thunder. "No explanation, no warning," she continued. "I was in the middle of a class, and one minute my heart was beating, and the next...it wasn't. I just, slumped down in my desk, and fell to the floor. A classmate tried to wake me by hitting my face, but of course I didn't feel it because I was somewhere else."

"Where?" the boy asked, pushing his hoodie off his head, suddenly interested.

"I was in a house," she smiled. "And there were kids running around. I'd never been there, but something about it was familiar. It wasn't until those children stopped running around and looked at me, did I know why. It was my house, and they were my kids. I could feel it in my heart, which was beating strong and steady in my chest like never before."

Dinah paused and looked around the room. "I

never thought I'd have a future. I was born with a rare heart defect that made a normal childhood difficult. I didn't play sports. I didn't go out and do any of the things my friends did. I didn't live because my parents feared my death. In limiting the present for *them*, they limited the future for *me*."

Dr. Forester reached for Dinah's hand, and she continued. "I didn't ever plan to go to college. I didn't believe a normal life was in my future, so didn't want to waste what time I did have living, in a classroom. But when I died that day, and went to the future, and met the children that would one day be mine, I knew with every fiber in me, it wasn't just a vision of what the future could be, but what the future *was*. That was my gift. Dying, showed me I was going to live."

Goosebumps again pricked my skin. Our experiences were similar; showing her the life that awaited her was the gift of her near-death experience, just as showing me the love that waited for me, had been mine.

"I was once like you," Dinah turned her attention to the boy as Dr. Forester let go of her hand. "I was skeptical of what happened, but I knew something *did* happen. To see my future would be full of life, not death, had been the reason I died that day. And when I came here and listened to Dr. Forester and met others like me...like you...it changed my life. I made friends and signed up for college. I even graduated with honors and began a career dedicated to helping others like me. I started my future, and I have never looked back."

I sat back, and looked to Mary, who shook her head, eyes wide. "Unbelievable," she mouthed.

"I know," I mouthed back, nodding. The similarity of our experiences was profound beyond words, and I wanted to talk with her more.

Dr. Forester thanked Dinah for sharing her story and then stepped forward. "That is what this session is all about...teaching you how to explore what you experienced on a deeper level so that you might find the gift that was meant for you. We will also go over techniques to help you explore your experience, and we will discuss the role of dreams and the subconscious, and we will also provide you with tools that can help you communicate with family and friends, about what you experienced."

Everyone began to clap again—even the boy in the hoodie, and the older man—and I knew in that moment, I had made the right decision. Everything she said, was exactly what I needed to hear, and I was grateful to be here.

"Before we dive in," Dr. Forester continued, "I'd like to go around the room and have each of you introduce yourself. If you could please start," she pointed to the man in the front, "and then work your way around the room in a clockwise fashion."

Ten-minutes later, after we'd finished with introductions, Dinah announced we would take a five-minute break before diving into the core work. Deciding to stretch my legs, I stepped into the hall and sent Evan a text.

(ME) Hi.

(Evan) How's it going?

(ME) Haven't run out yet.

(EVAN) LOL.

(ME) Actually, it's pretty amazing.

(Evan) Yeah?

(ME) Yes! Doctor is great.

(Evan) Better than the first?

(ME) Ha! No contest.

(EVAN) Good. Remember what I said…

(ME) I am.

(EVAN) You got this.

(ME) Thx babe.

(Evan) Love you.

(Me) Me too. Gonna run.

(Evan) Call me when you're done.

(Me) Will do. xo

"Well," Mary asked when I returned to my seat. "What do you think so far?"

"I'm pleasantly surprised."

"Same," she shook her head in agreement. "Ready for what comes next?"

I still hadn't made up my mind as to whether I was comfortable sharing my own experienced, but I was eager for the session to continue.

"I don't know," I admitted. "You?"

"We're all in the same boat. Can't be too bad, right?"

"True."

"Okay," Dr. Forester cleared her throat once everyone was back in their seats. "Let's get started," she rubbed her hands together. "It's time for the real work to begin."

Dr. Forester spent the next couple of minutes outlining the ground rules, reminding everyone of the most important—this was a safe space, and no one should feel intimidated or embarrassed. If anyone broke that rule the consequence was simple: they would be asked to leave.

When she asked for the first volunteer, a couple of people laughed nervously when no one raised their hand. But then the boy in the hoodie stuck up his hand and Dr. Forester nodded at him and told him to begin when ready.

He shared his story quickly. Six months ago, he'd overdosed, and when his heart stopped, he saw his grandfather who had passed away the year before. While a team of EMTs tried to restart his heart, he the two played a game of catch and talked about everything that had happened in the year he'd been gone.

Dr. Forester asked the boy a series of questions and slowly, his demeanor began to change. He unzipped his hoodie and brushed the hair from his eyes, and when they'd finished, he was smiling.

Something told me the boy had begun to use drugs to cope with the death of his grandfather, but hoped after today, he'd find comfort in in the game he'd once enjoyed with the man he obviously adored, instead of the drugs that nearly ended his life.

Surprisingly, the older man with the glasses went next. His near-death experience happened last year, when during what was supposed to be a routine surgery, his heart stopped. While it flatlined, he saw his young daughter that had died in a freak accident decades earlier, and the two walked in a garden and talked about the man's life since her passing.

Dr. Forester talked with him delicately, sharing in the memories of his first child, and when she walked over to where he sat, and reached for his hand, holding it tight, it was as if decades of remorse had lifted from the man's chest.

When it was time for the next person to go, I surprised myself again, when I raised my hand. "I think I'd like to go next," I said, when Dr. Forester called on me.

Seeing the impact of her conversation with the boy in the hoodie and the older man, I wanted to share my story, in hopes it may lift an unknown weight from me, too.

"Excellent," she smiled. "You may begin whenever you are ready."

The room was quiet as I thought about where I should start. "Two years ago," I said finally, "I was in a car accident. It was a pretty bad accident, actually. Three of my friends died, and...I lived."

I looked around the room—the weight of more than a dozen sets of eyes, bored into me—and when I got to Dr. Forester she smiled and nodded with encouragement for me to continue.

My heart pounded, as the words I'd only ever said to Evan, dangled on the tip of my tongue. "They weren't just my friends," I took a deep breath, the faces of Caleb, Timmy, and Lisa, flashing in my mind. "They were my best friends. We did everything together." I stopped to catch my breath, my heart pounding against my ribs. "This is harder than I thought."

"You're doing fine," Dr. Forester nodded with encouragement. "Just, take your time."

"I was injured in the accident," I said when I was able to continue. "My heart stopped. And when it did, I went...well, home. Only, it wasn't. It was a version of it, only, upside down. Nothing made sense, and my friends were gone, and Ev—"

I stopped myself before finishing his name, looking down at the ring on my finger. No matter the version of Evan that existed, I loved him and wanted to protect him. And the Evan of my near-death experience that had abandoned me when I'd needed him most, hadn't really. He just needed time because I'd forgotten him...forgotten us. Who was to say I wouldn't have done the same?

"Someone I'd always relied on," I corrected. "They were absent. Strangely so...because they'd never been. They'd always been there for me." The words rushed out of my mouth, as if caged up for too long, and finally being set free. "It angered me. To have everything taken, and the one person I believed would always be there for me, gone, too."

I'd remembered the night at *Jasper's*. The way Evan came from nowhere and rescued me, protecting me from myself. And then I'd remembered the night that followed, when he kissed me, and the pieces of that strange world, began falling into place.

"It felt so real," I said softly, focusing on the flame of the candle on the table in front of me.

"That's because it was," Dinah responded, looking at me with a warm smile. I could see by the look in her eyes, she too, felt a connection in our similar experiences; each tumbling down a rabbit hole—me, to an alternate present, and she, the future. Only, she had made it out of Wonderland, and if my nightmares were any indication, a part of me was still trying to.

"The accident changed everything," I swallowed. "But I thought I'd accepted what happened and moved on. I guess, I haven't."

"Why do you say that?" Dr. Forester asked.

"I've been having these nightmares."

She came over to where I was sitting and kneeled, eyes wide with interest. "Tell me more?"

"There's not much to tell because they're nothing, really. They're just…darkness. At least, they were. They've changed recently."

"How so?" she asked, rested her elbow on the arm of the chair.

"The darkness is gone and now there's this…wall."

"A wall?" she asked.

"Yes," I nodded. "And the darkness is behind me."

"Do these nightmares frighten you, or are they troubling?"

"Not really," I replied, trying to find the word to describe how they *did* make me feel. "They did at first because of the way they came out of nowhere. But now they're more confusing than anything."

"Distressing dreams, nightmares ... these are considered intrusive symptoms, and common in those who suffer from posttraumatic stress disorder. It is why PTSD is often used to diagnose near-death survivors as many cite nightmares as an affliction."

Dr. Forester's language mirrored that of the paper I'd found online. I knew PTSD was a common misdiagnosis of those who had a near-death experience and was anxious to hear more about their connection.

"While science would like us to put near-death experiences into a box," she explained, "the reality is...it's just not that simple. Given your experience, it sounds like these nightmares are more of an avoidance symptom, like anxiety or fear, which are highly common in near-death survivors."

"But why now?"

"Dreams are the canvas of our subconscious.

Often, those things we fear or are nervous about, lie far beneath the reveries we see when we sleep. We must go beyond the dream, beyond that which our subconscious is showing us, to truly uncover what needs to be seen."

"I had them, too," said a man sitting across the room.

"You did?" I asked, surprised to hear him speak. He hadn't talked the entire session. Didn't even participate during introductions. And yet, now here he was, talking to me.

"They went away eventually, but Dr. Forester is right. There was so much more to the dream than what I was seeing."

"How did you get them to go away?"

"I took control."

"What do you mean?" I asked, wondering if I could do the same.

"I told the dream to bring it on. Whatever the darkness was trying to tell me, to just get on with it."

"But, how did you *know* it was trying to tell you something?"

"Darkness is never just itself. There is always something hiding in its shadows."

"And that's what made the nightmares go away?" I asked, leaning towards him, perched at the edge of my seat. "You confronted it?"

"They didn't go away," he shook his head. "They revealed what I needed to see."

"And did it make sense...what you saw?"

I felt as if I were standing on a cliff and whatever he said next would either keep me from falling or push me over.

"Not at first," he crossed his arms. "Then eventually...it did."

"What is meant for us, is meant for us," Dr. Forester responded, nodding at the man, and then looking back to me. "Just like what you experienced...what you are seeing in these nightmares, is meant for you."

"What do you mean?" I asked, curious by the specificity of her words.

"Is it possible these nightmares might be trying to show you something? Something you need to see, that perhaps you may be afraid to?"

I'd assumed my nightmares were trying to *tell* me something about the gravity of what happened to me that night. A darkness left behind from those seconds I walked the line between life and death. It didn't occur to me they might be trying to *show* me something.

"Earlier, I mentioned dreams are the way our mind processes fear and anxiety. Is there something from your experience that you might not remember? Something, perhaps you were not ready to face then, but perhaps, may be ready to now?"

"I remember all of what happened to me when my heart stopped," I considered her question. "There isn't anything else. If there were..."

"If there were, what?" she asked gently.

"If there were, it would flip everything on its head."

"That's good," she smiled.

"Why would that be good?"

"Because only when we challenge what we believed, can we discover what is."

Was Dr. Forester, right? Were my nightmares trying to tell me something ...something else about that night, I needed to know?

Something my father said once in my near-death experience came to mind. *All truths are easy to understand once they are discovered; the point is to discover them.*

"What do I do next?"

"Start with the dark."

"The dark?" I swallowed.

"Yes," she nodded.

"Why?"

"Because there, you will find the light."

CHAPTER TWENTY-ONE

ONCE THE SESSION ENDED AND MARY AND I exchanged phone numbers, I lingered behind as the room emptied, so I could speak with Dinah. I wondered if there was anything she could share that might help me make sense of Dr. Forester's advice.

"What did you think?" she asked when I finally exited the room.

"It was good."

"But?"

"But...what?"

"I get the sense there is something more you'd like to say?"

"Well," I bit my lip, wondering if I should be honest. "It was better than I expected. Definitely easier than the therapist I once saw. And...it was nice to meet others like me."

"But?" she said again and smiled.

"Well, to be honest, I was hoping to leave with more answers."

"Ah," she nodded.

"Don't get me wrong," I added quickly, not wanting to sound ungrateful. "It was helpful to talk about my experience, without fear or judgment. But…" I paused, trying to figure out how to explain what I was feeling. "I didn't think I'd have to go back to the accident to find the answers I've been looking for about my nightmares."

"Do you think the work Dr. Forester suggested is asking that?"

"I think if there is something from my near-death experience I might not remember and need to, then yes, going back to the accident is unavoidable."

"What makes you say that?"

"Well," I took a deep breath. "The purpose…the gift, of my near-death experience was always obvious to me. Why I went through what I did in that world I was in. But if I have to go back and look deeper, that road, starts with the accident."

"And you don't think you can do that?" Dinah asked, eyes sympathetic.

"I don't know," I admitted, fragments of the past, slicing through my mind. No matter how long it had been, that night was, and always would be, painful.

"Maybe it's not about going back," she suggested. "Maybe it's about seeing it differently."

"How do you mean?"

"When you think about that night, is there one emotion...one moment...that is key?"

"Yes," I replied, without hesitation. My fight with Lisa. It was the catalyst for everything. And the regret, and guilt I carried from it, I would always feel.

"So, what if *that* moment was no longer the heaviest. What else might you be able to see that you had not before?"

"I don't know," I said with all honesty. Breaking my heart in two...losing my best friend...how much heavier could that night be?

"I'm doing my thesis on the subconscious," Dinah continued. "And I've learned that it is the puppet master of our psyche. Dr. Forester is right. Dreams are the canvas of our mind. But our subconscious is its guardian. It wants to protect us...revealing what we need to know when it believes we are ready."

"But that's just it...I've thought about my near-death experience dozens of times. There is nothing I need to remember about it, or the accident, for that matter."

"The brain is a powerful instrument and can do a great many things," she countered. "Including, condition us to see a memory as it wants us to, not as it was."

"Are you saying I think I may remember everything, when in reality, I may not?"

She pressed a finger to her chin, considering the question. "Many studies have examined the impact of trauma on the mind. One phenomena, state dependent learning, says that during times of trauma, the brain creates a memory to help cope with that experience. And the only way to recover that memory...that truth...is to revisit that trauma."

"And the darkness in my dreams?" I wasn't sure how I felt about the idea there could be something lying in wait in my subconscious. That the darkness in my dreams was something that I had yet to discover.

"It may not be darkness at all," she said simply.

"That's what Dr. Forester meant...by going into the dark."

"Yes," Dinah nodded. "Here," she reached into her pocket and pulled out a business card when I grew quiet. "My number is on the card. If you ever want to talk or need recommendations for specialists in traumatic recall, I'd be glad to put you in touch with someone."

"Do you think a specialist is necessary?"

"I think you have the power to do what needs to be done."

It was an answer, but not an answer. She too, could be a politician.

"Word of advice?" she asked as I reached for her card. "Don't be afraid of your dreams. They are simply manifestations. In you, lies the truth."

"Thank you," I clasped the card tightly. "For the talk...and the advice."

"My pleasure," she smiled. "It was good to meet you, Alaina. I hope everything works out for you."

After saying goodbye, I made my way down the hall and when I reached the double red doors, turned to look behind me. Dinah and the table were gone; the hallway empty, as if they hadn't been there at all.

Curiouser, and curiouser, I thought, as I turned back around and pushed through the doors.

In the past couple of hours, I'd learned so much, and yet, had more questions than ever. It'd been freeing to say aloud what I had kept bottled up inside me for so long. But also, a little troubling to learn there could be something about the accident, or my experience, that I'd not remembered.

What could my mind be keeping from me about that night? And whatever it was, did it even matter?

What was more important that the truth of my heart?

I thought about these questions as I made my way back to the hotel, and when I finally walked into the room, my mind was utterly exhausted.

"Hey!" Sam called from the balcony as the door closed behind me. "How was it?"

"Tiring," I set my stuff on the bench at the end of my bed, then kicked off my shoes and laid down.

"Well, that's no good," she padded into the room, wine glass in hand.

"Looks like you had a good couple of hours?" I propped myself up on my elbows, eyeing her enviously.

She laughed and sank down onto her bed. "That tub, is divine. And the candy…" she looked at the vases by the TV. "I may have put a dent in it."

"I can't wait to take a long, hot bath," I moaned at the thought.

"Too tired to go out?" Sam asked, eying me.

"No," I sighed. "I just need a few minutes to recharge."

"You know," she set her glass on the nightstand between our beds. "I wouldn't be opposed to ordering room service and making it a low-key night."

"Oh yeah?" I asked, trying to mask how good

the idea sounded. I didn't expect to feel as exhausted as I did and felt bad considering how I'd promised her we'd have fun this weekend.

"I've already made us reservations at the spa for the morning and have a list of stores for shopping in the afternoon. So really, all we have to do tonight is chill out if you want. What do you say...paint the town red tomorrow?"

"I'd say, I could kiss you."

"I'm taken, but I'm flattered," she grinned.

"Noted," I laughed back. I wondered if Sam could see how tired I felt. "Are you doing this for my benefit?"

"God no," she waved off the idea and laughed. "After a bath and wine...I'm wiped, too!"

"Are you sure?"

"Of course," she grabbed the room service menu. "Besides, they have some stuff I want to try. Like this skirt steak," she opened the menu. "Oh, and truffle mac n' cheese."

"Oh, that sounds so good," my stomach growled.

"And then for dessert, a big slice of chocolate cake?"

"Nice," I smiled. "Do they have red velvet?"

"They do."

"Then that's what I want."

"Why don't you go and soak in the tub and I'll place an order. When room service comes, I'll give you a shout.'"

I sat up and reached for my bag. "You don't have to tell me twice."

She laughed and picked up the phone, as I removed my toiletries and pajamas from my bag and headed into the bathroom.

After filling the tub, I peeled off my clothes and eased into the water—tension giving way as I lay my head back and closed my eyes. Thoughts from my conversation with Dinah lingered in my mind, but I pushed them aside, too tired to give them life.

Instead, I focused on the weightlessness of my arms and legs; imagining I was a bird, floating in the sky as clouds passed beneath me. Gone were all thoughts of the accident and what I'd experienced, the session and my nightmares. I felt nothing but the wind rushing beneath my wings, as the horizon stretched before me. It was freeing. Peaceful. I didn't have a care in the world. Then a knock at the door pulled me from the reverie.

"Laney," Sam called. "Food's here."

"Already?"

"You've been in there for twenty minutes," she laughed.

"Really?" I sat up, feeling the chill of the water.

"Yeah," she laughed again. "Did you fall asleep?"

"No," I called back. "Be out in a few."

Reaching for a box of soap at the edge of the tub, I ripped it open and turned on the water—rubbing the bar between my hands to create a lather, then ran it up and down my arms, and legs, finishing with a quick rub across my face. Once done, I rinsed off and drained the tub, stepping out and reaching for a towel to dry off.

"Something smells good," I padded into the room after changing into my pajamas.

Sam smiled as she shoveled a spoonful of mac n' cheese into her mouth. "And it tastes even better. Come…eat!"

After sitting down next to her at the makeshift table room service set-up with the dining cart, we dove into our meals, and when done, pushed the cart outside to the hall and curled up on the couch and watched a movie.

I was beyond tired by the time we crawled into bed and fell asleep as soon as my head hit the pillow. I hoped the weight of the day would pull me down into a deep, dreamless, sleep that even my subconscious couldn't reach. But it wasn't long before I found myself in my nightmare.

I tried to remember what Dinah said—that it

was nothing more than a manifestation of my mind—but as I stood there staring at the wall before me, fists clenched in defiance, the darkness, as if calling my bluff, came from behind and wrapped its arms around me, and pulled me awake.

Shooting up in bed, my pulse raced, and I reached over instinctively for Evan, the feel of him steadying me, always. Then I remembered where I was and pulled my hand back and looked over at the bed next to me and saw Sam sleeping soundly.

Relieved I hadn't woken her, I got out of bed and walked to the balcony, the cool night brushing against my skin as I stepped outside.

Leaning my elbows on the railing, I took a deep breath and looked up. The moon, only at first quarter, wasn't bright enough yet to dim the light of the stars; the two existing in delicate harmony filled the sky with light.

How did one go into the dark? Or could I even do so, if my subconscious were at war with itself—the darkness, and wall, both ally and adversary—one wanting to reveal, and the other wanting to protect?

Or was I thinking about it the wrong way? I'd always viewed what happened before the accident and the near-death experience as one event. One happening, leading to the other. But what if the nightmares were also part of it? A third angle of a triangle.

What if there was something about that night I couldn't remember — some kind of truth connecting the accident and the near-death experience, and trying to find its way to me? As much as I hated to admit it could be possible, I knew it was. I needed answers. Which brought me back to my original question — how did I go into the darkness?

Hadn't I heard Tony say at least a dozen times, the best defense was a good offense? I shouldn't go into it. I should let it pull me wherever it wanted. It was my mind, after all? Where could it take me but where *I* wanted it to go?

Heading inside, I closed the doors and crawled back into bed, and when I found myself again in the nightmare, instead of channeling strength or fear, I reminded myself this was just a dream, nothing more, and the darkness was neither friend, nor foe, but a part of me.

I stared at the muted green wall, eyes fixed, and despite the chill of the darkness as it encircled my waist, I did not flinch, or scream. I simply, yielded. And to my surprise, I did not wake. Instead, the wall vibrated, and the darkness hissed, as sinewy shadows reached up my arms and around my neck.

The darkness was like a feral cat, trying to

defend me from whatever the wall was protecting. But the wall pushed back, desperate to break through the shadow's hold; their combined strength and determination a force unlike any I'd ever felt.

Then I remembered what Evan said about the strength I was capable, and I remembered the darkness and the wall were a part of my mind. *I* did not answer to *them* — *they* answered to *me*.

I closed my eyes and searched within, and when I felt the strength that Evan thought I was capable firm in my gasp, opened them and reached out, pushing at the wall with both hands.

The darkness released its hold and the shadows retreated as the wall began to shake and break. One by one the pieces fell, until the wall had crumbled to dust, revealing what had been hiding behind.

A box hovered in the space, dimly lit by a light from behind, with patches of contrasting black and white. It looked like a film negative that had not yet processed, but as I stared at it, and the light grew brighter, an image began to take shape. Two lines started apart on the bottom, and ran upward, growing closer at the top, while dark shapes, like blotches of ink, grew from large to small on either side.

I held up my hand as the brightness intensified, light seeping through my fingers, as a noise from beyond the box, pricked at my ears. Something was coming and while the duality of fight and flight pulled at me, I reached into me again for the power I'd used to break down the wall and grabbed hold of it. I needed to know...*had to know*... what my mind was trying to show me, and I would not run.

The noise grew louder — a familiar, thunderous clanging that intensified as it approached — sending an electric shock through me, igniting every nerve. It took every ounce of strength I had to not give in to the force trying to pull me away. Just a few more seconds, and the image would fill in and I could see what the wall had been protecting. Then without warning, a tap on my shoulder pulled my attention and I woke up.

I sat up and looked around, the room dark, and Sam, asleep, just as she had been earlier. But this time, I couldn't shake the chill in the air, or the alarm that I felt, deep in my bones.

Dinah was right. The nightmare was neither about the darkness, nor the wall, but something else entirely. I pulled the covers to me protectively and recalled everything I'd just seen, committing it to memory; something telling me it wasn't only important, but key to everything.

CHAPTER TWENTY-TWO

I DIDN'T SLEEP THE REST OF THE NIGHT, BUT AS WE GOT ready the next morning, I'd decided to push everything about yesterday's session and the nightmare out of my mind. I'd promised Sam we were going to have fun, and that's exactly what we were going to do. Everything about the session and what I'd learned could wait until I was back home.

That afternoon we made our way through about every shop in Bangor, laughing and buying whatever we saw, and it proved the perfect antidote to the weight of the past twenty-four hours. Being out in the fresh air was a kind of therapy of its own, and when we finally arrived at *Forevermore*, arms full of shopping bags, I was beyond ready to see the gown I'd been coveting.

Sam and I marveled at one another as we entered the boutique. Finely polished wood floors extended the length of the space, while rows of gowns on wooden hangers, lined the walls. It smelled of jasmine and baby powder, and soft music filled the air.

"Oh wow," she marveled as we closed the door behind us.

"I know," I nodded. Sam didn't have to say anything because I knew exactly what she was thinking. The boutique was the perfect blend of comfort and elegance, and I know my mother and Evelyn would've loved it.

A young woman in a beautifully tailored black suit and hair twisted into a bun, greeted us. "Ladies," she smiled, revealing perfect white teeth, framed by light pink lips. "Welcome to *Forevermore*."

"Hello," Sam and I greeted her in unison, returning her smile with our own.

"How might I help you?"

"We have a reservation," Sam responded.

"We do?" I asked, looking at her, confused.

Sam winked at me and continued. "I spoke with Marie yesterday. She is expecting me."

"Of course," the young woman clasped her hands together. "You must be Sam. And you," she lowered her head and smiled, "must be the bride-to-be."

"Yes," I smiled, my cheeks warming.

"I'm Marie," she extended her hand, giving mine a shake, and then Sam's.

"Oh," Sam smiled sheepishly. "I'm so sorry. I should have recognized your voice."

"Oh heavens," Marie shook her head. "Please, do not worry. Let us take care of those," she clapped, and two salespersons who seemed to appear out of nowhere, reached for our bags and took them away.

"Thank you," I exhaled as the weight I'd been carrying for the last couple of hours, lifted.

"My pleasure," Marie smiled as a third, carrying a silver tray and two glasses of champagne, handed Sam and I each a glass.

"Thank you," I smiled politely.

"Now this, I could get used to," Sam clinked her glass to mine.

"Are you going to tell me what's going on?"

"I booked the place," Sam smiled.

"What?" I asked, eyes widening.

"From now until closing, myself and the team are at your service," Marie nodded.

"It's just you and me, and a thousand gowns," Sam grinned.

"You're kidding me."

"I would never kid about that," she laughed.

"If you ladies would follow me," Marie turned.

Sam and I followed, flutes in hand, as we made our way through the boutique into a private parlor, where a bucket of champagne, bowl of chocolate covered strawberries, and vase of pink roses sat on a low white marble table, in front of a set of tufted armchairs.

"I understand there's a special gown you're interested in," Marie stopped next to a dressing room with a linen panel, pulled back by an iron tieback in the shape of a leaf.

"Yes," I looked from her to Sam. "How did you know…"

"I might have told her," Sam reached for a chocolate covered strawberry.

"But, how?" I asked, still stunned.

"I have my ways," she grinned, taking a bite.

"The dress is hanging up, right in here," Marie pointed to the dressing room.

"What?" I asked, my stomach tumbling excitedly.

"Whenever you are ready," Marie smiled widely. "And if there are any other dresses you might wish to try on, we can bring them in as well."

"I can't believe it," I swallowed over the lump in my throat.

"Why not?" Sam asked.

"You did this for me?"

"Of course," she smiled. "You're getting married. You deserve to be spoiled!"

"We've put some gowns aside for you, as well," Marie said to Sam. "I selected a few, but of course, let us know if there are others you might be interested in, and we can get those for you, too."

I looked over at Sam, eyes wide. "What?" she asked with feigned innocence.

"Trying on dresses?" I asked, suggestively. "Are you preparing for something?"

"Honey, I've been preparing since I was six."

We both laughed and the salespersons that had taken our bags earlier, entered with a rack stuffed full of dresses of every color.

"I also understand the two of you would like to have some fun," Marie continued. "So, we've pulled a selection of dresses I think will be perfect for that as well."

Judging by the look on Marie's face, she'd obviously encountered her share of wedding parties, with the same idea.

"Those are amazing," Sam eyed the rack with approval.

"But before you dive into these," she turned to me and smiled. "Shall we get you into that dress?"

"Yes," I nodded excitedly.

"Great," Marie extended her hand to the dressing room. "Shall we?"

"I'll be here," Sam reached for the bottle of champagne on the table and refilled her glass.

"You have wonderful taste," Marie said as we'd stepped inside the dressing room and pulled the panel closed. "This gown is beautiful. Simple, yet elegant."

"Simple?" I asked nervously, wondering if that was bad.

Marie reached for the hanger, holding the dress up, and fanning the skirt out with her hand. I stared at it, speechless, still not believing I was seeing it finally in person.

"Simple, is perhaps one of the most important tenants in bridal gowns," Marie smiled. "When you have exquisite artistry, there is no better way to display it, than a simple, yet elegant canvas."

I touched the dress delicately. It was flawless. Not a mar on the smooth fabric.

"It's a ball gown silhouette," Marie continued, "with a chapel length train."

"Is that long?"

"No," she shook her head. "It is the perfect length and a common choice for brides. It adds just enough length to the gown's skirt, without overwhelming the dress, and looks beautiful in any setting. It will work for both indoor and outdoor settings. Do you know what kind of ceremony you will be having?"

"We are having the ceremony on a boat, and the reception at a hotel."

"Lovely," Marie smiled. "Spring or summer?"

"Spring," I nodded.

"Very good," Marie placed the hanger back on the hook. "This dress, should you choose it, would be perfect. Some gowns can be quite heavy, but not this one, and the sleeveless, deep v neckline, make it ideal for warmer weather."

"Is this white...or ivory?"

"It is ivory silk with an embroidered lace overlay. I particularly love the draped midriff. It creates such a lovely silhouette and allows for beautiful movement in the skirt."

I knew my mother would be nodding along, understanding everything Marie was saying. But I didn't have to understand design to know the gown was stunning. I loved it even more in person and couldn't wait to try it on.

"Are you ready to try it on?" Marie asked, almost reading my mind.

"Yes," I smiled.

"Would you like me to step outside, or would you like me to help you?"

I looked to the dress and wondered where to begin. "Would you mind helping me?"

"It would be my pleasure," she flipped the hanger, revealing the back of the dress, and placed it back on the hook. "I've placed some shapewear over there," she pointed to a small table in the corner of the room as she unzipped the dress. "Choose whichever one you like best. It's complimentary."

I eyed the garments on the table. There was such a variety, and I had no idea which to choose.

"Why don't you try this one," Marie reached for a nude-colored bodysuit with a low plunge in the front, and clear straps.

"Do I have to wear one of these?"

"You can wear whatever you like," she smiled. "It's your day, and you should feel comfortable. Given the cut," she looked at the dress, "you might not need anything."

"I like the idea of keeping it simple."

"Well then," she clapped her hands together excitedly. "That's the way it will be. Shall we?"

I smiled and turned around, slipping out of my clothes while watching Marie in the mirror's reflection, unzip the back of the gown. When I was ready, I turned around, holding my hands protectively over my chest.

Marie held the skirt of the dress open. "All I need you to do is step in and I will do the rest."

"That's it?"

"That's it," she nodded.

"Okay," I inhaled, "here it goes."

I placed one foot into the skirt, then the other, and Marie pulled the dress up slowly, holding each of the sleeves so I could slide my arm through the openings. Once the straps were over my shoulders, she zipped up the back; a delicate row of pearls that ran down my back, concealing the zipper.

"How does it look?" I asked nervously when she finished.

"Why don't you see for yourself," she nodded to the mirror.

I turned around slowly, keeping my eyes down for a second, before looking up. The dress wasn't everything I thought it'd be. It was more.

The silk was weightless, shifting delicately as I turned my head from shoulder to shoulder, and the overlay airy, like fine spun sugar. The deep cut in the front, while dramatic, was no more revealing than the halter tops I preferred in the summer; the straps resting perfectly between my neck and shoulder.

This was the dress I would wear when Evan and I said our vows. I could feel it in my heart. And I couldn't help but think of Lisa; how this was a moment I knew no matter where we were in life, neither would've missed. I hoped she was looking down on me, wistful tears in her own eyes.

"Would you come on already?" Sam called from the parlor. I sniffed and straightened my head.

"Ready?" Marie asked.

I opened my eyes and nodded, and she pulled the panel to the dressing room back, then hurried around to the train, and lifted it up and held it while I walked.

Sam's mouth fell open as I stepped through, walking slowly to the carpeted platform in front of a floor-length, tri-fold mirror.

"You're not saying anything," I said uneasily as I stepped up carefully onto the platform.

"Because I can't," Sam said as Marie let go of the train.

"Is that a good thing, or bad?"

Sam smiled as she made her way over to me, while Marie adjusted the skirt, so it fell in perfect waves to the floor.

"It's...perfect," Sam whispered.

"You think?" I asked, turning around to look at her.

"Yes," she smiled.

"Do I look like a princess?" I asked wryly. The

old habit of using humor to deflect being in the spotlight, still very much a part of me.

"No," she shook her head and smiled. "You look like a queen."

I turned back around and smiled. "Do *you* like it?" Marie asked as I stared at the dress, admiring every detail.

"I love it."

"Are there others you'd like to try on?"

"No," Sam and I said in unison.

"This is it," I said with confidence.

Marie's lips pulled into a big, beautiful smile, as she stepped back and crossed her arms, studying the dress with an analytical eye. "We will want to take it in a bit, but the adjustments will be small. A bit at the waist, and shoulders…our tailor will take full measurements, of course, and make the necessary adjustments. But otherwise, it looks as if it were made for you."

Marie was right. The dress did feel like it was made for me.

"How much is it?" Sam asked.

"I don't need to know," I stuck my hand up before Marie could answer. She looked at Sam with a curious expression. "My mother said when I found *the* dress I'd know, and that I should get it. No matter the cost. So," I turned back to the mirror, "that's what I'm doing. I'm listening to my mother and buying the dress."

"Regardless of whether she and Evan's mom have seen it?" Sam asked, lifting an eyebrow.

"Regardless," I nodded, knowing well that my mother and Evelyn would be upset with me for robbing them of the chance of looking at wedding dress with me. But I also knew their disappointment would be short-lived once they saw the dress.

"Alright then," Sam turned to Marie and lifted her champagne glass. "Looks like she's made her choice!"

"Excellent," Marie clapped.

"Evan is going to fall on the floor when he sees you," Sam grinned.

I knew no matter what I wore, Evan would think it was perfect. But there was something about this dress that was ethereal, and dreamy, and hoped he would be speechless, the moment he saw me in it.

"Now," Marie looked to Sam. "You're up."

"Oh," Sam smiled mischievously at the rack of colorful dresses. "How about we dive into that rainbow over there?"

"What?" I turned from the mirror. "I thought you wanted to try on wedding dresses?"

"There will be plenty of time for that in the future," she waved airily. "Today, is about you. But that rack of confectionary perfection over there," she laughed. "I'm all about that."

"Well," I turned to Marie and smiled. "I guess it's time for me to turn back into a pumpkin."

"Nonsense," she winked. "This dress is part of your fairy tale, now. It will stay with you, long after midnight."

"Right," I looked back to the mirror; never caring much for fairy tales, while also finding it hard to deny somewhere out there, some kind of fairy godmother was looking out for me.

"Let's get you out of this dress so you two can have some fun, and while you're doing that, I will schedule your fittings."

"Which one should I try on first?" Sam asked, holding up a blue dress with one hand, and pink with the other.

I laughed and pointed to the blue one, then lifted the front of the skirt of my dress so I could step down off the platform. Once I'd made it safely down, I stopped and turned to look in the mirror one last time.

"It really is exquisite," Marie smiled at me in the mirror. "You are going to make a beautiful bride."

"Thank you," my cheeks warmed.

"How many months until the big day?" she asked as we made our way back to the dressing room.

"Six months."

"Oh, that is plenty of time," Marie smiled, pulling the linen panel open so I could step inside.

"I wish it were sooner."

"Trust me," she leaned in once I'd begun to get out of the dress. "When you're in the middle of planning, you'll wish it was further out."

I looked at her and smiled, knowing there may be some truth to her words. I could only imagine how much work it would be and was thankful my mother and Evelyn would be involved. But I also knew I wasn't the only bride-to-be counting down the days to their wedding. I was, however, the only one that was counting down the days until she married Evan Davies.

***

An hour later, Sam and I were back in our dressing rooms, trying on another dress. We'd made it through half of the rack, and my stomach hurt from laughing.

Trying on the dresses of bridesmaids' past, was as fun as I imagined it would be. There were leather dresses, and taffeta, latex, and lace. There was even a tube dress that looked more like a sock, made of a material I couldn't place.

And the colors... it wasn't just pastel perfection. It was Crayola heaven. There were pink and green, blue, and red, even black dresses. And they were each a different length and style. But of all the dresses I'd tried on had paled in comparison, to the utterly ridiculous dress I was about to take off.

The lemon-yellow taffeta creation was brighter than the sun, with a big sunflower on the waist, and lace collar that looked like a doily. I felt like Little Bo Peep, and I could honestly say, it was by far, the most bizarre bridesmaid's gown I'd ever seen. Well, alongside the red metallic gown Sam had just tried on, with oversized puffy sleeves and lace hem on the skirt.

"Shoot," I muttered as I struggled with the zipper.

"Everything okay over there, Pineapple Dream?" Sam called out from her dressing room.

"Zipper's stuck."

"Need help?"

"I think I can get it," I took a deep breath, and reached up again, pinching my shoulder blades together as I tried to grab the zipper. "Darn it," I fumed under my breath, wiping my brow when I failed. Between the weight of the dress, the lights overhead, and three glass of champagne I'd consumed, I was beginning to sweat.

"You sure?" Sam asked.

"I'm...good," I lied, trying the zipper again.

I took a deep breath and reached around my back, closing my eyes while pushing my hand up towards the zipper. Ignoring the pain in my shoulders, I pushed my hand further until a burst of light flashed under my lids.

I winced and dropped my hand, as a bead of sweat rolled down my temple.

"Did you say something?" Sam knocked on the wall between our rooms.

"I'm good. Just...this dress zipper won't budge."

"Do you need to be cut free?" she laughed.

"I hope not," I laughed back and tried again.

I did the same as before, closing my eyes and reaching my hand as far as it could go, and as I pushed past the point of comfort, pain shooting down my arm, light flashed under my lids like lightning in a storm, and illuminated the darkness.

To my surprise, the image from my nightmare flashed in my mind, and I dropped my hand and opened my eyes quickly—an imprint of it floating around in my line of sight for a couple of seconds, before fading from view.

No, I begged, wanting it to come back; wondering if when I broke the wall in my dream, had I done so in my mind.

Wanting to recreate what I'd done seconds earlier, in hopes it would bring the image back into mind, I took a deep breath, closed my eyes, and pushed my hand further up my back until a bolt of pain shot through my shoulders. The light again flashed, and the image appeared. But instead of dropping my arm to ease the pain, I kept it there, holding it firm, using it to light up the dark under my lids.

As the pain increased, the light got brighter, and filled in the image, and as a picture took shape, a flash of memory came to mind, and I knew what it was I was seeing. It was my view through the windshield of Caleb's car the night of the accident, in the seconds before the logging truck struck us.

I squeezed my eyes tight, channeling the strength I'd used to break down the wall last night, and allowed myself to be pulled into the memory. And as the lights and engine of the truck, got brighter, and more deafening, I *was* back in time, in those last seconds.

Yet, despite the intensity of the moment, I felt no fear, and when I looked down, I knew why. Lisa had grabbed my hand in hers, and locked her eyes on me, stoic, in that moment of terror; eyes filled with neither panic nor worry, but beautiful acquiescence, as a silent apology passed between us. It filled me with love and peace as our friendship flashed before my eyes, and then everything went dark, and silent.

I remembered it now...that lost moment, left in the void, and understood why my mind had been keeping it hidden. It was painful and perfect, and I wouldn't have had the strength to remember it until now. But a tug in my heart told me there was more—something greater than those seconds—so I continued staring into the darkness, searching for what else I needed to see.

After the two cars collided it was quiet. As if everything in the world had stopped, taking all light and sound with it. But through the broken glass and twisted metal, I remembered not something, but someone. The driver. They'd gotten out of the truck and stumbled towards me, but I did not see their face; the world faded from view as they approached.

I dropped my hand from my back as everything faded; layers of chiffon and tulle, puffing up around me as I dropped to the floor.

All this time, it wasn't the accident my nightmare was protecting me from. It wasn't even that last precious moment with Lisa. It was the driver. The one piece of the puzzle that had never been found.

I never knew their name. Neither it, nor a photo, had been in any of the news stories. And honestly, it never really mattered. The police had ruled the logging truck had not been at fault and the driver's identity did nothing to change the fact that my friends were not coming back.

Then, I realized, I wasn't the only one to survive that night. They, too, had lived through the accident, and their life changed. Albeit, differently than mine, but changed, nonetheless. *That* was the truth I was meant to discover. I knew this, because now that I had discovered it, I could feel it.

I rocked back and forth, tears filling my eyes. Lisa's forgiveness had freed me from the guilt I'd carried since that night, and as it lifted, I knew I needed to do the same for the driver. They too, needed an absolution, and it was me, the only survivor of that night, who could grant it.

"Everything okay?" Sam asked again, this time from the other side of the panel.

"Mm-hmm," I mumbled softly, throat thick with tears.

"Did the fabric swallow you? I can barely hear you," she laughed.

"I'm…. fine."

"Are you sure?"

"Mm-hmm."

"Mind if I come in? Are you decent?"

"Sure," I wiped the tears from my cheeks.

"Well, aren't you a ball of sunshine," Sam said wryly as she stepped into the dressing room. But it quickly faded when she saw my tear-stained cheeks. "Hey," she sat down next to me, puffs of red fabric billowing up around her. "Are you okay?"

I couldn't carry this weight alone. Not anymore. The time had come to tell those I cared about, the truth about that night.

"I...need to tell you something," I picked at a piece of lemon-colored tulle.

"Okay," she said slowly.

"But if you don't want to listen, I understand."

"Hey," she placed her hand on my arm. "Whatever it is, you can tell me."

"It's about the accident," I looked up.

"Go on," she nodded for me to continue.

I wondered how I should explain the real reason we came to Bangor. "The thing I went to yesterday. It wasn't for work. It was for me. A session...for near-death survivors."

I braced myself, waiting for her reaction, and when she said nothing, and instead, nodding with encouragement, I continued. "The night of the accident...I died. And I don't mean a piece of me, but my heart...it stopped."

Sam looked at me, eyes soft and accepting, and it gave me the strength to tell her everything.

Twenty-minutes, we sat side by side, surrounded by fabric, and Sam knew everything.

"I'd always assumed since there was no fault with the driver, there was no reason to find them. But that's what all this is all about. It's about them."

"Well," Sam took a deep breath, and I could see she was processing everything she'd learned. "Lucky for you, there's an ace reporter in your corner. I'll help you find them."

"How?" I asked, amazed by her acceptance and support.

"We dig. And when we hit a wall, we dig some more."

"But why?" I asked.

"Why...what?"

"Why get involved in all this?"

"Laney," she gave my hand a squeeze. "That's what friends do. I'm in your corner, always."

I leaned in and gave her a hug; grateful to have a second chance at having the kind of friendship I not only wanted but needed. "Thank you," I whispered. "I don't know what I did to deserve you."

"Fate," she pulled back and smiled. "It shines down on us every now and then. And boy," she looked around at the heaps of yellow fabric around me. "Is it shining down on you now."

I looked down and grabbed handfuls of the yellow taffeta. "It's awful, right?"

"It's the worst," she laughed. "Please do *not* make me wear something like that."

"I would never," I laughed softly, and Sam laughed, too.

"We'll figure it out," Sam said after the laughter had subsided. "I promise."

I hugged her again, the rustling of our gowns, filling my ears. "Thank you."

She hugged me back and when Marie called our names, from the other side of the dressing room, we both stood up quickly.

"Ladies, is everything alright?" Marie asked

"We're good," Sam called back.

"I thought I might steal Laney for a couple of minutes so we could get her fittings scheduled."

"Oh...right."

"And pay," Sam whispered.

"Shhh," I smiled and turned my back to her. "Will you help me with this?"

"This dress is awful," she yanked the plastic zipper and I exhaled with relief as it broke free.

"Thank goodness," I exhaled, relieved to be free of the confining fabric.

"Marie," Sam asked.

"Yes?" she answered from the other side.

"Could we get one last glass of champagne?" Sam asked as she stepped through the panel to go back to her own dressing room. To her surprise, Marie stood there with two glasses on a tray. She smiled and reached for one, then turned and winked at me. "It's like you have a chip in my brain."

After slipping out of the yellow dress, I put on my clothes and then stared at my reflection in the mirror. My mind felt free, and everything was so clear now.

It *had* been keeping a truth from me. Until I was ready. Until I was strong enough to remember and forgive myself, so that I could grant it to another. And now that I knew what I needed to do, I felt a powerful sense of purpose. I knew what I had gone through after the accident, and the dark place it had taken me to. I just hoped I wasn't too late to save another from going there, too.

CHAPTER TWENTY-THREE

THE REST OF OUR TRIP WAS A SUCCESS. AFTER WE LEFT the boutique, we had a great dinner in town, followed by drinks in the hotel lobby—and that night when I fell asleep, I had nothing but sweet dreams. My mind, having broken through the wall in my nightmare, was at peace with itself—the darkness, no longer present—and I woke by only the light of morning.

Despite Evan's unfailing support of me, a part of me always felt alone when it came what happened. We'd both lost our friends, but I was the one who was in the car. I was the one whose heart stopped. To know someone else had been on that road that night and shared those seconds and carried a similar weight, was a kind of comfort.

I believed more than ever, I had to find the driver, and as Sam and I checked out of our room, loaded up the car, and began the long drive home, I thought about all I'd learned. It wasn't until I found myself at the end of Sam's driveway, however, staring at the road, that I realized just how big a weekend it had been.

So much had changed in twenty-four hours, and the idea of going somewhere quiet to process it all, sounded good. Evan wasn't going to be home until later, so there was time. But I didn't know where to go. No one was ever really alone in a small town, especially ours, and I wanted to go somewhere different than usual. Then then I got an idea.

Jasper's!

It came to me out of nowhere and I'd laughed it off at first. The bar was not a place I'd consider going to ever before. Yet…it had been there for me once. What's to say it couldn't be again? That part of the coast *was* remote and quiet. I could easily go there for a bit, spend time with my thoughts, and be home before Evan even walked through the door. Deciding it was as good an idea as any, I pulled out of Sam's driveway, and headed up the coast.

I'd always wondered what the real *Jasper's* looked like. Of course, I'd driven by the bar countless times over the years, but I'd never gone inside. When I was finally old enough to, it was no place the five of us would consider going to whenever we were back home.

When I finally arrived and saw it was nothing like it'd been in my near-death experience, I was disappointed. It was dark and quiet—sparse of both furniture and people—and not at all warm or cheerful like the *Jasper's* of that world had been. But then I reasoned, it was just as well.

The reason it had looked the way it did in that world was because it served as a place of light when everything was dark. But now, in reality, that I didn't need the visage of comfort, rather, a quiet place where I could be alone, this *Jasper's* appeared as nothing more than what it was—a quiet bar, on a remote part of the coast

"What'll it be?" the bartender greeted me as I approached the bar.

I slid onto a stool and debated what to order. It was happy hour somewhere, right? "Beer will be fine."

"Draft or bottle?"

"Bottle."

"Coming up," he nodded.

Both establishment *and* bartender were different in reality. He was tall and strong, and while I got the impression, he was only a couple of years older than me, fine wrinkles flanking the corner of his eyes indicated he'd already lived more than his years.

"Here you go," he set a bottle down on the bar in front of me.

While this bartender may have looked different than the one that walked me through my first shot of tequila, he did sound similar. Then again, the accent of a Mainer mid-coast was distinct.

I lifted my bottle and took a sip, looking around. There was no trophy case or jukebox playing old records; no booths lining the walls, or tables and chairs, dimly lit by small red jar candles. *Jasper's*, in reality, wasn't a place you shared a drink with friends after a long day at work. It was the kind of place one would go to hide from the world. *Like that guy* I thought as I turned my attention to the end of the bar, stopping for a second to do a double take, before realizing it was Dean.

He looked a million miles away—staring down into a glass full of what looked to be whiskey—and I wondered whether I should say anything. Deciding a quick hello was the polite thing to do, I set my bottle down and cleared my throat.

"Dean?" I asked, knowing well it was him.

He looked up, surprised to hear his name. "Oh, hey," he lifted his chin in acknowledgement after turning to look at me.

"Hi," I smiled awkwardly.

"You two know one another?" the bartender asked.

"We do," Dean nodded.

"Small world," he laughed.

You can say that again, I thought, reaching for my beer, taking a sip. I'd come all the way out here to not run into someone, and then wound up doing exactly that. And Dean, of all people.

"Another drink, buddy?" the bartender asked him.

Buddy? I stared over my bottle at the two men, wondering if the reference was a term of familiarity, or bar colloquialism.

"Thanks man," Dean pushed his empty glass towards the bartender.

"Are you sure you don't want to slow down?"

"I'm fine, Jasper," Dean tapped the glass.

I lowered my bottle slowly, the name making the hair on the back of my neck stand up. "Your name is Jasper?"

"That's what the sign says," he laughed.

It wasn't too weird a coincidence; names, like family businesses, passed from family member to family member in these parts. But if the bar *had* looked the same, that would've been hard to ignore.

"And you two... you know one another?" I asked Dean, ignoring the decidedly not so odd similarity of the bartender's name.

The two exchanged a glance and Dean responded. "We, um, met at the VA."

"The VA?"

"Veterans Administration...in Bangor."

"Ah," I nodded.

"Jasper was in the service, too," he added.

Similarity number two, I thought. Again, weird, but not unusual. Young people in rural communities signed up for the service, anxious to see the world.

"This old goat served before my time, though," Dean cracked a smile.

The bartender removed the towel slung over his shoulder and smacked Dean on the arm. "Six years," he laughed. "I am only six years older than you, brother."

"Well," I cleared my throat, and held up my bottle. "Thank you both, for your service."

"Thank you," the bartender nodded in appreciation and Dean held up his glass.

"So," the bartender continued, "how do you two know each other?"

"We went to high school together," I replied politely.

"Oh yeah?" he leaned back and propped a foot up on the bar.

"Yup," Dean nodded. "Feels like a hundred years ago."

"It does," I agreed.

"Far from home, aren't you?" the bartender asked.

"Hey," Dean cut in before I could respond, shaking his head.

"What?"

"It's none of our business."

"Just making conversation."

"Well, sometimes people don't come here for small talk."

"Speak for yourself."

"Sometimes, people just want to be left alone, Jasper."

"Alright," the bartender held up his hand in apology. "Sorry, didn't mean to pry."

"It's fine," I held up my hand. "No apology necessary."

He nodded and rapped his knuckle on the bar, then made his way to a back room, leaving me alone with my drink, and Dean with mine.

He looked down, again lost in the amber liquor, and as I watched him sitting alone, carrying what looked to be the weight of the world, I realized what had driven me to *Jasper's* once, was in contrast to what I needed, now.

That night in my near-death experience when I'd run to *Jasper's*, I'd felt lost and alone, and my future uncertain. But now…I had a family, and a fiancé, and a future filled with light. And there was someone out there I needed to find, so they could be set free from whatever guilt they had been carrying, and have their future, too.

Realizing this was the last place I should be, I finished my beer, placed a five-dollar bill on the bar, and then slid off the stool, slipping out the door without anyone noticing.

After getting into my car, I called my mother, staring out across the water as I waited for her to pick up. "Hey honey," she answered.

"Hi," I sat back, watching the waves roll effortlessly.

"To what do I owe the pleasure?" she asked happily.

"Just got back into town and thought I'd stop by."

"That's right. Girl's weekend. How was it?"

"It was good. That's actually why I'm calling. I was planning to come by and fill you in."

"Sure honey. I'd love to see you. You're welcome anytime, you know that."

"I know," I smiled and looked down.

"Are you on your way now?"

"I'll be there in a bit."

"Okay, honey. We'll see you when you get here."

"See you soon."

After hanging up with my mother I started my car, then backed out of the parking lot, and watched *Jasper's* disappear in my rearview mirror as I made my way home.

***

When I walked into my parent's house half an hour later, my mother greeted me with a big smile and warm hug.

"Hi sweetheart," she squeezed me tight.

"Hi," I laughed squeezing her back.

"So," she grabbed my hand, leading me into the kitchen. "Tell me all about your weekend."

"Before we talk about the weekend, there is something else I need to tell you."

"Okay," she stopped at the counter. "Can I get you something to drink? I was about to make myself some tea."

"I'm fine," I smiled. "You go ahead."

"Okay," she removed the kettle from the stove and filled it with water, then placed it on the burner, and turned it on. "Now," she smiled. "What was it that you wanted to tell me?"

"I...found a dress."

"A dress?"

"Yes, a dress," I said again.

"You mean, a wedding dress?"

I nodded, waiting anxiously for her response. But instead of saying anything she came around the counter and gave me a hug.

"Oh honey, that's wonderful!"

"You're not...mad?" I asked as she shook me excitedly.

"Mad?" she stepped back, eyes glistening. "Why would I be mad?"

"Well, I know you and Evan's mom were looking forward to shopping for a dress with me."

"Oh heavens," she waved off the thought. "While, yes, I would've loved to go shopping with you for your dress, you should do what you want because it's *your* day."

"You mean it?"

"Yes," she laughed. "But I do have one question?"

"Yes?" I asked, wondering what kind of bargain I was in for, in exchange for robbing her of the joy of shopping for a dress with me.

"Is it what you wanted?" she asked, surprising me with the easiest question possible.

"It is," I smiled.

"Then that's all that matters."

"Well that certainly makes the next part easier."

"Did you and Evan elope?" she asked, eyes wide.

"No," I laughed. But the idea of being Evan's wife as soon as possible didn't sound too bad.

"Okay," she exhaled, visibly relieved.

"Do you think we'd do that?" I smiled.

"Well," she looked at me, considering my question. "I think when it comes to you and Evan, either one of you, would do just about *anything*, to be with the other."

"Well, you have a point," I blushed. "But no, we aren't going to elope. It's unrelated to the wedding, actually."

"Okay," my mother turned off the burner as the kettle began to whistle. "I'm listening."

"Remember that day in your shop, when you said I should consider seeing someone?" I asked, watching as she reached into the cabinet for a cup and then dropped in a teabag.

"Yes," she slipped on an oven mitt, reached for the kettle, and filled her mug with hot water.

"Well…I took your advice."

"Oh?" she asked, clearly surprised.

"That's where I was this weekend. It's the reason

I went to Bangor."

"Oh sweetheart," she replaced the kettle to the stove, and then turned to her cup, lifting the teabag in and out of the water. "How was it?"

"Honestly...it was good. Revealing, actually."

"Yeah?" she brightened, lifting the cup to her lips.

"Yes," I nodded. "That's why I stopped by."

"I'm so glad to hear you followed your old mother's advice," she smiled.

"Well, there's more."

"There is?"

"Maybe we should sit," I suggested. She eyed me carefully as I made my way to the kitchen table and pulled out a chair to sit down. "It's just...time that I filled you in."

"On?" she walked to the table, tea in hand.

"What happened the night of the accident."

"Honey," she set her cup down and sank into the chair opposite me. "You don't have to—"

"I know," I cut her off. "But I want to. I've not said anything to you about what happened that night because I couldn't before. But I can now. And I have to because I might need your help."

"How can I help?"

"Well," I sat back and began to tell her everything, starting with the argument Lisa and I got into that night at the campsite, and ending with what happened in the dressing room at the boutique yesterday.

When done, my mother sat back, quiet. There was two years' worth of information to digest, and I knew it was a lot to take in. "Well," she said finally. "It certainly explains a lot."

"How so?" I asked, curious.

"Why Evan's so protective of you. And, why you're so protective of him. You two have always been close, but these last couple of years....it now makes sense."

"Are you mad?" I asked for a second time since arriving, hoping she understood why I had only told him all this time.

"No," she reached for my hand. "He's the one you trust most in this world. I'm glad you have him. And, that you got the help you needed. But...I'm not sure how I can help?"

"The driver. I need to find them."

"Find them?" she asked.

"That's what all of this about," I nodded with determination. "I can't explain it, but it's like...we're connected. And I get the feeling the weight of that night...it's swallowing them whole."

"But I don't understand how I can help."

"Do you know anything about them?"

"No," she shook her head and released hold of my hand. "After the accident, we tried to find them, but once the police ruled them out for being at fault, the driver disappeared, and we didn't try to find them."

"Didn't you think that was weird that they just...vanished?"

"Not really," she shrugged. "People process tragedy differently. And an accident where three young lives were lost..." she trailed off.

"But that's just it. What if they have been struggling with what happened all this time, alone? What if I can help?"

"Who's to say they want to be found?"

"You have a point," I chewed my cheek.

"Thank you for telling me," she said after it had grown quiet as I considered her question. "It sounds like...quite an experience."

"So, you believe me?"

"I believe anything is possible," she nodded.

"Well, whatever might be possible, I do know one thing for sure, about that night."

"And that is?"

"Evan saved me. He's what brought me back."

She gave my arm a squeeze and smiled. I was grateful and relieved for her unconditional support.

"Alright," I smiled once she'd finished her tea.

"I'm going to get going."

"Say hi to your father on the way out. I'm sure he'd love to see you."

"I will," I leaned in to give her a hug. "See you later."

"Bye honey," she smiled and watched as I headed down the hall, then turned around and made herself busy in the kitchen.

"Yes?" my father called when I knocked on the door to his study.

I pushed open the door and stepped inside, looking around at the familiar space. On one side of the room was a large wooden desk, and the other, a tufted leather sofa in front of a fireplace. Bookshelves lined the walls, and French doors on the far side of the room opened up onto a side yard.

"Hi honey," he greeted me warmly, removing his reading glasses, and setting them on the desk.

"Anything good?" I eyed the stack of manuscripts on his desk.

"A couple look promising," he got up from his chair and came out from behind the desk to give me a hug. "What brings you by?"

"Just got back into town and wanted to say hi."

"Well, that's nice," he smiled. "It's good to see you. Did you and Evan go somewhere to get away for the weekend?"

"No, me and Sam."

"Oh," he shoved a hand in his pocket. "That sounds fun."

"It was. Most of it." My father tipped his head, curious at my choice of words. "It's a long story."

"I've got time," he leaned back against his desk.

"Well," I crossed my arms. "That's good, because that's why I came by."

"Oh?" he walked over to the sofa and sat down.

"There's a lot I need to tell you."

"About?"

"The accident."

"Ah," he leaned back and crossed one leg over the other.

"Still have time?"

"For you my daughter, always."

I took a deep breath and sat down on the other side of the sofa, then told him everything, just as I'd told my mother.

"Wow," he whistled when I'd finished.

"Sound crazy?" I asked.

"Not at all. Quite the contrary, actually. Near-death experiences have popped up in literature for centuries."

"The session host said something similar," I nodded.

"Evan knows, I assume?"

"Of course. But don't be mad at him for not saying anything. I swore him to secrecy."

"I would never be upset with Evan for protecting you."

I nodded and looked down, understanding well, my parent's affinity for Evan.

"I guess…I didn't want to worry you," I looked back up. "That night was already difficult enough as it was."

"You are braver than you believe, stronger than you seem, and smarter than you think," he smiled.

"What does Winnie the Pooh have to do with it?" I laughed at my father's quote of choice.

"Don't ever question your choices. You did what was best for you until you were ready."

"Even though it took more than two years?"

"You could've waited until I was eighty. I would've understood."

"Thank you," I leaned in to give him a hug.

"Can I ask you something?" he asked when I pulled back.

"Sure."

"What was it like?"

"The session?"

"No," he smiled. "What you experienced."

"Surreal…and confusing."

"I bet," he listened, with wide, curious eyes.

"You should write it down."

"Write it down?"

"Words can be a source of catharsis…and study. I've kept a journal ever since I was in college. You should give it a try."

"Maybe," I considered the suggestion.

"So, what are you going to do?"

"About the driver?" I asked and he nodded. "Sam is going to help me look into it."

"That's good," he crossed his arms. "Reporters have a keen mind for digging."

"That she does," I agreed.

"And you and Ev…things are good?"

I got up from the couch and made my way the bookshelf. "Things are great. There is something I am curious about though."

"That would be?" he asked, watching as I ran my hand along the top shelf. When I found what I was looking for, I grabbed the book's spine and pulled it out.

I turned around, holding up a worn copy of *Arabian Nights*. "I can't believe he read this for me."

"I'm not," he smiled.

I placed my hand on the cover, wondering how many nights Evan held the same book in his hands.

"And I am surprised you never said anything."

"It wasn't my secret to tell. He's quite the young

man, though."

"He is," I agreed, my cheeks warming.

"You two have been through a lot these past few years. More so than I had by your age, that's for sure."

"Didn't you and mom have a kid when you were my age?"

"I guess we did," he laughed. "Still, that does not compare to the trials you two have had."

"Well," I held the book against my chest, "you know what they say...out of adversity comes opportunity. Although...somehow, I don't think any of the last few years, is what Benjamin Franklin was talking about."

My father got up from the couch and made his over to where I stood. "I think, to have gone through what you have, and come out the other side, and use it for good to help another, is pretty remarkable."

"All truths are easy to understand once they are discovered; the point is to discover them, right?"

"Good advice from Galileo," he smiled.

"I just feel like I have to. There's a reason. But I won't know until find them. Does that sound weird?"

"Not at all," he shoved a hand in his pocket.

I looked to the stack of manuscripts on my

father's desk. "Well, I'll let you get back to work."

"Okay sweetheart," he smiled at me warmly.

"Do you mind if I borrow this?" I looked at the book in my hands. "I'll return it. I just…"

"No need," he smiled and held up a hand. "I've been holding it for you. I figured you'd want it one day…once you knew."

"Thank you," I pulled it to my chest. "And thank you…for all of those years with Evan."

"Oh honey," he exhaled. "I've never wanted more than the world for you. And Evan, always wanted to give you that world. That book was my way of making sure he was ready."

"It's pretty amazing to think he was reading it all those years for me."

"It is," my father nodded. "But I've always known there is nothing he wouldn't do for you. He would move Heaven and Earth if asked."

"I know," I admitted, knowing well the lengths Evan would go for me.

"You're both lucky to have what you do. Honor it. And cherish it."

"I will," I leaned in to give him a hug, eyeing the closed dartboard on the wall. "How about I swing by later in the week for a game?"

"I'd love that," he nodded when I pulled back.

"Good, then. You're on. Get your money ready."

"Noted," he laughed and walked me to the door. "And Laney…"

"Yes?" I stopped before stepping into the hall.

"Think about what I said."

"About?"

"What happened to you…consider writing it down."

"Catharsis?"

"And…it would make one heck of a story."

Write it down I thought as he walked back to his desk and sat down. *Maybe someday, I would.*

CHAPTER TWENTY-FOUR

WHEN I MADE IT HOME, I WAS RELIEVED TO SEE EVAN'S car in the driveway. Between my trip to *Jasper's* and the visit with my parents, I was anxious to fill him in on everything. Not to mention, I missed him like crazy.

Surprisingly, the house was quiet when I finally walked through the door. Setting my bags down on the floor, I dropped my keys on the table and made my way to the kitchen. Taking a quick look outside, I found Evan standing at the edge of the property, looking across the water.

We both loved this time of day—when the sun-bathed the world in a soft warm glow—and the secluded beach attached to the house, offered a breathtaking view of the light washing over the cove. It was one of the main reasons we decided to rent this place instead of something in town.

Another, being that the owner was interested in selling eventually and we'd hoped to make it ours, someday.

"Well, hello," I said, coming up behind Evan, wrapping my arms around him.

"Hey," he turned around and smiled. "When did you get in?"

"Just now."

"Didn't hear you drive up."

"You must've been deep in thought."

"That I was," he smiled softly, gold specks in his caramel-colored eyes, reflecting the sun's light.

"Anything you'd like to share?"

"How about I show you?"

Evan leaned down and kissed me, and the anxiousness in me dissolved, as he held me close.

"Well, that's one heck of a way for a girl to be welcomed home," my lips tingled as we parted.

"Not just a girl," he winked. "*The* girl."

"That's right," I gripped the front of his vest jokingly. "And don't you forget it."

"You got it," he smiled and kissed me again. "Have a good weekend?" he asked when our lips again parted.

"I did. You?"

"It was good to be with the guys."

"Did you miss me?" I asked cheekily.

"Do you even have to ask?" He laced his fingers through mine, and pulled me to him, wrapping my arms around his waist.

I tipped my head up, knowing well his answer. "I missed you, too."

"And the session...was it helpful?"

The gravity of the weekend felt too important to share on the phone or in text, so I'd promised to fill Evan in on everything as soon as I was home.

Part of me felt bad that I'd already shared what I'd learned with Sam and my parents, when Evan had been my only confidant for so long. But I also knew Evan wouldn't mind. He just wasn't that kind of person.

"I have *a lot* to tell you."

"I can't wait to hear."

"How about we order some takeout and I tell you over dinner."

"Good idea," he scooped me up in his arms. "That way, we can make up for lost time now."

I laughed as he carried me into the house, kissing me as he walked. "I should go away more often," I teased as we tumbled down onto the bed once upstairs.

"I missed you," he hovered over me, eyes on mine.

I reached up and stroked his cheek gently. "And

I, you."

"I'm glad you're home."

"It's good to be home."

"Can I tell you a secret?"

"Of course."

"I found a dress."

"Yeah?" he asked, eyes widening.

"And not just one. *The one*."

"I can't wait to see it," he beamed.

"Well, you'll have to because you're not seeing it until our wedding day."

"No private preview?"

"Nope."

"Even if I beg?"

"Not even if you were on your hands and knees," I grinned. "But..." I smiled coyly. "I do have a little something for under the dress that I *can* show you?"

"Oh?" he raised an eyebrow.

"Wait right here," I slid out from under him.

"Where are you going?" he propped himself up on one elbow, watching as I jogged out of the room.

"I'll be right back," I called out as I jogged down the stairs.

"What's this?" he asked when I came back into the bedroom a minute later, and set a small box tied with grey satin ribbon down in front of him.

"There's no way you're going to see me in my dress before the big day. But, if you're good, I might let you see me in this." Evan smiled as he grabbed the box and untied the ribbon. "Something new," I explained, as he removed the lid and pulled the tissue paper back carefully.

"You're not playing fair," he looked at me, a wicked smile pulling at his lips.

"No?" I asked innocently.

"No," he removed the white garter that was inside, and twirled it around his finger.

"There's more," I smiled. "And if you're good, maybe I'll show you that, too."

"Promise?" he pulled me to him, eyes on fire.

"I do," I fell into his arms, smiling.

"Until death do us part?"

"Even longer."

We kissed, longer and deeper than before, making up for the long, yet short weekend apart.

***

Later, after the sun set, we made our way downstairs and curled up in front of the fire in the living room with containers of takeout spread out on the coffee table, and I filled Evan in on everything.

"So," he reached for a container of sweet n' sour chicken. "Fill me in. And don't hold anything back."

"Well," I grabbed the box of noodles and spooned a bit onto my plate. "It was totally unexpected."

"Unexpected in a good way?" he asked, reaching for the pot stickers.

"In the best way."

"How so?"

"Well," I lifted my noodles and took a bite, then proceeded to fill Evan in on everything—the session, the nightmare that first night in Bangor, and the vision I had in the dressing room the next day.

"You're not saying anything," I set my chopsticks down once finished.

"I'm processing."

"Are you okay?"

"I'm fine. Are *you* okay?"

"It's a lot," I confirmed.

"That's one way of putting it," he took a deep breath. "I mean, that's...intense."

"It was," I agreed.

"Are you okay, really?" he asked, reaching for my hand.

"Knowing Lisa and I shared that moment and that she'd forgiven me," I paused, my eyes welling up. "It gave me peace, and closure. Knowing she wasn't angry with me...that was a gift I never expected to receive."

"Maybe that was the point of the nightmares, and not the driver," he said gently. "Maybe, it was as simple as absolving you of that grief?"

"I thought that at first," I nodded. "But it's greater than that. Because she forgave me, I am the one that has to grant *them* forgiveness. The driver is the missing piece. I can feel it."

"Are you sure?"

"I'm positive," I insisted.

Evan let go of my hand and studied his plate for a moment, then pushed up from the floor.

"Where are you going?"

"Come," he held out his hand.

"Where?"

"There's something I need to show you."

"What?" I set my plate down and got up as well, following him into the room he'd taken over as an office.

"Something told me I should hold onto this," he said as he walked over to the desk, and pulled open a drawer, reaching inside. "I guess my gut was right."

"What is it?" I asked, watching as he came back around to where I stood, and held a folder out to me.

"I looked into it once. The driver."

"You…what?" I reached for it, tentatively.

"After the accident," he leaned back against the desk and crossed his arms.

I looked down to the manila folder in my hands, stunned. "But, why?" I looked up, stunned.

"After the accident," he paused and looked at me, his eyes dark with remembrance of that night. "I wanted the driver to pay…for what they did to you…and them."

"But it wasn't the driver's fault."

Lisa had been driving erratically that night. I remembered this, not to mention, it'd been determined Caleb's car had veered into the path of the logging truck.

"I know," he nodded. "When you were out of surgery and we knew you'd be okay, I went to the police and asked about the driver. But they didn't tell me anything. They only said that they hadn't been at fault, and that was it."

Feeling the folder's weight in my hand, I wondered what was inside.

"I talked to the Sherriff first," Evan began, and I opened the folder, finding a police report staring back at me. "I thought, given his friendship with my father, and yours, he may be willing to help out.

But, according to him, it was an open and shut case. Driver gave a statement and it corroborated with the scene of the accident. He did say something didn't feel right. It's why he gave me the report on top, but the rest is from my own digging."

I looked through the folder's contents in disbelief. There had to be more than a hundred pages of reports and newspaper clippings...even a background search on the logging company.

"I can't believe it," I shook my head and looked up.

"I'm sorry I didn't say anything before," Evan exhaled. "I just...didn't want to cause you any more pain or regret or...I don't know. Give you false hope."

"False hope?"

"I didn't only want to make the driver pay, Lanes. I wanted to exonerate her...for you. I knew how important it was to you that people remember Lisa as you did. But I didn't want to get your hopes up that I would be able to do that, so I didn't say anything."

I hated the articles that ran after the accident. Story after story painting Lisa as less than, and Caleb and Timmy the innocent, beloved sons of Lake Haven.

"That's why you did all of this?" I asked, my

eyes filling with tears.

"When you love someone as I do you, Alaina Thomas, you will do anything for them. Even if it means, helping clear the name of their best friend that you didn't always see eye-to-eye with."

I jumped into Evan's arms, smashing the folder between us. "If there is anyone I believe in Laney, it's you," he wrapped his arms around me and buried his head in my neck. "And if you think we need to find the driver, then we'll find them."

"Thank you," I whispered.

"For?"

"Believing in me."

"I will always believe in you."

We stood there holding onto one another; nothing but the sound of our breathing in the quiet room.

"This is really helpful," I said once we pulled apart. "It's going to help her so much."

"Her?" Evan raised an eyebrow.

"I told Sam everything."

"Everything?" he asked, eyes wide with the realization of what that meant.

"Yes, everything. About the accident, what happened when my heart flatlined, and my nightmares. And after all that, she offered to help me find the driver."

"That's great," he nodded with encouragement. "She's a good friend."

"She is," I agreed.

"You know, it was never about me not liking Lisa," Evan looked at me, eyes full of love. "She was one of us, and if anyone would've hurt her, I would've hurt them. It's just...all those years, I loved you. And that's what I wanted more than anything. You...and your happiness. That's why I looked into the driver. To grant your heart the peace it deserved and let her memory rest."

I dropped the folder and again leaped into his arms, my love for him stronger and deeper in that moment, than it had ever been.

The answer to the mystery of the driver was hiding somewhere in the pages on the floor around me. And tomorrow, I'd start digging until I could find them, and close that chapter of our lives. But with only one piece left to find, it wouldn't be long until the next chapter began — the chapter that was Evan and I and the rest of our lives — and I didn't see any reason that couldn't start, tonight.

CHAPTER TWENTY-FIVE

As promised, Sam began looking into the driver as soon as she got to work on Monday, and when I stopped by her office later that same day to drop off the folder Evan had given me, she seemed as surprised by its contents as I was.

"I found something," Sam said excitedly when she called me at work later that week.

"What?" I asked anxiously, turning around in my chair to look out the window.

"I can't say...yet. But it's promising. I'm looking into it now, and when I have more, I'll let you know."

"Okay," I sat back in my chair, bummed she couldn't say anything else.

"I promise," she added, sensing my disappointment.

With Sam focused on tracking down the driver,

there was nothing I could but wait and I was feeling restless. I could feel a truth, not yet discovered, reaching out, begging to be set free, and it was growing heavier by the day.

"How's the dance?" Sam asked, changing the subject.

"It's good," I glanced down at my watch, expecting Niña for our weekly appointment any minute.

The dance was only days away, and all of the students were talking about it. I'd heard plenty of conversations in the hall at school, around who was wearing what, and I knew the Social Committee was working hard to live up to the hype.

I'd also seen Dean at the school a couple of times. He'd nod, and I'd nod back, but that was it. Neither one of us said a word about our run-in at *Jasper's*. And I found it interesting, he hadn't said anything to Evan, either. It reminded me of Tony's comment that day at the house and wondered if what he said was true—Dean knew I was what made Evan tick and didn't want to lose the project by causing any problems.

In a way I'd put what happened with Dean in my near-death experience behind me. While I'd told my parents and Sam about what I'd experienced, I'd kept him out of it, just as I had when I first told

Evan. His presence was no longer significant, and I planned to take the secret to my grave.

"And the wedding?" Sam continued, bring me back to our conversation.

"Oh," I exhaled. "Well, you know…the mania has officially begun."

Sam laughed. I'd been filling her in on my mother and Evelyn's sudden focus on the wedding, so she knew exactly what I was talking about.

Having found a dress, our mothers had dived head-first into planning the reception; Evan's mom starting a text thread with me, my mother, and herself, to share ideas and pictures.

The two had been sending texts nonstop, to which I'd respond with a smiley face, or a thumbs down. Last night, I'd shared a screen shot with Sam, of a particular hot button topic that had come up earlier in the day — party favors — to which Sam replied with a crying emoji. It had only been a couple of days, and I couldn't imagine what it would be like in a couple of months.

Hearing a knock on my office door, I turned, and seeing Niña on the other side, waved for her to come in.

"Hey, Sam, my next appointment is here. Keep me posted?"

"Absolutely. Cross your fingers this lead pans

out."

"They're crossed," I confirmed.

"Talk later," she replied, and we hung up.

"Busy?" Niña asked after I'd put my phone down on my desk.

"Not at all," I motioned for her to take a seat. "How are you? How are things going with the dance?"

"Good," she sat down and dropped her backpack to the floor.

"Everything is coming down to the wire I bet."

"I never imagined it would be this much work," she leaned back and ran her hands, down the arms of the chair, dramatically. "I can't believe it's in two days."

"Are you excited?"

"I am," she said, with a hint of reluctance.

"Do I sense some hesitation?"

"No. I just...need some advice."

"About?"

"What to wear."

"Oh," I sat back.

"What?" she asked with a dubious expression on her face.

"Well, I'm...not very good about that kind of thing."

"What?" she asked, sitting up.

"It's true."

"Are you sure?"

"Pretty sure," I smiled. "I've never been much into fashion."

Niña reached across my desk and tapped her finger. "I think you're wrong."

"What?" I looked down, not sure what she was doing. Then I saw what she was referring to.

On my desk was the picture of my wedding dress that I'd been carrying around; visible lines etched into the paper, from my endless unfolding and unfolding.

"How'd that get there?" I grabbed it, slightly embarrassed.

"It's...always there," she smiled.

"Sorry," I folded it up and tossed it into the top drawer of my desk.

"Don't be."

"It's my wedding dress."

"I assumed," she smiled. "It's beautiful."

"Thank you," I smiled appreciatively. I knew Niña's compliment was sincere. The aloof girl, with the dark make-up and hard exterior, had warmed up to me and I felt a genuine respect from her.

I was, however, still, clueless about her family situation. The town grapevine was unusually quiet when it came to talk of anyone new in town, and I was, admittedly, curious. But we'd come far, and I decided not to pry too much.

"So," Niña continued. "With your amazing taste in mind, what should I wear?"

"Well, maybe someone at home could help?"

"No," she tensed. "I think I will keep her out of this."

Her? It was the most Niña had said about family, but it was enough to pique my curiosity.

Seeing this, she cleared her throat and looked down. "I just…I could use advice."

"Well," I watched her curiously, the way she appeared to retreat into herself, concerning. "What would be appropriate?"

"I was planning to paint my face like a calavera," she looked up, the tension in her shoulders, beginning to ease. "But I'm torn on the actual outfit."

"Well, what is customary?"

"A dress. Something bright, or something black."

"Bright?" I questioned, imagining black to be the color of choice on a day honoring the dead.

"Oh yeah," she nodded, a smile pulling at her lips. "The streets in Mexico City during Día are just beautiful. So colorful, and it smells amazing, with the air filled with candles and flowers. It's what I

384

imagine the afterlife looks like."

"Really?" I asked, surprised.

"The afterlife is a party."

"I would've never thought that."

"Religious?"

"No," I shook my head once.

"No church wedding, then?"

"Nope."

"Anything?" she asked, curious.

"My father believes in books, and my mother…" I paused, thinking of the crystal she wore around her neck. "I'm not sure what she believes."

Well, I believe in Santa Muerte," Niña said with conviction. "And I think, she wants to see color."

"Then that's your answer. Wear something bright."

"Yes," Niña pressed her fingertips to her chin. "You're right."

"But you'd better hurry. You only have two days."

"I know," her smile faded. "And getting something shipped overnight is dicey."

"Overnight?" I questioned. "I don't think anything you order now will arrive in time. I'm sure you could find something in town. Or take a drive to Eastport."

"No offense, but flannel isn't really what I was

thinking."

"There's more than flannel in the stores, here," I smiled.

"Sure," she nodded. "There's ugly Christmas sweaters."

She had me there. Fall barely had a chance to hit the shelves, before the Christmas invasion begun. But that wasn't just Lake Haven. It was the case everywhere.

"Good point," I agreed.

Niña reached into her back pocket and pulled out a cell phone, swiping and typing, then replacing it to her pocket a minute later.

"Hopefully, it will arrive on time."

"You just ordered something?"

"That's the beauty of mobile shopping. Point, click, buy."

"So," I shook my head, marveling at her ability to solve a problem in a matter of minutes. "How is everything else?"

"Good," she said simply.

"Classes, okay?"

"They're fine."

"And Lake Haven...you seem to be adjusting well?"

"This place isn't so bad."

"Well, I'm glad to hear."

We stared at each other, the clock overhead, skipping forward one tick.

"Ms. Thomas?" she asked.

"Yes?"

"Never mind," she looked down.

"What's on your mind?"

"It's nothing," she inhaled.

"Are you sure?"

"Yeah," she looked back up. "It's... nothing."

"We have another minute or two if there's something on your mind."

"No," she reached for her backpack and stood up. "I'll figure it out. I've gotta run. Committee needs me."

"Alright," I got up to walk her to the door. "I'll see *you* on Friday. I'll be the one under the papel picados," I laughed, knowing how awful my Spanish must've sounded.

"You're going to the dance?" she stopped.

"I was asked to chaperone. Figured, why not."

"You don't have to. I think we have enough."

"Really?" I crossed my arms. "Shelley asked just yesterday."

"Oh," she bit her lip. "Well, I'm sure you have better things to do on a Friday night, then spend it at some high school dance."

"I won't bother you," I smiled. "I promise.

Besides, I want to see all of this work everyone has been doing and could use a night out."

Niña started to respond, but the ringing bell overhead cut off her words. "See you on Friday," I nudged her gently.

She walked out of the office, stopping to look back at me just before she reached the door to the hall, then turned around and disappeared.

What's gotten into her? I wondered as I made my way back to my desk and sat down.

I didn't like the way Niña said *her*. Or the way she appeared to want to say something, and then quieted. I hoped whatever was going on she was okay, and it didn't set her back. She was doing well, and I believed she could flourish here.

Maybe she was just going through typical teen stuff—curfews, or too much time on her phone. Or perhaps she was nervous about the dance. I could only imagine how demanding the most popular kids in school could be.

Regardless, I made a mental note to look into her home situation. In the meantime, with my schedule clear for the rest of the afternoon, I found myself now wondering, what *I* was going to wear to the dance.

The irony I'd thought about clothes more in the last month, than I'd ever had, wasn't lost on me. It was hard to believe, all the hours I'd spent watching Lisa flip eagerly through fashion magazines, were catching up to me.

I'd never paid attention to the glossy spreads in the clothing magazines Lisa coveted; the preening models in dramatic outfits that looked neither practical nor comfortable had always made me laugh, while she'd stare at them for hours, dreamily.

The Social Committee had encouraged dressing in theme. Surely that meant chaperones, too. It could be fun to dress up for the night, and wear something out of character.

I opened my laptop and did a quick search to get some ideas, then called around to the few shops in town I thought might have something. One had new inventory, another was out of everything after a bunch of students came in the week before, and a third hadn't gotten anything new for weeks.

After grabbing my bag and coat, I stopped by Janie's desk to let her know I was heading out a bit early, then went into town to look in the one store that sounded promising. If I didn't find anything there, I'd have to go to Calais or Eastport.

As I looked through a sales rack in the one store with promise, I started thinking about the fit of the spandex dress I'd tried on in the boutique in Bangor. I remembered that while the design was horrible, I actually liked the way it hugged the curves I did have and wondered if I could find something with a similar fit, but more tasteful design.

Seeing nothing remotely close to that dress on the racks, I went home and called around to a couple of stores in Eastport. After confirming with a salesperson at one store, they had a couple of dresses that sounded like a match to what I was looking for, I made plans to go there after work the next day. It would be cutting it close, but it was the only real option.

Turns out, Eastport was more fashion-forward than I'd remembered. There were a few shops with options and one in particular, which had a dress I fell in love with and wound up buying. It was tasteful and hinted at the look and feel of the dresses worn during Día de los Muertos celebrations.

After buying shoes for me, and a top-hat and a cane for Evan, I made my way home, excited about the dance. Sure, we'd been to dances together in school, but it was always as a group. Friday would be the first time I'd get to go to a dance as Evan's date, and I couldn't ignore the butterflies that idea stirred.

We may be engaged and be one another's future,

but every now and then, there were firsts—
moments we'd never experienced together before—
and in those moments, I remembered how lucky I
was to have another chance at life so that I *could*
have them.

Then again, when you had a love like ours,
second chances weren't luck. They were part of
something bigger, beyond us, like Sam suggested.
Something written in the stars.

CHAPTER TWENTY-SIX

EVAN WHISTLED AS I WALKED OUT OF THE BATHROOM, adjusting the backing to one of my earrings.

"You like?" I smiled.

"Like is not the word."

I still couldn't believe I'd found a dress in Eastport. With an off the shoulder neckline, and long, lace sleeves, it was exactly what I'd been looking for.

It fit like a glove down to the knees, with the skirt cutting high in the front and flowing long in the back. All I had to do was pull my hair into a low bun, place a decorative flower above my ear, and apply a bit of eyeliner around my eyes, and I had a look that was appropriate, but not a costume, which is exactly what I wanted.

"What would the word be, then?"

"How about..." he came over to where I stood

and whispered in my ear.

"If you say that again, I won't make it out the door," I blushed.

"Doesn't sound so bad," he grinned.

"Because you have a meeting to go to, and I, am needed at the school."

"I think you meant, you have to get to the school, and I need you."

I laughed, shaking my head, adjusting my beloved locket so it lay flat. "You're impossible."

"That I am," he wrapped an arm around my waist and pulled me to close.

"What are you doing?" I smiled as he grabbed my hand with his free one and held it against his chest.

"Getting in a dance with you now," he grinned.

I placed my hand on his shoulder and looked up as he began to move me back and forth. "This is nice."

"It is," he smiled. "How come we don't go dancing more often?"

"Or ever?"

"Or that," he winked.

"Not sure. But we should."

"Agree," he smiled, and I leaned against his chest.

"You're a good dancer."

"You can thank my mom. She and my aunt made Tim and I take classes when we were kids."

"She did?"

"Six months," he nodded, holding my hand tighter.

"Well, I'll have to thank her."

He swayed me back and forth, humming a bit, and then continued. "I'm sorry I can't make it tonight."

"It's fine."

"It's not. I promised I'd go, and I broke that promise."

"This dinner is important," I looked up, staring into his eyes. "You need to be there. You're not breaking a promise."

Shortly after walking through the door, Evan received a call from Councilmember Evers. There was growing interest in speeding up the project timeline, and he'd invited Evan to discuss the idea over dinner. Evan was about to raincheck, but I'd insisted he go—the project at the hotel, more important than a high school dance.

"I'll come as soon as I can," he said for the fifth time.

"Take your time," I insisted. "You don't want to disappoint The Council."

"Are you sure?"

"I'm positive."

"Maybe Sam can join you?" he suggested.

"She's got a full plate right now. Between work and looking into the driver for me."

"How's that going?" he asked, pulling back to twirl me under his arm.

"She has a lead," I smiled as we came back together.

"Oh yeah? Anything interesting?"

"Truthfully, I don't know. We haven't talked much, but we're getting coffee tomorrow. Hopefully, I'll know more, then."

"That's good," Evan nodded. "Maybe the four of us can have lunch after. Tony and I have some stuff to go over in the morning, and who knows what else after tonight's dinner."

"I think that can be arranged. Hey...speaking of Tony, did you fill him in on everything?"

"Everything?" Evan asked, slightly puzzled.

With my parents and Sam now aware of everything that happened, Tony was the only person in my inner circle that didn't. But he'd become like a brother to me, and I wanted him to know.

"The accident, my experience...the driver."

"Ah," Evan nodded. "I haven't, no. I wasn't sure if you wanted me to."

"Sam knows. He should, too."

"Well, Tony adores you, and would want you to tell him. You should."

Evan was right. I should be the one to tell him. "I'll tell him," I agreed.

"He'll probably think it's cool how close we were with he and Sam in what you experienced."

"Probably," I agreed. "I'm glad that came true. And us."

Evan adjusted his hold on my waist and locked his eyes on mine. "Lanes, we came true long before that."

Evan was right. We were the truest truth there ever was. "You know we've been dancing this whole time with no music."

"Who needs music when you have the song of our hearts," he leaned down and kissed me softly, careful not to smudge my shiny, red lipstick.

"That's so cheesy," I grinned after he pulled back.

"Read it in a greeting card," he laughed.

"Is that what I have to look forward to? A husband who speaks his heart through greeting cards?"

"I will never need a card to tell you how I feel, Alaina Thomas. I love you. Always have, always will. You can look forward to that."

"That sounds like happily ever after to me," my chest tightened.

"Our life together is going to be amazing. I can't wait for what the future brings."

"Me too," I smiled. "But first, I let go of his waist, "the present. You need to get going, and so do I."

Evan sighed, then lifted my hand and kissed the back. "Thank you for the dance."

"The pleasure was all mine," I curtsied.

"I am the luckiest man on the planet," he grinned, the fire in his eyes undeniable.

"Stop," I blushed.

"No, I mean it."

"Ev...it took me a long time to pull myself together for tonight."

"And?"

"And, if you keep saying things like that to me, neither of us are leaving this house tonight."

"Well, maybe we should just stay here for the night, in our own world, just you and me."

"As much as I like the sound of that, you know you shouldn't keep The Council waiting. And I want to go to the dance and show my student support. She's worked hard and she should know someone cares."

"Now see, *that* is why I love you. Whether it's

Millie and her pies, a student, or the driver, you want to help people."

"That's me, Alaina Thomas, patron saint of do-gooders."

"You're more special than you even know," he reached for my hand, eyes serious as he grew quiet.

"You, okay?"

"I'm fine."

"You sure?"

"I was just thinking."

"About?"

"How I wish it were possible."

"How you wish *what* were possible?"

"You and me...being in our own world."

"Well," I smiled. "In a way, we are."

"You know what I mean," he said softly.

"Hey," I pressed my palm to his chest as he looked at me. "You, okay?"

"It's nothing."

"You sure?"

"Yeah," his face brightened. "Go and have fun."

"I'll be home before you know it," I leaned in to kiss him goodbye, and he wrapped his arms around me, holding me tight.

I kissed him gently, careful not to smudge my lipstick, and then grabbed my bag and coat and turned for the door.

"Laney?" he called just before I reached the hall. I stopped and looked back at him, over my shoulder. "I love you."

"And I you, always," I winked. Then headed down the stairs and out the door.

***

When I arrived at The Conservatory, I couldn't believe my eyes. The Social Committee had outdone themselves. The space had totally transformed and looked exactly as I imagined Day of the Dead would look, based on everything Niña had told me.

The twisted limbs of the woods outside, cast eerie shadows through the translucent ceiling above, while the flowers scattered all around, bright, and vibrant, filled the space with light. It felt as if I'd stepped into a world of both life and death; a dance of the macabre, of that which is real, and that which lies beyond.

Large potted trees, with sweeping moss that fell to the ground, flanked the main doors, while marigold garlands adorned the walls, and dozens of candles on gold pillars, sat atop tables draped with thick red and gold velvet, flickering with light.

Making my way through the main entrance, I found myself in the gift shop, which had turned into a parlor for the night, with half a dozen tables filled with food. There were cookies and cakes and food of all kinds piled high on colorful plates and bowls, and a table with flower headbands for the girls, and top hats for the boys.

Leaving that room, I made my way into the greenhouse and looked up at the domed ceiling. The moon was high and shining bright.

"You're here!" Niña called to me from the other side.

"Hi!" I called back, following the green velvet ropes that had been set up to keep students from veering off the path into the plant and flower beds. "That entrance is incredible," I said when I finally reached her.

"Wait until you see the rest. Come," she waved for me to follow, and we left the greenhouse and walked out under the tent that had been set up over the terrace.

A large dancefloor filled the center of the space, with a DJ stand on one side, and photo area, including professional photographer and photo booths, on the other.

"This is amazing," I nodded with approval.

"It's not too bad," she smiled.

"All of this is just incredible. You should be proud."

"Speaking of incredible," she smiled, looking me up and down. "You said that you didn't know about clothes but look at you."

"Thank you," I adjusted the flower behind my ear. "You didn't do too bad yourself. You look terrific."

Niña looked great. She wore a long red dress, pulled down on the shoulders, and a headband in her hair, adorned with yellow and orange flowers. And she had applied her makeup expertly, painting red circles with rhinestones around her eyes, and a light coat of black powder brushed underneath for a shadow effect. But I loved the way she'd painted her nose — two delicate triangles on the tip — and the thin strips of black across her lips that mimicked stitching.

"Everything is just magical. I see your influence, everywhere."

"Now do you understand why I love Día so much?"

"I do," I nodded. And I meant it. It was hard not to feel the power of life, in this celebration of the dead.

"Come," she motioned for me to follow her again. "I want to show you something."

Niña led me to back of the tent, where a structure shrouded in large swaths of fabric stood tall.

Pulling one section of fabric back, we stepped under the cloaking, and I saw then, that it was a giant altar. It was tall, about fifteen or twenty feet high, with dozens of shelves, and on each shelf, sat dozens of pictures in hand-painted frames and a small tea candle in front.

"The candles are battery operated. Fire ordinance or something," she shrugged. "Same with the ones in the main entrance. It's cool, though. They look real."

I listened as she talked excitedly, looking at the pictures, realizing this must've been what Dean had been working on the last few weeks—then froze when I saw one photo, in between a handful of others. It was of Lisa, Caleb, and Timmy.

"I hope you don't mind," Niña eyed me carefully, as I stared at the picture. "This night is about everyone we've lost...so they can hear and feel our love. I just, wanted to make sure we included those you lost, too."

I reached out, pulling the picture to me. "I've never seen this before."

"That's because I did some photoshopping. See," she pointed down at the image.

As I stared at the picture more closely, I realized it was one from my desk. Only, Evan and I were gone, as if we hadn't been there that day at all; the three of them appearing natural, as if it were how the photo was originally taken.

I placed my hand on the picture, not sure what to say. It was good to see them together, happy and smiling.

"Is it okay?" she asked.

"Yes," I nodded, and meant it. It was beautiful to see them this way, and I hoped wherever they were now, they were together.

"Good," she exhaled as I replaced the picture to the shelf.

"You've been so kind to me. I just...wanted to do something for you."

"It means so much to me," I smiled, wiping away a lone tear. "Thank you."

"My pleasure," she smiled.

"Well," I pressed the corner of my eyes as a pre-emptive strike against any other tears that threatened. Any minute, students would begin to arrive, filling the room with excited chatter. "It's time for me to go, and you, to start having fun."

"Where will you be tonight?" she asked

"Refreshments," I confirmed. "Main entrance."

"Oh," her face fell.

"It's fine," I looked at all of the speakers and could only imagine how loud it would be out here, shortly.

"Are you sure?"

"Of course," I laughed. "You don't want me watching over you."

"You're not so bad," she said simply.

"Well thank you," I laughed. "But there will be plenty of chaperones out here. How else are they going to stop the kids from messing around in the greenhouse?"

"Yeah," she rolled her eyes. "We were warned about that. The school had to sign a dozen papers. We had strict instructions to use the front entrance, and back. Nothing in the greenhouse."

"Go have fun," I looked around as we stepped out from under the cloak. "I'll see you later."

"Okay," she waved reluctantly, as I made my way back to the greenhouse and to the main entrance.

***

An hour later, the dance was in full swing. The students were having fun and I enjoyed watching them wander around, eyes wide with excitement, at the world they'd stepped into for the night.

After being relieved from the drinks table by another chaperone, my phone rang. Seeing it was

Sam, I stepped outside where I could hear to answer it.

"Hey," I picked up, glad to hear from her.

"Lanes...where..." she started to say, but her voice cut out.

"I can barely hear you," I pressed a finger into my free ear, trying to concentrate on her voice. "I think we have a bad connection."

"Don't...go..." she continued, static breaking her words.

"Where are you?" I shouted. "I can't hear you very well."

"I'm.... going...be..."

"Sam," I shouted again, obvious she couldn't hear anything I was saying. "Call me when..." but the line went dead before I could finish. "Shoot," I clasped the phone in my hand and spun around, bumping into Dean.

"Sorry," we said in unison; his eyes widening when he saw it was me.

"What are you doing here?" he asked stiffly.

"Phone call," I held up my phone. "Bad reception, though. You?"

"Altar," he said stiffly. "Sticking around, should they need anything with it."

"Right," I nodded. "That altar is incredible."

"It's the least I could do," he shrugged.

"Honoring those we lost is important."

"It is," I agreed. Dean's cell phone rang, and he reached into his pocket and answered it, turning his back to me, and speaking into the phone low so I couldn't hear.

"Everything okay?" I asked when he turned around.

"No," he said tersely, shoving his phone into his pocket. "That was um... Shelley. She thinks a student went to The Boneyard."

"The Boneyard?" I asked, surprised. "But how? There are chaperones, everywhere."

"She didn't say. Just that she heard a few kids talking about going over there."

I looked across the street, The Boneyard was pitch dark. "Why did she call you?"

"Not sure," he shrugged.

"Did she say who it may be?"

"Um...the girl who planned the dance?"

"Niña?" I asked; my voice elevated.

"Yeah," he nodded. "That's the name. She asked me to go over there and check it out."

"I'm coming with you."

"No," he protested. "You're not."

"Yes, I am."

"You're not dressed for that."

"Who cares what I'm wearing?"

"That place is old and rotting."

"Look, there's no use arguing with me. I'm coming."

"Laney," he pushed back.

"I'm coming," I said again.

"You won't take no for an answer, will you?"

"Nope," I said with finality, looking inside. There were more than enough chaperones. I could go and come back, and no one would miss me.

"Do you at least want to grab a coat?"

"No," I said quickly. "Let's just go."

"Alright," he held out his hand in exasperation. "After you."

We made our way across the street, entering through the only way you could get in and out of the abandoned ruins.

I hoped Niña wasn't here. It was in worse shape than I recalled, and the aging structure was no place for students.

Dean used the flashlight on his cell phone to help us manage through the maze of fallen boards and litter, and I wondered if I should have taken his advice and grabbed my coat. It was cold, with the ocean below, and my heels kept poking through the rotting floorboards.

"So, you know this student?" he asked as we walked carefully, from one room to the next.

"I do," I wrapped my arms around me, trying to shield myself from the cold.

"Is she a good kid?"

"She's...special."

"How so?"

"I don't know...I feel like I know her."

"That makes sense," he mumbled.

"What do you mean?" I asked as he came to a stop next to me and turned off his phone.

"We have to talk," he said, ignoring my question.

"About?" I looked around, trying to think of which way we should go next.

"You and me."

"What?" I whipped my head around; not sure I'd heard him right.

"You and me," he said again.

"What are you talking about?"

"We're connected, Laney. And you feel it, too. Don't you?"

"Connected?" I asked, confused.

"Yes," he nodded. "And you need to know why."

With my eyes now adjusted to the dark, I could see Dean's eyes focused on me. "There's no time for whatever it is you're doing. We have to find Niña."

Dean looked down and I closed my eyes

realizing this was all a ruse. "She isn't out here, is she?"

"I needed to get you away…from the dance."

"What are you talking about?" I stepped back, his words sending a chill down my spine.

"You needed to be somewhere safe."

"Why?"

"So, no one could find us."

Every suspicion, every fear, every notion I ever had about Dean Danvers, slammed into me. "I knew it," I shook my head, angry with myself for letting my guard down.

"Knew what?"

"You tricked me!" I seethed, eyes narrowing.

"What? No, I didn't trick you."

"Damn it!" I shook my head angrily. "I could kick myself for being so naïve."

"You're not naïve," he held his hand out.

"Don't touch me!" I shouted.

"I can explain."

"Save it," I said angrily. "I'm not interested in whatever game you're playing."

"Game?" he took a step towards me. "Laney, this isn't a game. You need to listen to me."

"I'm done listening to you." I pushed past him and began to walk as fast as I could on the lifting floorboards, in my heels.

"Laney?" a voice called up from below.

"Sam?" I called back, surprised to hear her voice.

"Laney, thank God," she shouted. "Where are you?"

"Up."

"Where?"

I looked around, trying to make sense of the dark. Rusted hooks, dangled loosely from the ceiling. "The packing room, I think."

"Stay there!" she shouted.

"Laney," Dean came up behind me. "You need to be careful. This place is dangerous."

"No," I shouted back. "You are. Stay the hell away from me!"

"There you are," Sam ran into the room, slightly out of breath, holding a flashlight.

"What are you doing here?" I asked, relieved to see her, but also, confused.

"One of the chaperones said they saw you two come out here."

Thank God I exhaled. Someone knew we were out here. If Dean tried anything...

"And you," she shook her head, looking at Dean.

"Look," he held his hand out to Sam.

"No," she stepped back. "Get away from us."

Dean ignored Sam's interference and looked to

me. "Laney, you have to listen to me. We are connected, and you have to know why."

"No," I swallowed, Tony's story that night at *Fiero's*, about me having a fan club in high school, rushed into my mind. "Whatever you think you feel for me…"

"Feel for you?" he straightened, puzzled.

"You and me," I said bitterly. "It's never going to happen."

"You don't understand," he closed his eyes. "If you would just listen to me…"

"Stay away from her!" Sam shouted.

"Laney doesn't need to be afraid of me," Dean shot back angrily.

"That favor you asked me to do," Sam continued, holding out her hand to keep the space between us and Dean. "I have an answer."

"What?" I asked, confused why she was telling me this here and now.

"I know everything," she said pointedly, looking at Dean. "That's why I was calling earlier."

"You can fill me in later," I shivered.

"No, you need to know, now."

"Why?"

"It's important. But I think he should be the one," she looked to Dean, eyes narrow.

"You know," Dean said to Sam, matter of fact.

411

"I...know...everything," she crossed her arms. "So, tell her. Or I will."

"That's what I've been trying to do!"

"What's going on?" I asked angrily.

"Are you going to tell her, or shall I?" Sam crossed her arms.

"Whatever you think you know..."

"Oh, I know," she spat back.

"You don't know everything!" he said, irritably.

I listened to Sam and Dean argue, my eyes darting back and forth as if I were watching a tennis match.

"Enough!" I shouted when I couldn't take it anymore. Sam and Dean whipped their heads in my direction, eyes wide. "What do I need to know?" I demanded.

"There are things you should know," Dean said, the urgency in his voice clear. "And I will tell you. But we need to get you somewhere safe. She would want me to do that."

"Who is she?" I asked, looking from him to Sam.

His eyes were wide, and then with each second of silence that passed, they changed, from urgency to acceptance and then finally, to sadness.

"Lisa," he said finally, voice cracking.

"What?" I asked, my own catching in my throat.

"This is about her."

"What is about her?" I whispered.

"It was me," he said sadly. "I killed her. I killed all of them."

CHAPTER TWENTY-SEVEN

THE ROOM SHIFTED AS A WAVE OF CONFUSION CRASHED into me, knocking me off balance. I stumbled backwards, teetering in my heels.

"What?" I asked, trying to catch my breath, sure I'd heard him wrong.

"It's true," Sam nodded, looking at Dean accusingly.

"H...how do you know?" I stammered, my ears starting to ring.

"I did what you asked me to do," Sam answered. "I found out who the driver was. It was Dean," she pointed. "*He* was the one driving."

"No," I rubbed my arms, the cold getting harder to ignore. "A logging truck hit us."

"I know," Dean responded, finally speaking. "I was driving it."

"Why would you be in a logging truck?"

"I was just starting my business and got a tip on some cheap lumber," he began, looking at me, eyes hollow, as the rhythmic pounding of waves crashed against the rocks below. "I thought I could save some money. Rent a truck, and do the haul myself, instead of paying a team money that I didn't have." He stopped and looked down, kicking a piece of debris with the toe of his shoe. "I never should have taken that damn truck up there. But she was so upset..."

"She?" I asked.

"Lisa," he looked up.

"Lisa?" I repeated, surprised to hear her name a second time. "Why would she call you?"

"She always called me."

"What?" I asked, confused. Lisa didn't know Dean. At least, not well enough to call him on the phone.

"That's what we did when we weren't together. Talked on the phone. Sometimes, all night."

"Wait," I held up my hand. "You were friends?"

"You can say that" he smiled somberly.

"But I never saw her talking to you."

"I know," he said simply. "She wanted it that way."

"She didn't want me to know you two knew each other?"

"She wanted to keep us a secret."

"Why?"

"Our relationship was special."

"What relationship?"

"The one we were in."

"You two were *not* dating."

"You're right," he crossed his arms.

"Thank you," I exhaled, hoping he'd stop whatever game he was playing.

"It was more than that," he continued. "So much more."

"You're lying," I shot back angrily.

"I'm telling you the truth," he replied evenly.

"It's not possible."

"Why not?"

"I never saw you two…together."

"I know."

"If you were together, I would've known."

"Look," he said gently. "She had her reasons for keeping us quiet."

"When?" I asked, trying to make sense of what he was saying.

"When, what?" he asked, tilting his head slightly.

"If you two were together, when did you see each other?"

"Whenever we could," he smiled with the

response. "We were together that week...before the accident."

"No," I said icily. "She was taking a seminar."

"No," he corrected me, gently. "She was with me."

"Where?"

"In Bangor."

"Bangor?" I repeated.

"I lived there at the time."

"This doesn't make any sense," I looked away, my mind reeling.

"It wouldn't...to you. But together, we did." I turned back to him; the warmth of his voice hard to ignore. "She wanted to tell you, but she was nervous."

"Tell me what?"

"About us."

The familiarity in which Dean spoke of Lisa was hard to ignore. "Why wouldn't she want to tell me?"

"She didn't want it to cause any problems that first weekend you were back together."

The irony of his response was eerie. I'd requested the same of Evan that weekend and it had put me on edge those first hours we were all back together.

I was anxious Lisa would discover the secret I

was hiding, and my nerves had been on edge. It never occurred to me the tension I felt between us could've been because she, too, had a secret. *But Dean?* I looked to him, the idea hard to believe.

Or was it? She had been unusually cool that night, and I'd assumed it was because she had grown tired of the trip that we'd taken every summer since we were kids. Had her coolness actually been, nervousness?

"Sometimes it feels like she's been gone forever," Dean continued. "And then other times, like she was just here."

I watched him carefully; observed the way in which he spoke, and how his eyes lit up when he mentioned her.

"I would have known," I looked down, trying to find the truth among the scattered debris on the aging wooden floor. "She would have told me if you two were together."

"Not if," he corrected. "We were."

"But she told me about every guy she dated."

"I was different."

"How so?"

"Laney," he said, his voice even, face serious. "I loved her. And she loved me."

Lisa, in love? It was impossible to imagine. Then again, she did everything full throttle. Even love. If she fell for Dean, it would have been hard, and fast. I would have questioned her because that's what I did. I was her best friend, and I protected her, even when it was from herself.

But when Lisa dug her heels in on something, she could be stubborn. It's what *she* did. If she were with Dean, and felt I wouldn't have approved, she'd have kept it a secret in fear of my telling her, 'I told you so.' She would've made up her mind, and nothing would've changed it.

"What was she proudest of?" I asked, looking to Dean.

"What?" he asked, clearly confused by the question.

If anyone knew Lisa it was me. I could call his bluff, here and now, with one simple question. "If you knew Lisa...really knew her. If you were with her, and loved her, you would know the answer. So, I'll ask the question again...what was the one thing, she was proudest of?"

Dean smiled sadly. "I knew her, Laney."

"Don't know?" I countered.

"I know," he said simply.

"Then what's the answer?" When he didn't respond, I answered for him. "Homecoming Queen," I laughed dryly. "Her proudest accomplishment was that stupid crown she got in high school. She even bought a cover for her phone with a rhinestone studded crown on the back, to remind her."

I thought back to the night she'd once told me had been the best of her life. The night she was queen, with Evan by her side.

Even now, despite the fact I knew Evan loved me, and always had, I could feel the familiar flame of jealousy licking at me; the two people I loved most, standing side by side — no two people looking more beautiful, or perfect together.

Every time I saw her phone, I could feel the jealousy I felt that night, flicker. Until the accident, her greatest night had been my worst, and I hated the way the crown on that damn phone, reminded me of that night, and how inferior I'd felt.

"You're wrong," he said softly.

"I'm not," I crossed my arms, the chill biting at me.

"You are," he nodded sadly.

"They what, pray tell, was her greatest accomplishment?"

"You," he said flatly, eyes locked on mine. "Her greatest accomplishment, was you."

"What are you talking about?" I asked, my throat dry.

Dean reached into his front pocket and then

removed his hand, holding it out to me. "Lisa told me she got these when you first moved to California," he said, opening it slowly. In his palm lie a keychain in the shape of a license plate, with *California* LISA engraved.

"Where did you get this?" I whispered and reached for the trinket I thought was long gone.

She loved that thing," he smiled. "I gave her a key to my apartment, and she put it on that keychain so she would have the two things she adored most, side by side."

Holding it in my hand, I closed my eyes, as the memory of the day she'd bought them for us, flashed in my mind.

"She was going to move home so we could be together," Dean continued. "But she hated the idea of not being with you and knew how angry you'd be since she was the reason you went to California to begin with."

"She told you that?" I opened my eyes, the promise I made to Lisa as a girl, echoing in my mind.

"We talked about everything... her dreams, her friends...*you*. She said you were like her sister. That you never abandoned her, even though she'd given you more than enough reasons to over the years. That's why you were her greatest accomplishment.

Her friendship with you, was the thing she was most proud of, Laney."

Pain, like I'd been punched in the gut, ripped into my stomach, and I doubled over, feeling like I was about to be sick.

"Laney!" Sam ran over to me. I put my hands, on my knees, taking one deep breath and then another. "Don't listen to him. He's lying."

"I'm not lying," Dean insisted.

"Stay back!" Sam shouted. "You've done enough!"

*Lisa and Dea*n? I gasped, holding the keychain tight.

My knees were shaking, and I was numb thanks to the cold. But as the nausea began to wane, I felt a spot in my chest start to thaw. It was my heart, and it believed what he was saying. But my head…it was cautious and needed to understand.

"Why was she afraid to tell me?" I swallowed, straightening slowly.

"She knew the five of you were drifting apart, but also knew how much that weekend meant to you," Dean said carefully.

I studied his face, looking for a sign that what he was saying was a lie. A sick, twisted play on my memories about that night. But how could he know a truth that was so intimate, so personal, that I'd

422

never even said it aloud?

I considered every scenario, but as I ran his words over in my mind and he watched me anxiously, waiting for my response, I finally saw in Dean, what Tony and Tyler had all this time. Melancholy — the kind born from loss — poured out of every part of him, and it was then, my mind, like my heart, knew he was telling the truth.

Lisa had kept a part of herself hidden from me, just as I had from her, because we were each too afraid of what our revelations would mean to *us*. We had grown apart. It happened to the best of friends, and it had happened to us.

In finding another with whom we felt complete, we'd become different people, and trying to comprehend what that might do to a friendship that had been part of our hearts for as long as it had, was hard to comprehend.

I remembered how it felt that night of the accident, as if each of us would rather have been somewhere else. It never occurred to me it might have also been with some*one* else.

I turned my head, tears I thought had long-since run dry, pricking the corners of my eyes. The irony, the loss, the misunderstanding…it was too much to bear.

"I would have understood," I wiped away a lone

tear that broke free. "If only we'd just trusted each other."

Maybe, deep down, a part of me knew all this, and when my heart stopped, the world I went to, was a way for the part of me that knew the truth — about my feelings for Evan and the changes between Lisa and I — to reveal itself to the part of me that hadn't been ready. The depths of my mind, safeguarding my naïve heart, until it was.

"She hated lying to you," Dean cleared this throat. "I think that's why she called me that night."

"She called you?" I sniffed, my voice barely a whisper.

"She did," he nodded gently. "A few times. But every time I answered, the call would drop."

The reception at the campsite had been horrible. The only way you could get a signal was by calling from the clearing the next campsites over. But to get to it, you had to follow the trail through the trees. The trail I took to gather firewood. The trail Evan had followed me on to steal a moment alone, away from the others.

That's what she was doing, I realized, my heart sinking. In trying to get a signal to call Dean about not liking keeping secrets from me, she saw I had been keeping one from her.

"She found out I'd been lying to her." I took a

deep breath, the truth heavy, even now. "That's why she was calling you. She wasn't the only one keeping secrets. And when she found out, we got into a fight. A really big one."

"That's why she sounded so upset the one time I was able to hear her on the other end."

"Because of me," I said sadly, our argument that night, echoing in my mind. *It wasn't about Evan. It never was.*

His eyes darted back and forth, and I could see he was back in the memory of that night. "She sounded so upset, but the call cut off before I could ask her what was wrong. I started having all these crazy thoughts...was she hurt? Had one of you gotten hurt? When she didn't call back, that's when I decided to head up there. I didn't care she may be angry with me for ruining her weekend with you. I just wanted to make sure she was okay."

"This doesn't make any sense," Sam cut in. "Why would you drive a logging truck up there?"

"I'd rented the truck for the weekend from a vendor out of town," Dean explained. "I was going to do the hauls while she was away for the weekend, and then drop it off before picking her up when she was back. But... when I picked up the truck, I left my car in their lot. There was no time to get it. The trailer was empty, and I thought it'd be just like towing a boat."

"Are you buying this?" Sam asked, incredulous.

Everything Dean said lined up. Both what he knew about Lisa and that night. He even knew intimate moments that only she and I shared. But it wasn't this, which told me he was telling the truth. I saw it in the way he carried himself—shoulders pushed down as if he were carrying the weight of the world. A weight I too, had carried.

"Yes," I confessed.

"Laney," Sam closed her eyes.

"No," I implored, needing her to hear me. "I believe him," I confirmed, looking to Dean. "I believe you."

We stared at one another—the wind whipping off the ocean, whistling through the broken boards—and as it hummed its haunting elegy, I felt all of my fear and skepticism for him lift, and carry to the sea.

"After I got out of the service," he said softly. "I did everything I could *not* to feel. The things I saw ...it turned a part of me off. But the night she walked into the bar, so full of life and color...I felt alive. I never expected to feel that way again. She changed my life that very moment that she stepped into it, and I fell in love with her before I even realized that I had."

I smiled, remembering the way I too, had fallen in love with her, that day she walked into my classroom in elementary school.

"I still can't believe it," I whispered sadly.

"Why?" he asked pained. "Because it was me?"

"It has nothing to do with you," I said sadly. "It has to do with *who we were*."

To know Lisa and I had grown so far apart that we were afraid to tell each other the truth, and yet also knowing she *had* found love, was bittersweet.

"I've wanted to tell you for so long, but it never felt right."

"When?" I asked.

"When did I want to tell you?"

"No," I shook my head, needing to know more about their beginning. "When did it start...you and her?"

"The winter before the accident," he recalled. "I was renting an apartment over this hole in the wall bar in Bangor. One night I couldn't sleep, so I went downstairs for a drink...and there she was."

"Was she alone?"

"Caleb was with her for a bit, and then he left. We talked until the bar closed and when I walked her back to the hotel, she wrote her number on my hand with a pen from the concierge desk in the lobby."

My mind reeled, as years of assumptions began to unravel.

He met her when we were in town for my birthday weekend; the night she and Caleb got ridiculously drunk.

That's why, despite finding her in bed with Caleb the following morning, she mumbled angrily at me when I pulled her fully clothed, into the shower. And, why, the night of the accident when we'd argued, she'd said Caleb and she weren't the same as Evan and me. That's because they weren't. They hadn't gotten together.

She'd never given anyone her number. They always asked. But she had given it to Dean that night they met in Bangor. And that's why she was so angry with me. She wasn't the horrible person I thought she was, but she couldn't fight back the way she wanted. She was desperate to protect *her* heart, just as I was desperate to protect mine.

"She loved that bar," Dean smiled. "Called it our place. Whenever she came to town, we'd end up there until it was just the two of us."

That must have been where Tyler saw Dean. It sounded like the kind of place he too, would have gone for privacy. And the girl he assumed Dean had been with ...it was Lisa.

"She was never going to agency meetings, was

she?" I asked, remembering all the trips to New York she started taking after that winter break.

"No," he admitted. "She was coming to see me."

"I thought her sudden interest in modeling seemed was odd."

"We happened kind of fast. Spent whatever time we could together. It may not have been long to others, but it felt like a lifetime to us."

Who was I to judge how and when people fell for one another? Six months may not have been a long time, but for Lisa, it would have been the longest she had dated anyone. Not to mention, she was planning to move back, and knowing how badly she wanted to get out of Lake Haven, I couldn't imagine she would do that for just anyone. She would only have done it for *the one*.

"Was she happy?" I asked, needing to know Lisa's last days had been filled with joy.

"She was," he smiled.

"Good," I nodded, eyes filling with tears.

While I couldn't believe Lisa had kept her heart from me all those months, I reminded myself that I had done the same, for much, much longer. Our hearts were ours and ours alone.

"How did you do it?" Sam asked.

"How did I do what?" Dean shot back.

"Keep your name out of the news." I looked to

him, wondering now myself, how he had kept his name out of the newspapers. "I read the reports," she pressed. "You don't match the description of the driver."

"They talked with someone who *said* they were the driver. But it wasn't me."

"Who was it?"

"A friend."

"A friend?" Sam shot back. "Why would a friend lie about something like that?"

"When I first came to after the crash, I didn't know what happened. I thought I was back in a war zone. The smell in the air...the acrid taste of blood and oil," he lifted his hand to his mouth as if the memory had triggered his senses. "After pulling myself out of the cabin, I could see someone on the road, and knew they needed help. But flashes of red and green...car and Humvee...kept slicing through my mind, making it hard to walk. I reached for my phone to call for help, but instead of it being a military satellite phone, as I thought, I'd called the emergency contact on my cell phone. Jasper. He told me to get out of there, but I wanted to see if they were..."

"Okay," I said, finishing his sentence.

"You remember?" he asked, eyes wide.

The memory I'd seen in the dressing room that

day in Bangor, played like a movie in my mind. And I now saw who the driver was. It was Dean. He stumbled towards me, blood running down his face, and he held a phone, and someone—Jasper—was shouting at him, telling him to leave.

But Dean refused. He kept saying over and over, he just wanted to see if I was okay. The same words he'd screamed at Evan during the argument they'd had the night of the ball in my near-death experience.

Dean's need to see me…that dazed look in his eyes, as he stumbled towards me on the dark mountain road…it was the last thing I heard, and saw, before the darkness pulled me under, and I lost consciousness.

It wasn't about me. He was trying to get to whoever was in the car. And that urgency I remembered had followed me into that world I went to when my heart stopped.

"You left her in the road to die?" Sam screamed, pulling me from revelation. "What in the hell is the matter with you?"

"I didn't know," he begged. "I did what I was told to do. I got out of there. It was only as I ran away, did I start to remember where I was, and who I had come for. Only, then, my vision started to blur, and my legs grew heavy, and then I passed out. I had no idea I had run away from her, not to her," he hung his head, voice grave.

"You could've saved them," Sam said angrily. "But instead, you—"

"No," I cut her off.

"What?" she turned to me, shocked by my response.

I remembered those seconds before the truck hit, when Lisa grabbed my hand as if she had already let go. "He couldn't have saved them," I swallowed. "It was…instant."

Dean's eyes filled with tears. "If I'd known, it was you on that road…and her in that car…."

We *were* connected.

Everything about *that night*, was connected.

What happened to me when my heart stopped, was meant to remind me of its truth. But all of what had happened since then—the nightmares and finding the driver—was meant to help me discover Lisa's.

I wondered if in her own way, she had done all of this. If in death, Lisa had reached out to the living, to help us discover the truth and grant those who loved her, the peace they needed.

Sam opened her mouth to speak but I held my hand up to stop her. There was nothing left to say. We could not change what happened.

"It wasn't until I woke up in the hospital that I learned what happened," he wiped his nose. "Jasper was at my bedside and told me everything. About my calling him, and where he found me. He was also the one that told me you all had been in the car, and that Lisa had died. After he told me, they had to sedate me, and while I was out, *he* gave the police his report…as the driver."

"What kind of friend does that?" Sam asked, disgusted.

"One that took an oath."

"An oath to evade the police and falsify information?"

"You have no idea what guys like me have been through," he said angrily. "Or what we would do to help one of our own."

"You don't have to be in the service to know right from wrong."

"Look," Dean replied with sudden urgency. "Don't worry about why he did, what he did. All you need to know is it was me, and that I've lived with this secret, every minute, of every day, since it happened."

"But why not come forward?" she pressed.

"How could I admit to the world what happened, when I could barely admit it to myself?"

"That's not a reason to—"

"It was an accident," I said before she could finish.

"Laney," she turned to me. "Come on."

"It was an accident," I said again. "And we both played a part."

"No," she shook her head. "It's his fault. He left the scene. That's a crime."

"I'm the reason she got into the car, Sam."

"You may have been the reason she got into the car," Dean refuted. "But I'm the one who was driving the truck. If only I'd borrowed a car. But I didn't, and I couldn't get out of the way fast enough," he said angrily, clenching his fist. "It's because of me that she's gone...that they're all, gone."

"No," I remembered that night; the horses under the hood of Caleb's car had been a power Lisa could not control. "The police...they ruled it was Caleb's car that veered into the other lane."

"It doesn't matter if the car was in my lane. *I* killed her," he pointed at his chest. "That's why it has to be me."

"That's why *what* has to be you?"

"I need to make this right."

"How?"

"By turning himself in," Sam answered.

"What's the point in doing that now?"

"Because it's the right thing to do," Sam crossed her arms.

"This has nothing to do about the police," Dean cut in. "It has to do with—"

"Ms. Thomas," Niña ran into the room, slightly out of breath.

"Niña?" I asked, surprised to see her, then remembered the reason Dean and I had come here to begin with.

"Well, this is interesting," Sam looked from Niña to Dean. I looked to Sam, confused by her comment. "That's the second bit of information I came to tell you."

"What...information?"

"Why don't you tell her who *you* are?" she looked at Niña, eyes hard.

"There's no time for this," Dean said quickly.

"Don't talk to me that way," Sam sneered.

"I can explain later," Niña said urgently. "Right now, we *have* to go."

"Why?" I asked.

Dean and Niña looked at one another; a silent conversation passing between them.

"Yes," a voice said coolly from the shadows. "What's the hurry?"

"It's too late," Niña said, eyes wide. "She's here."

CHAPTER TWENTY-EIGHT

DEAN STEPPED IN FRONT OF ME, STICKING HIS ARM OUT protectively. Looking around him, I strained to see in the dark, but the depth of the shadows and echo of the cavernous space, distorted both view and voice. It wasn't until the person began to approach, that I finally saw whom the voice belonged.

"Lila?" I asked, surprised to see Lisa's mom emerge from the shadows.

"Hello," she said coolly.

"What brings you out there?" I pushed past Dean, glad to see the woman that had been like a second mother to me, and also slightly concerned— The Boneyard no place for her.

I'd not seen Lila since moving back to Lake Haven. Whenever I called, she didn't answer, and the times I did stop by, no one was home. I was beginning to wonder if she was avoiding me, or, even worse, if Lisa's death had plunged her into a dark place from which she had never returned.

But as Lila approached, I saw the latter didn't appear to be the case. She looked less frail than I remembered, as she deftly navigated the debris littered floor, and she looked good; hair pulled back into a tight bun, revealing high cheekbones and bright eyes.

When she reached Dean, she stopped and smiled, placing her hand on his arm. The gesture indicated familiarity, and it confused me at first. But then I realized, of course they knew one another. Lisa may have kept Dean a secret from me, but she would never have from her mother. Especially if he were the reason she was planning to move home.

I could see, however, the gesture made him uncomfortable, and his response confirmed this. "Why are you here, Lila?" he asked crisply.

"You do not think I would let my niece come here alone, do you?" she removed her hand from his face and looked to Niña, smiling.

"Your…what?" I followed her eyes.

"The second, bit of information I discovered," Sam crossed her arms.

"And you are?" Lila looked at Sam with antipathy.

"Niña is her niece," Sam continued, ignoring

Lila's question.

"You're...Lila's niece?" I asked Niña.

"Yes," she responded, lowering her eyes.

"Omigod," I covered my mouth, goosebumps pricking my skin. That made her...*Lisa's cousin*.

I stared at the girl, shocked by the revelation, and then, as if seeing her for the first time, I now detected the similarities. They had the same spirit — the same passion for that which excited them — and while Niña's eyes were heavily painted, and hair adorned with flowers, they were the same depth and brilliance as Lisa's, despite their color difference.

"Why didn't you tell me?" I asked, the affinity I felt for the girl since that first day in my office, now making sense. I wanted to throw my arms around her as if it were Lisa, herself, standing in front of me.

"I really wanted to. I just, didn't know how."

"Nonsense," Lila waved her hand, dismissively. "You didn't tell her, because you didn't want her to know."

"My thoughts, exactly," Sam said.

"But why?" I asked, not understanding why Niña would want to keep it a secret.

"I wasn't sure what to say," she looked down.

"So that's why you're here?" I nodded, now

understanding why no one in town had been talking. Lila had always kept to herself, and since Lisa died, had become more or less invisible.

"Niña came to stay with me while her parents are traveling," Lila explained.

"My father is a historical linguistics expert," Niña added. "He travels all over to host seminars and do research."

"Ah," I nodded; her strong knowledge of history and languages making sense.

"I've been traveling with my parents since I was young, but this time my mother insisted I stay with my aunt."

"I'm so glad she did," I smiled. I had so many questions. Why hadn't Lisa ever told me she had a cousin? And knowing that Niña lived in Los Angeles…why hadn't I ever met her? "Did you and Lisa ever see each other when we were in California?"

"No," Niña said sadly. "I was living with my parents in Spain at the time. We only moved back last year."

The heaviness in my heart from my conversation with Dean started to lift; this new revelation filling me with hope.

"There is so much I want to tell you about your cousin," I said excitedly, deciding my question about why she hadn't told me she was Lisa's cousin, could wait.

"I'd love that," Niña brightened.

"Wait," Sam looked from me to Niña. "You're okay that she didn't tell you? I mean, don't you think that's a little odd?"

Sam's question was valid. But seeing the look of worry in Niña's eyes, I knew why she hadn't said anything.

Niña knew what Lisa meant to me. I'd talked about her in a couple of our check-ins. She'd obviously decided against telling me she was Lisa's cousin because she didn't want to hurt me. What other reason could there be?

"Anything my niece needs to know about her cousin, *I* can tell her," Lila said tersely.

"Oh..." my smile faded slightly. "I didn't mean—"

"A mother knows her daughter best, no?"

"Of course," I nodded. Lila was protective of her daughter's memory. I couldn't begrudge her that. "Niña," I turned back to the girl, changing the subject. "You shouldn't be out here. It's dangerous."

"I could say the same for you."

"We came out here to look for you."

"Dean knows I can take care of myself."

"Wait," I looked to Dean. "You two already

know each other?" Then I realized, of course they did.

"Yes," she shifted nervously from one foot to the other.

"I met Niña when she moved to Lake Haven," Dean confirmed.

"Why didn't you just ask him to help you?" I asked, curious why Niña asked me for a carpenter recommendation, when she already knew one.

"I didn't want to be a bother," Niña said simply.

"Oh, my dear," Lila smiled sweetly. "You are no bother. You are family."

"That's why the dance was so important to me," Niña explained. "Día has always been a part of my life, thanks to my father. But I didn't really learn about the deities and their power until we were living in Oaxaca. I thought it would bring my aunt some peace."

"That's why I helped," Dean cleared his throat. "If there is a chance that Lisa can hear us...*hear me*...I needed to take that chance."

I looked from him to Niña. "I think it's a wonderful idea."

"Yeah?" Niña asked, smiling for the first time.

"Sure," I nodded. Who was I to say the dead did not hear the living? I'd done my fair share of talking to Lisa since she died, and believed, sometimes, she

441

not only heard me, but responded.

"So, you believe in the power of tonight?" Niña asked.

"I do," I confirmed. The tension in her shoulders eased, but I could still see worry in her eyes.

"I'm glad we're all here," Lila clapped her hands together. "It makes things easier."

"It does," I agreed. Everyone who loved Lisa was in this very room, and tonight, we would honor her memory, and remember her life.

"Tell me, Alaina," Lila continued. "What would you do?"

"If what?" I asked, keeping my eyes on Niña, still in shock she was Lisa's cousin.

"What would you do if you knew the truth?"

"About?"

"Your daughter's death."

"What?" I asked, my heart thumping deep in my chest in response to the question.

"What would you do, if you knew the truth about the night your daughter died?"

I looked to Dean, every ounce of elation from the last few seconds, draining out of me. "I don't—"

"Do not try to deny it," she said bitterly, cutting me off. "I know the truth about that night."

"That night," I turned to her, my mind racing with where to start.

"That night I lost my daughter," she said coldly. "And I lost her, because of you."

"Lila," I gasped as if I'd been bit.

"Don't Lila me," she admonished.

"I can explain."

"I do not *want* your explanation," she looked at me, eyes narrow.

"But I need—"

"Your needs, do not matter to me."

"You have to know what really happened."

"Did you two not fight?" she asked.

"Yes," I admitted, the truth hurting, even now. "But it's not what you think."

"It is exactly what I think, because I heard you."

"I don't know what you think you overheard Dean and I talking about, but—"

"Not you and Dean," she hissed and leaned in. "You and my daughter."

"What?" I looked at her, confused.

Lila reached into her coat pocket and removed a cell phone, tapping her fingernails on the cover, just as Lisa used to.

"Where did you get that?" I swallowed, easily recognizing the rhinestone bejeweled crown on the back.

"After the accident, when the police first dropped off the box of Lisa's belongings, I couldn't bear to look inside," she said, somberly. "It's a strange feeling…to see that life which you brought into the world, and once held in your arms, relegated to a box."

Lila closed her eyes, her words heavy and Dean too, closed his own, visibly upset by what she'd said.

"I didn't open it for a long, long time. But one day, out of fear and desperation that I was forgetting my own daughter, I did." She opened her eyes and continued. "Thanks to a small extension of grace, her clothes still smelled like her. And her handbag," she smiled, wistful at the memory. "It was stuffed with all kinds of stuff…receipt and lipstick and her compact. Those small items of hers brought me such joy, but they were nothing compared to what I felt when I found this," she pulled the phone to her chest, holding it tight.

A tear rolled down Lila's cheek, and mine, too. The love of a mother was one that I did not yet know. But I understood its power and could not imagine, the unbearable pain of having lost a child.

"She used to send me these little videos from California," Lila continued. "Of the sky, and ocean…even the palm trees. I was always so excited whenever I checked my email and got those little videos from her. On those days, I felt so close to her, and it made me so happy to know she was living the life she always wanted."

Lisa loved California. She felt alive there. And knowing she was moving back to be with Dean, meant he made her feel alive in the way she most needed.

It was easy to see the effect Lila's words were having on Dean. His eyes were dark, and his shoulders slumped, shrinking his bulky frame by two sizes.

"So, you can image," Lila continued, the coldness of her voice raising the hair on the back of my neck. "What it did to my heart, to hear this," she stopped and tapped the screen. At first, I couldn't hear anything. Only the sound of static. And then Lisa's voice filled the air, and seconds later, mine.

I'd replayed the night of the accident in my mind countless times, and no matter the crispness of the memory, it was nothing compared to hearing it again. It felt as if I'd transported back in time, back to that night—our voices, filled with hurt, and anger.

"She must have been trying to call me," Dean looked at the phone, haunted by the sound of Lisa's voice. "And when she shoved it back into her pocket, she hit record."

"Turn it off," I closed my eyes, the hurt and

resentment in our voices, too hard to hear.

"Is it uncomfortable for you to hear?" Lila asked.

"Yes," I nodded numbly.

"Does it hurt?"

"Yes," I said again, a tear breaking free.

"How could you!" she screamed. "She trusted you!"

"I'm sorry," I sobbed, unable to look her in the eyes.

"Look at me when I'm talking to you," she demanded.

"I never meant..." I opened my eyes, searching for the words to apologize for what I'd said to Lisa that night. To say I was sorry that it'd been me, the best friend who swore to protect her, who hurt her most in the end.

"That's the problem with you, Alaina Thomas," Lila said, eyes flashing. "You never, mean, anything. You just breeze through life, everything falling into place perfectly."

"My life is not perfect," I shot back, hurt, and angry at Lisa's death, all over again. "I lost her, too. But she forgave me," I remembered that beautiful moment we shared. "She knew how much I loved her."

"No!" she hissed. "We are the ones that lost. He lost the love of his life," she looked to Dean. "And

I," she turned her attention back to me. "I lost my daughter. My daughter!" she screamed. "I will forever have a hole in my heart that nothing...nothing can fill. And it is because of you. You are the reason she is gone! And I will never forgive you."

"It was an accident!" I screamed back hysterically. "You have to forgive me. You have to forgive us."

"Dean does not need my forgiveness. He was only in that truck because of her. But she was in that car *because of you*. Why do you think he is here, if not for her?"

"You're wrong," he shot Lila a dirty look. "I'm here to protect her friend. It's what I know Lisa would want me to do."

"Don't tell me what my daughter would want!"

"I knew her heart," Dean pushed back, ignoring Lila's rage. Dean had found his strength and was again standing tall. "I know she would not want this. You got your confession, now let it go!"

"My confession?" I looked to Dean. "You knew she was coming here?"

"Of course, he knew," Lila said, indignantly. "As did my niece."

I looked from Dean to Niña, the feeling of betrayal stinging. "You were in on this, too?"

"We weren't in on anything," Dean renounced. "Tell her the truth, Lila."

"I can't do that," she said simply. "Both of you were an important part of my plan."

"What did you do?" I asked Niña.

"She's lying," Dean said with urgency.

"I didn't do anything," Niña said, her voice panicky.

"I was kind to you," I said in disbelief.

"I know you were," she reached out and I flinched. "You don't know how much that meant to me."

"What did you do?" I asked again.

"She told me you and Lisa were close and if I wasn't going to try and be happy here, then at least I could get to know my cousin." Niña looked at Lila, the fear in her eyes undeniable. "So, I did. I got to know her through you. But then I found this bulletin board in Aunt Lila's room...with all these photos," Niña was beginning to speak faster, her words rushing out, tripping over one another. "At first, I thought it was some kind of scrap book. But then I saw it they were all pictures of you, and Evan."

"Dean was very informative," Lila smiled, seeming to enjoy herself.

"You gave her information on me?" I asked,

turning to him. It felt like I'd been slapped.

"No," he said, face serious.

"That's why you came back to town...to spy on me...for her?"

"It wasn't like that."

"You son of a—" Sam cut in, stepping between Lila and Dean. I'd forgotten that she was here and was relieved to have someone in my corner.

"Why don't you tell me what it is like, then?" I shot back.

"It doesn't matter because I only did it once."

"What did you do!" I yelled, clenching my fists tight.

"Okay," he held up his hands. "I came back to town because Lila was having a tough time. She felt like people were still whispering behind her back, blaming Lisa for killing Caleb and Timmy. I knew Lisa would want her mother to be at peace, so I told Lila what happened. That it hadn't been Lisa, that it was me. I didn't care if she hated me. As long as it gave her peace. But instead," he paused to take a deep breath, "in exchange for her forgiveness, she asked me to pay you a visit. She said she couldn't bring herself to do it but wanted to make sure you were well. So, I told her I would. You were Lisa's best friend, and the ask made sense."

"That's why you were at my mother's shop that

day?" I grabbed my stomach, the nausea returning.

"Yes," he nodded. "But—"

"I knew it," I croaked. I had been right that day on the running path, when Evan proposed, and I saw Dean's car parked in the overlook. I'd gotten the feeling he was here for me. And I'd been right. He was. Only, the reason was more nefarious than I'd imagined.

"Lila began to act really strange," he continued. "She kept asking me for information on you and Evan, and it made me really uncomfortable. Then Niña told me what she'd found, and none of it felt right. That's why I decided to submit a bid for the hotel project, so I could keep an eye open for any trouble. And that day at your house, when I saw your pictures on the wall...it felt like Lisa was telling me I was where I needed to be. That I needed to watch over you. I never planned to hurt you, or Evan. He's a great guy. I meant every word I said at that City Council meeting. You have to believe me."

"If that's true, then why didn't you tell me?"

"I didn't know how to. I mean, what would I have said, 'Your best friend's mom wants to hurt you?' You never would've believed me."

I considered his response, and he was right. I wouldn't have believed him. "And tonight?"

"When Niña text me and said Lila was coming

to the dance, I made up an excuse to get you away from there. She'd been acting really weird the last few days, and I could feel that something was up. That's why I wanted to get you out of here."

"You hate me that much," I turned to Lila, "that you were going to what...out me with that recording at a high school dance?"

"I don't hate you," Lila said, devoid of emotion. "I feel nothing for you. That's what makes this easy."

"Makes what easy?"

"To break your heart, like you broke mine."

"Laney," Sam stuck her hand out to me. "You don't need to deal with this. And you," she pointed at Lila, "consider yourself served tomorrow with a restraining order."

"You may go," Lila agreed, keeping her eyes on me. "She, however, cannot."

"Okay," Sam rolled her eyes. "Laney?" she held out her hand. "Are you coming?"

"I am not telling her what to do," Lila looked past Sam, keeping her eyes locked on mine. "It is her heart that will keep her here."

"Laney," Sam said again.

"What do you want?" I asked, eyes firmly on Lila.

"Your life."

"My life?" I scoffed. Clearly Lila was delusional; lashing out, saying things she didn't mean.

But as we stared at one another, I could see that she meant it. Lila's world didn't just go dark when Lisa died. She'd completely lost her mind. And any connection we once had, was gone. I was nothing to her now, but the person that took her daughter away.

"Okay, Lila," Dean cut in. "That's enough. You aren't going to take anyone's life."

"Oh," she laughed viciously. "You misunderstand me. I am not planning to take her life. I'm going to take *away* her life. There is a difference."

"What are you talking about?" I asked icily.

"You always thought you were better than my daughter," Lila pushed past Sam, closing the space between us. But for each step she took forward, I took one back; floorboards creaking underfoot as my weight shifted from aging board to aging board. "You and Mr. Davies, have this whole town wrapped around your fingers. But soon, that will no longer be the case."

I looked her, the realization of what she'd meant, becoming clear. Evan. She was after Evan. I narrowed my eyes and tightened my fists, prepared to do whatever was necessary to keep him safe.

"Lisa always said to me you and he were like one person," she continued. "And based on what I have seen, she was right. Without one, the other has no life."

"Leave him alone," I said through gritted teeth. Gone was any fear, or guilt, or feeling of betrayal. All I felt was my raw and primal need to protect Evan.

"The way to make you pay was right in front of me, this whole time."

"Lila, I swear…if you touch him…"

"You'll what?" she asked, shaking the phone at me. "You are in no position to make threats, Alaina. This recording proves you are responsible for her death. And when I share this with the Sheriff, everyone else will know, too."

"We got into an argument. I didn't push her into the car."

"With a little editing, it could sound like you did," she countered.

"They know she was driving."

"It will not matter if she was forced into the car."

Lila wasn't playing games. She had planned all of this. In the grief of losing her daughter, she'd lost her mind, and she wanted me to feel that pain. She wanted to take away someone I loved, more than anything.

"Sam," I looked past Lila, ignoring her threat. I was no longer angry. I was beginning to panic. "Call Evan."

Sam reached for her phone and held it to her ear. "He's not picking up."

"Try Tony."

"Tick Tok Ms. Thomas," Lila clicked her tongue against the roof of her mouth.

"He's not answering either," Sam said, eyes frantic.

"What did you do, Lila?"

The floorboards under my feet shifted; my weight causing the aging wood to pull away from their rusty nails.

"Laney, get off those boards," Dean ordered.

"She will go nowhere," Lila stared at me, emotionless.

"That's enough, Lila!" Dean shouted. "Laney," he said again with greater urgency. "Get off those boards."

"Sam, go find Evan, now," I commanded as the wood continued to give. "Tell him—" I continued, but before I could finish, the boards popped and then snapped.

"No!" Dean screamed as I fell through; knocking into Lila as he ran over to where I had fallen through the floor.

Pieces of fabric from my dress, clung to the edge of the splintered wood of the hole's perimeter, as I clawed at the floor trying to keep myself from falling.

"Give me your hand!" Dean commanded.

I strained to hold on while reaching, but my hand was slipping. "I can't."

"Try again," Dean urged, laying down on the floor, stretching out his arm further, the aging wood creaking under his weight.

"Get back!" I kicked my feet, and a heel slipped off, plunging to the sea. "You're too heavy."

"I'm not...leaving you," he reached for me again; his fingertips brushing mine.

My pulse raced as I tried to push my arm as far as it would go. "I can't...reach."

Dean felt around the floorboards, searching quickly for one that was strong enough, and when he found one, pushed against it and reach out for me again.

"It's no use," my voice quivered, fear setting in.

"No!" he stretched his hand our farther. "You have to do it."

"Dean," I looked up, finding his panicked eyes on mine. "You're going to fall. You need to let me go."

His face grimaced as he strained to grab my

hand again, and when he clasped it around mine tight, a wave of relief washed over me. But as he began to pull me up, the boards under him popped and broke.

Niña and Sam screamed as we fell through—air swirling as we plummeted to the cliffs below—and as the sea approached, spraying my arms with salt and surf, I looked to the moon. Like Lisa had the night of the accident, two years earlier, the moon looked at me—and I felt neither sadness, nor fear, but a peaceful acquiescence, as I closed my eyes and thought of Evan.

D.M. Simmons is a writer of Young Adult and New Adult fiction. She studied literature, creative writing and communications at University of the Pacific and has published several short stories in anthologies. She lives in the San Francisco Bay Area with her family where she is a PR consultant and writer. For news and updates visit www.dmsreadwrite.com.

Printed in the USA
CPSIA information can be obtained
at www.ICGtesting.com
LVHW030915021124
795449LV00014B/200

9 781737 630220